SUMMER MAGIC

"Caryn?"

She went completely still. There was only the sound of her breathing. She wanted to tell him she wanted him, she needed him, and that she did not want to be alone.

"Are you all right?"

"Yes." She remained in the same spot as she heard him move off the bed. Then he was beside her, the heat from his body nearly suffocating her when he pulled her naked body against his.

Holding her gently in his strong embrace, Logan lowered his head and dropped a kiss over her ear. "I'm going back to bed," he said softly. "And if you come with me, then I can't promise you I won't make love to you."

Her fingertips inched up his bare chest to his lips. Rising on tiptoe, her mouth replaced her fingers and answered his challenge. "Then don't promise," she whispered. . . .

Other Books by Rochelle Alers

Happily Ever After
Hideaway
In the Holiday Cheer Anthology—"First Fruits"
Home Sweet Home
In the Love Letters Anthology—"Hearts of Gold"
Hidden Agenda
Vows
Heaven Sent
Summer Magic

SUMMER MAGIC

ROCHELLE ALERS

BET Publications, LLC
www.msbet.com
www.arabesquebooks.com

ARABESQUE BOOKS are published by

BET Publications, LLC
c/o BET BOOKS
One BET Plaza
1900 W Place NE
Washington, D.C. 20018-1211

First Printing: May, 1999
10 9 8 7 6 5 4 3 2 1

Printed in the United States of America

Nothing is concealed that will not be revealed, and
nothing hidden that will not become known.
—Mathew 10:26

Chapter One

The sun reached its zenith at the same time Caryn Edwards steered her car onto the private road along Marble Island. The blinding rays fired salvos of near-ninety-degree heat, and she found it hard to believe that the sultry summer temperature had not abated even though she was near the ocean. Challenging the speed limit, it had taken her less than five hours to crisscross the state of North Carolina while it had taken nearly three weeks for her to agree to her best friends' offer to use their beachfront home for a summer vacation.

Marcia Crawford taught art at the same high school where Caryn taught life and career skills, and the two of them had become fast friends from the first day they attended a faculty orientation together. Both women had been newlyweds, Marcia having married her architect husband within six months of her college graduation, Caryn marrying Thomas a week after her own graduation. The two couples bonded quickly, and most of their social events were planned around one another's schedules. The foursome ended when Caryn left Thomas, but her close friendship with the Crawfords continued.

A bleached wooden marker along the side of the road pointed the way to Watermelon Patch Lane and the Crawfords' beachfront home. Switching off the air-conditioning, Caryn rolled down the driver side window and inhaled a lungful of saltwater air.

Stress, anxiety, and fatigue flowed from her tense limbs as she anticipated spending two months in a house with the beach and an ocean as her backyard. Terrence and Marcia Crawford had used the house as their summer getaway for the past four years; but this summer they decided to vacation in Europe and offered her the opportunity to occupy their retreat for the months of July and August.

A glimmer of anticipation lit up her eyes behind the lenses of a pair of oversized sunglasses. As a high school life and career skills teacher, she never taught summer school classes, however, the months of July and August were usually divided between a trip to Philadelphia to visit her brother and his family and an annual sojourn to Atlanta to see her retired parents. This year would be the first time since her divorce that she would get to spend her entire vacation alone.

She'd married Thomas Duff at twenty-two and divorced him at twenty-six. Tom had made all of her decisions for her, and after the divorce her family pulled her to their bosoms, believing she had to be consoled because her "perfect" marriage had failed.

What they did not know was that the marriage had been less than perfect from the very beginning. Only Caryn chose not to admit it to herself until it was too late.

She had accepted the Crawfords' offer to open the beach house because she needed to be alone to think—think of what she wanted to do with the rest of her life.

Steering her four-year-old Toyota sedan over a narrow, sand-littered patch of ground, she parked in front of the last house on the dead-end road. She pushed open the door and stepped out into the oppressive southern heat.

She stared up at the Louisiana low-country house and smiled. It was perfect!

Walking up the steps to a spacious veranda, she noticed the house wore a recent coat of gleaming white paint. There was no evidence of peeling or cracking from the hot sun and salt water. The broad shaded porch with electric ceiling fans was noticeably cooler, and she knew it would be the perfect place to have her breakfast.

Returning to the car, she started it up again and drove around to the back of the house. Terrence Crawford had designed an exact replica of a Louisiana low-country plantation house, even down to a complex two-story double stairway at the rear.

She mentally ran down a list of things she had to do: air out the house, take a shower, then find the nearest grocer where she could buy enough food to get her through the next three days, knowing instinctively it would take her three days to settle in and feel comfortable in her temporary home.

She unlocked the front door and opened it slowly. The yawning entry opened out to a dining room and another the Crawfords had set up as their living room. A layer of dust had settled onto the exquisite pine floors, but she was grateful that all of the furnishings were concealed under dust covers.

To the left of the dining room was a modern state-of-the-art kitchen with a functional cooktop island, which served as a partition between it and the family room.

Making her way past the staircase for the upper level, she walked into the master bedroom. The expansive room was painted a pale pink, and here as in the other rooms in the raised plantation-style house, the tongue-and-groove plank ceiling was high enough to allow the heat to rise and escape through the many generous windows and French doors. The master bedroom on the house's main level provided easy access to the veranda.

She was impressed with the design of the main level with the front of the house set up for formal entertaining and dining, the rear with a family room/kitchen/eating area just off an outside porch, and the main-floor master bedroom suite.

Making her way to the second story, she felt the enveloping heat cloaking her like a blanket. A hall divided two large bedrooms with ample closet space from two other rooms the Crawfords elected to use as a library/sitting room and a storage area. The larger upper-level bedroom claimed an adjoining full bathroom while another full bath was situated near the top of the staircase.

Caryn turned on the faucets in the sinks and tubs until the water ran clear and the pipes stopped wheezing and groaning.

She also flipped wall switches in each room and checked that electricity flowed through the overhead light on the second-story hallway.

She returned to the first floor and checked the built-in refrigerator-freezer. Several containers of baking soda had kept the interiors odor-free. At least she wouldn't have to give it a major cleaning before she went to the store to buy milk, eggs, butter, fresh fruits and vegetables. Plugging in the refrigerator, it, too, started up with a soft humming. Much to her delight, she discovered an area off the kitchen where a pantry was stocked with row upon row of canned foods.

Testing the wall phone in the kitchen, she smiled as a distinctive hum came through the line. Everything was in working order, and she decided to take the larger of the two bedrooms on the upper level.

It took three trips before she emptied all of the luggage from her car. She finally returned to the bedroom she had selected as her own during her stay with a small travel case and extracted bottles of shampoo, conditioners, lotions, and bath oils. It took only fifteen minutes for her to put her indelible trademark on the room she had decided to call the sunny garden.

The bedroom and adjoining bath were decorated in a soft lemon yellow, the wallpaper in the bathroom, a yellow and white stripe, while the bedroom claimed a floral background with tiny purple flowers.

Stripping off her shorts, tank top, and underwear, she walked into the bathroom and stepped in a shower stall and turned on the water.

Undoing the thick, curling black plait falling down her back, she let the warm water sluice down her body. She turned her face into the spray, luxuriating in her good fortune. For the next two months she would not have to adhere to clocks, rush-hour traffic, or boisterous high school students, whose intention it was to test every teacher's patience whenever they were given a fleeting opportunity. No more detention slips, no more lesson plans, and no more endless faculty meetings.

She showered and shampooed her hair, but before stepping out of the tub she realized she didn't have a towel. Dripping water onto the bricked-tiled floor, she paddled over to a closet. Towels and facecloths were carefully stored in rectangular plastic containers filled with small cheesecloth sacks of dried spices and fruit peel. The fragrance of orange, lemon, and cinnamon wafted throughout the space.

Caryn had just wrapped her hair in a towel and secured a second one over her breasts when she heard a thumping sound. Going still, her large gold-green eyes widened. It sounded as if someone was walking around downstairs.

Cursing under her breath, she realized that she hadn't unpacked her clothes. She couldn't afford to waste time rummaging through her bags to find something to put on. There came another thump, then the distinctive sound of a man's voice.

She raced down the hallway and leaned over the banister at the top of the staircase. Standing below her was a tall man with hair the color of a raven's wing. Even from the distance she could see it was blacker than her own, which tended to pick up dark red highlights in the sun.

Holding the towel over her breasts in place with one hand, she took a step, her heart beating loudly in her ears.

Who was he? She thought she had locked the front door. And if she hadn't, why had he just walked in?

"Who are you? How did you get in here?" she called out.

"Caryn Edwards?"

"How did you get in here?" she repeated, her voice rising slightly.

"Are *you* Caryn Edwards?" the man asked, not answering her question.

"Who's asking?"

"Logan."

He started up the staircase and she retreated one step. How did he know her name? She'd been on Marble Island less than an hour and some man, a stranger, knew her name.

"I . . . I don't know you, Mr. Logan."

He continued his ascent, and Caryn's eyes were wide and filled with fear. *Stalker!* The single word rendered her immobile. She'd been stalked in the past by a male student who had become obsessed with her. She had done nothing to encourage his attention. In fact, he hadn't been in any of her classes. It had taken legal procedures to finally have the student removed from the school, but her fear never vanished completely.

The man stopped a step below her, and still he towered over her by four inches. The towel she held to her breasts almost slipped when she saw his face, and she sagged against the banister.

Her gaze examined his features one at a time: a wide, sensual mouth with a full lower lip; a strong straight nose; and a pair of black eyes, as black as his hair, burned her with their intensity. A stubble of an emerging beard darkened his lean ebony jaw, making him look even more sinister. His towering height and the unleashed power in his arms and large hands made her shrink further against the wooden banister. His tall, muscled body reminded her of a statue of a polished ebony African totem.

He was casually dressed in a white T-shirt, faded jeans,

and a pair of running shoes, and she wondered if he had just wandered onto the island. Marcia had related stories about most of the twenty-odd people who lived on Marble Island year-round, and she could not remember whether Marcia had mentioned a Logan. But, then, it was the summer and like herself many outsiders came and went until the Labor Day weekend signaled the end of another summer season.

"Marcia called you about me," Logan said, his deep voice rich and caressing.

The towel cradling her wet hair fell to the floor, but Caryn ignored it, as curling black strands cascaded over her shoulders.

"When?" she questioned.

Logan, sensing her anxiety for the first time, smiled. The gesture transformed his face, softening the lines along his jaw and around his eyes and mouth.

"Did you check the answering machine?"

She shook her head. She had checked to see if the telephone was working, but she hadn't looked for an answering machine.

"Marcia said she was going to leave a message on the answering machine to let you know I was coming."

She noticed his gaze inching from her face and down to her chest, and in that instant anger overrode her fear. "Coming here for what!" she snapped.

Logan, watching the color rise in Caryn's delicate khaki-brown face, was transfixed. She looked very young, too young to be twenty-eight. And there was no way she could stand in front of a classroom of high school boys and not have them try to come on to her.

She was average height and very slim, and he concluded that there wasn't much of her hiding behind her towel. His gaze had taken in everything about Caryn Edwards in one sweep, but it came back to linger on her eyes. They were an odd shade of green-gold brown. Barely tilting his chin, he dismissed the notion that Caryn Edwards was cute; very, very cute.

"You and I are going to share this house for a few weeks."

Her jaw dropped as she stared at him in disbelief. He was lying; he had to be lying.

"I spoke to Marcia before she and Terry left for Europe, and not once did they indicate that I would be sharing this place with anyone," she protested.

"I spoke to her *after* she and Terrence arrived in England, and she said she would call you at home. She said if she didn't reach you there, then she would leave a message on the answering machine here at the beach house," Logan countered.

Caryn would not relent. She did not want to share the house with anyone, even a man as attractive as Mister-whatever-his-first name-was-Logan. "When did you talk to her?"

"Early this morning."

"I left Asheville at six."

"And I spoke to Marcia at six forty-five."

Running a hand through her damp, naturally curly hair, she wagged her head. "I don't believe this."

All warmth in Logan's black eyes vanished. "I'm going back downstairs to get my things. I suggest you check the answering machine to confirm what I've been telling you, then put some clothes on."

Turning, he made his way down the stairs, leaving Caryn staring at the top of his midnight hair. He had ordered her about before dismissing her like an annoying child.

But if what he was telling her was the truth, then her time on Marble Island would not have the magic she had anticipated.

Fastening the towel around her body, she retreated to her bedroom and flung open bags. She finally found her underwear. After slipping into a pair of pale pink panties and a matching bra, she withdrew a crinkle-cotton sundress in a darker rose-pink and pulled it over her head. Not bothering with shoes, she raced down the staircase and into the master bedroom. A telephone on the bedside table sat beside an answering machine, and Caryn noticed the flashing red light on the machine for the first time. Someone had left a message.

She pressed a button and listened as Marcia's laughing voice come through the speaker: *"Hi, Caryn. I tried calling you, but you must have either gone out or you'd already left for Marble Island. My brother's friend needs a place to chill out for a few weeks. His name is Logan. He had a confrontation with his fiancée a week before they were to be married and the wedding was called off. He's gotten a lot of flack from her family, so I offered the house because there are not too many places he can go where people won't recognize him. His photograph and the story made all the major dailies. I hope you won't mind putting up with him until he's back to normal. He's a great guy. I know you'll love him. Bye!"*

"No," Caryn whispered as the tape stopped then rewound itself.

She was not going to love him, or any man, and she intended to establish from the onset what she would put up with and not put up with.

He could *not* bring women into the house!

He could *not* have any parties!

And he could *not* invade her personal space!

If he adhered to her demands, then she would find the magical summer she was searching for. If not, then he could leave because she had arrived first; after all, he was the interloper.

Chapter Two

Caryn returned to her bedroom, closing the door behind her. Catching a glimpse of her reflection in the mirror on the back of the door, she groaned. Her damp hair hung around her face and shoulders like streamers of curling ribbon. She swore softly under her breath. She still had to find a comb.

Logan's arrival had turned her plans upside down. She had wanted to take her time settling in. She no longer had three days because now she had to scramble to get dressed, comb her hair, and meet with Logan to outline the limits of their sharing the house.

Retreating to the bathroom, she found a large-tooth comb and pulled it through the long black curly strands before braiding it quickly in a thick plait.

Her face was flushed with high color by the time she left the bedroom and made her way down the staircase. She met Logan as he walked through the front door, two bags cradled under each arm.

Folding her hands on her hips, she glared up at him. "I've checked the machine and I'm dressed. Now we talk."

Logan blinked slowly, his black eyes examining her critically. What Caryn Edwards did not realize was that he did not want to share the house with her any more than she wanted to share it with him, but he wasn't given much of a choice.

It wasn't as if he couldn't fly out to the West Coast or down to the Caribbean for several weeks where he could forget about the fiasco that ensued after he'd called off his marriage to Nina Smith. What he wanted was to get away from people—lots of people who wanted to know the "real reason" he decided not to marry one of the most sought-after African-American women in the South. The Smiths were wealthy, powerful, *and* vindictive; his own family had fostered their own sphere of influence within the state of North Carolina, but he had promised himself that he would not tell anyone what he saw when he opened the door to Nina's bedroom a week before they were scheduled to exchange marriage vows.

The elder Smiths had been in Chapel Hill for a NAACP fund-raising event, leaving Nina alone with only the domestic staff when Logan decided to return to Raleigh a day earlier than expected; he wanted to surprise his bride-to-be with a bracelet she had tried on during a trip they had taken to New York City earlier in the year.

It was Nina who would have been surprised if she had known that he had opened the door to her bedroom and found her in the throes of passion with the man who was to be his best man. Neither Nina nor Wayne realized he witnessed their acrobatic encounter when he closed the door and left as quietly as he had arrived.

He waited until the following morning to contact Nina. He telephoned her, saying, *"I can't marry you."* Four words and all of the promises they had made for their futures ended abruptly.

After that one telephone call, all hell broke loose. The elder Smiths returned to Raleigh after Nina's frantic summons and descended on the Prescott household like blood-crazed sharks. They demanded to know why their daughter had been treated like a piece of paid goods. No man was going to use their princess then discard her because he deemed it. How could their Nina hold up her head?

Logan had sat quietly, wanting to inform the Smiths that Nina had no trouble keeping her legs up, but didn't because his parents were present.

He'd listened silently, waiting until the Smiths ended their tirade, then rose to his feet and politely asked that they leave his parents' home or he would call the sheriff and have them forcibly removed for trespassing.

An hour later he called all of his groomsmen and told them to meet him at his Raleigh apartment where he informed them that he had canceled the wedding. All were surprised by the announcement and visibly disappointed, including the man who had cuckolded him. It had pained Logan to even sit in the same room with the man who had been his friend since childhood.

The Smith-Prescott marriage had been billed as the African-American wedding of the year, and everyone who had received an invitation flaunted the coveted engraved parchment as if it had been a treasured relic.

Only Michael, Marcia's brother, remained behind after the other five left and suggested that he go away for a while. Logan shrugged off his suggestion but was forced to reconsider it a week later when the Smiths gave a conflicting story to the local newspapers, and to spare his family any further humiliation he accepted the offer to leave Raleigh for Marble Island.

Miss Caryn Edwards would not have to worry about him bothering her because what he wanted for the next few weeks was to be left completely *alone.*

"Let me take my bags upstairs, then we'll talk," Logan said, his midnight gaze burning her face with its fierce intensity.

Watching his retreat, Caryn shivered slightly in spite of the heat. There was something about the man that was dangerous and lethal. His height; lean, muscled body; black hair and eyes; smooth ebony-hued face; and the masculine voice which could soothe or cut without warning was unsettling. He was a little too attractive for her to ignore, and she had successfully ignored most men since her divorce. But what she did not want was the constant reminder of how sterile her life had become. She had recovered from the breakup of her marriage, and now at twenty-eight she needed to know what she wanted for the next ten years of her life.

Did she want to remarry? Did she want children? Would she continue teaching? Would she relocate?

These were the questions she wanted answers to; answers she hoped she would find before the end of the summer.

A soft whining came from the direction of the screen door, and Caryn glanced over her shoulder. Standing on the porch, his tiny black nose pressed against the screen, thin white tail wagging uncontrollably, was a Dalmatian puppy. Strategically placed black spots around its eyes made it look as if he were wearing a mask.

She opened the door, and the black and white puppy sniffed at her bare feet. Going to her knees, she smiled at the tiny dog. "Who do you belong to?"

"He belongs to me. His name is Domino," came Logan's voice behind her.

Caryn pushed to her feet, but before she could regain her balance Logan reached out and helped her to a standing position. For several seconds their gazes met and held, then dropped as his hand fell away from her elbow.

She inhaled deeply, her sensitive nostrils taking in the scent of Logan's sensual aftershave and the natural masculine fragrance of his warm body.

Arching a delicate black eyebrow, she tilted her chin. "So, I get to share this house with you, your dog, and who or what else?"

Logan crossed muscular arms over his white T-shirt as a slight smile played at the corners of his strong mouth. "There's only the two of us."

Caryn pushed her hands into the large patch pockets of her sundress. "I think we should establish a few rules—"

"Oh, I agree," he interrupted. "No loud music, and I

don't want a troop of guys coming and going as if this were a sports bar."

She couldn't believe his arrogance. Where did he get off thinking she slept around? What had or hadn't Marcia told him?

"I'll see what I can do about curtailing the number of men I pick up this summer, if you agree to the same with women." Her words were dripping honey while her eyes had lost all of their gold color, leaving them a frosty, brilliant green.

"I don't want any loud parties or strangers traipsing through here and invading my personal space. And there still is a matter of cleaning and cooking," she continued, not giving him an opportunity to respond. "I will not clean up after you, so make certain you don't leave dirty dishes in the sink."

"Anything else, Miss Edwards?"

Caryn decided to ignore his facetiousness. "Make certain you clean up after your pet."

Logan glanced down at Domino, who had flopped down on his sneakered feet and tucked his head against his ribs. The two-month-old puppy had fallen asleep. Leaning over, he picked up the dog and cradled him to his chest.

A bright smile transformed his stern features, making his face so attractive that her breath caught in her chest. She stared, stunned, as Logan's dark looks became a sensual feast. What had appeared dangerous was now seductive. He tilted his head at a slight angle, seemingly studying her in one swift glance.

"What you propose isn't unreasonable," he said quietly. "I will take my meals outside so you don't have to worry about dishes in the sink, and I'll make certain to clean up after myself and Domino. I don't plan to host any parties or have any female guests." His smile faded. "Is there anything else?"

She stared at the sleeping puppy rather than his master. "I think that's all."

"Good. I'm going to need the key for the house. I want

to have a duplicate made because it would make our living arrangement a lot easier if we both had a key."

It was only now that Caryn realized that she hadn't locked the door. She was lucky it was Logan who walked in and not someone else.

"I have to go into town to pick up a few things. I'll see if I can get it duplicated while I'm there," she volunteered.

"Why don't we go together?" he suggested. "It will save time."

She wanted to refuse his offer, but couldn't. He was right. Going into town together would save time for both of them.

"Okay."

Logan flashed his sensual smile, revealing a mouth filled with large, white teeth. "Give me about fifteen minutes to shower and change my clothes."

She returned his smile. "You've got it."

He opened the screen door and placed Domino gently on the porch before he went up the stairs to the bedroom he had claimed as his own.

Meanwhile, Caryn returned to her bedroom and used the time to unpack her bags. She put away her underwear, shorts, T-shirts, dresses, skirts, and shoes. She hadn't known why, but at the last moment she packed a few pieces that were more than casual. Marcia and Terrence both praised the island's only restaurant as one of the best along the North Carolina east coast, and she thought perhaps she would eat dinner there a couple of times before she returned to Asheville.

Slipping her bare feet into a pair of sandals, she picked up a lightweight leather-trimmed woven shoulder bag and her sunglasses. She glanced at the travel clock on the bed-side table. She had given Logan more than fifteen minutes.

She walked out of her bedroom at the same time Logan left his. He had shaved, showered, and changed into a pair of white laundered jeans, a navy-blue golf shirt, and had exchanged his running shoes for a pair of imported Italian loafers. His close-cut coarse black hair shimmered with a light layer of hair dressing. His blatant masculinity was shocking, and Caryn wondered about the woman who had let him get away.

The poor woman probably got tired of his tyrannical manner, she thought. It was good she got out of the union before it was too late. Unlike me, she mused. It had taken two years before she knew she could not continue in her own marriage, and another two before it was legally over. Thomas had not given up without a long, drawn-out legal battle.

She walked past Logan and made her way down the staircase, feeling the heat of his large body as he followed her. Seeing him, inhaling his sensual cologne and knowing they would share the house for at least a month created a feeling of uneasiness. She did not want a man—an attractive man—so close as to remind her of what she once had.

She had enjoyed being married and in love. Becoming Thomas's wife was the closest thing to being a complete woman. She had felt adored and protected. But in the end it was as if they were two strangers who happened to share a house. And that was what she and Logan were—two strangers who were sharing a house.

Caryn handed him the keys, and he closed and locked the front door. Leaning over, she picked up the sleeping puppy and cradled it to her breasts.

Logan pocketed the house keys and extended his arms. "I'll take him."

She tightened her hold on Domino. "I don't mind holding him."

"I don't want him spoiled."

A slight frown furrowed her smooth forehead. It had nothing to do with her spoiling Domino. How could she spoil the dog when he didn't know who she was? And in that instant Logan had just unwittingly revealed a lot about himself. He was selfish *and* possessive.

Wordlessly, she handed him the dog and turned on her heel. The boundaries had been drawn. There would be no connection, no communication as long as both occupied the house.

"We'll take my vehicle," Logan said, following her down the porch and around to the rear of the house where he had parked his black Jeep Wrangler.

Not waiting for him to help her up, Caryn opened the passenger side door and pulled herself up to the seat. He had removed the soft top from the two-door, four-wheel-drive vehicle, and the sun beat mercilessly down on her bared head. Reaching into her purse, she took out her sunglasses and perched them on her nose, while Logan attached a leash to Domino's collar and looped the end around the Wrangler's roll bar.

Logan swung his long frame up into the car in a smooth, graceful motion. He reached his sunglasses off the dash and put them on before shifting gears and turning on the ignition. The engine caught and seconds later he maneuvered the Jeep along Watermelon Patch Lane then out onto the main road.

A warm breeze lifted tendrils of hair about Caryn's face as they escaped the single braid resting between her shoulder blades. The searing sun beat down on her bare shoulders, and she berated herself for not applying a layer of sunscreen to protect her delicate skin.

Logan drove slowly, seemingly in no hurry to get to the hub of Marble Island's business community. He had lingered along the two square blocks of business establishments on the ride from Raleigh, cataloging the number of stores and what they offered the vacationers who swelled the normal population of twenty-six to a burgeoning seventy-five.

One building claimed the local post office, shoe repair, and locksmith. Another doubled as a Laundromat and dry cleaner. There was a candy store which sold everything from soda, newspapers, and magazines to video rentals, and a small supermarket. There was only one restaurant which served three meals a day, seven days a week, a nondenominational church, a service station offering gas and auto repairs, and a small pharmacy. The residents of Marble Island were adamant about not permitting a fast-food establishment on their island. They claimed it would destroy the ambiance of their laid-back ocean retreat community.

Once he'd left the city limits of Wilmington and headed south along Route 17, Logan felt as if he had shed all of the pain and bitterness that seeped into his being the moment he opened Nina's bedroom door to find the woman he had fallen in love with and pledged his future to in the arms of his best friend. What was deceit was magnified twofold. The people he had trusted most had the power to hurt him the most.

Once burned, twice shy.

It would never happen again. He would never trust another woman.

He pulled into a parking lot behind a row of stores, shut off the engine, and chanced a quick glance at Caryn. Her face was flushed with color, the tip of her nose bright red, and a sheen of moisture dotted her smooth forehead and cheeks. Wisps of black curls clung to her damp neck, bringing his gaze to the spot. The warm, clean feminine scent of her body rose sharply in his nostrils, reminding him that Caryn Edwards was the epitome of femininity.

He didn't know when he had mentally cataloged everything about her, but he knew without looking at her the delicate shape of her small hands and feet, the graceful curve of her neck which made her appear taller than she actually was, and the luminous glow of the gold-green eyes which seemed so incongruent to her black hair. But what he had consciously noticed was the lush fullness of her mouth. A mouth that pouted and one that curved in the most beguiling smile he had ever seen on a woman.

He stared at her mouth behind the lenses of his sunglasses, watching it move and form words. But it took several seconds before he realized Caryn was addressing him.

"I'm sorry," he apologized. "My mind was somewhere else."

"I said that I'm going to the supermarket. I'll meet you back here."

Logan nodded. "Okay." He leapt from his seat and came around the front of the Jeep and opened her door. His fingers curved around her waist, and he swung her effortlessly to the ground.

Caryn stared up at him, momentarily stunned by the gesture, then glanced over his shoulder. "Is there something you'll need that I can pick up for you?" His hands fell away from her body as he took a backward step.

"No."

Her eyebrows shot up at his sharp retort. What was it about him that made his moods so mercurial? The sooner she settled into the house and established a routine where she would not come into contact with him, the better.

Clamping her jaw tightly, she turned and walked away from him. She knew the heat scorching her back was not only from the sun but also Logan's burning black eyes. She took a quick glance over her shoulder and saw him leaning against the door to the Jeep, watching her intently.

The heat in her face increased when she realized she wanted him to watch her. As ill-tempered as he was, she wanted him to find her attractive.

He's dangerous, whispered a small voice in her head.

Shrugging a slender shoulder, she walked into the minimarket through the parking lot exit, temporarily dismissing the image of her summer housemate.

He was dangerous only if a woman chose to become involved with him, and she had no intention of becoming involved with him or any other man—at least not this summer.

Chapter Three

Caryn pulled a shopping cart from the stack of more than a half dozen lined up along the passage leading from the minimarket to the parking lot.

She walked up and down the narrow aisles, filling the basket with dairy products, flour, sugar, and several different varieties of fresh fruits and vegetables. Impressed with the appearance of what appearded to be quality meat, she selected packaged steaks, chicken, and hamburgers.

Steering the cart to the checkout counter, she quickly scanned her purchases, hoping she did not forget anything.

The tall, blond checkout clerk flashed her a winning dimpled smile. "Good afternoon."

She offered him a friendly smile in return. "Good afternoon."

"Are you here for the summer?"

Caryn continued to unload her shopping cart, placing her purchases on the counter. "Yes."

The sun-bronzed youth wiped his right hand down the front of his white apron, then extended it. "Chris Barnett."

She took the proffered hand. "Caryn Edwards."

Chris's gold-flecked brown eyes swept appreciably over her face and body. "If you need someone to show you where the *real* action is let me know."

Withdrawing her hand, she nodded. "Thanks for the offer."

He continued ringing up her order, his practiced smile in place. "Where are you staying?"

She knew if she didn't tell him, he would find out within an hour. "I'm staying at the Crawfords' place."

"Cool spot," Chris drawled. "If you need help settling in or if you get lonely sometime . . . call me. I work during the day, but I'm free at night." Reaching for a small paper bag, he scrawled a telephone number on it and handed it to her.

A large dark hand swept the bag with the number from her fingers before she was given the opportunity to glance at one of the digits. "Forget it, kid," Logan drawled, his voice low and threatening.

Caryn felt faint as her heart pumped wildly in an erratic rhythm. And judging from the loss of color in Chris's face, he also hadn't noticed Logan when he walked into the minimarket.

"Logan!" Her own voice was low and angry.

Ignoring her, Logan turned on the hapless young clerk. They were of equal height, but Chris had yet to put on the bulk of a man who had left adolescence behind fifteen years ago.

"Pack up everything! Now!"

Chris threw articles haphazardly into paper sacks while Logan reached into a pocket of his jeans and withdrew a gold monogrammed money clip. Tossing five twenties on the counter, he stacked the bags in the shopping cart.

He turned his midnight gaze on Caryn, and for a brief moment she saw a hint of rage lurking beneath the surface of his composed features. "Please go and check on Domino," he ordered quietly. "I'll bring the food out."

She vacillated, knowing Logan wasn't finished with Chris, and what she saw in the young man's startled gaze was fear. Managing a bright smile, she said, "It's been nice, Chris. I'll see you around."

Chris shook his head, but Caryn did not see his last gesture of desperation as she turned and walked out to the parking lot.

Logan waited until she disappeared before he leaned in close to the quaking store clerk. "Stay away from her," he warned, "or I'll show you what real action is."

Holding up his hands in a sign of surrender, Chris displayed his perfect white teeth. "Look, man, I didn't know she belonged to you. I . . . I was just trying to be friendly."

Logan's lips twisted into a cynical grin as he patted Chris's cheek. "No harm done, kid."

His head bobbing up and down like a buoy on the water, Chris totaled Caryn's purchases. He picked up the five twenties, handing two back to Logan. "You gave me too much money."

Logan, pushing the cart away from the counter, shook his head. "No, I didn't. It's a tip."

The fact that he had just faced possible bodily injury because he had come on to another man's wife faded quickly as Chris computed that the man Caryn had called Logan had given him a fifty-dollar tip.

"Cool, man," he shouted to Logan's departing back.

Yeah cool, Logan thought as he pushed the shopping cart out to the parking lot; what he had wanted to do was shake Caryn until her teeth rattled. He couldn't believe it when he saw her flashing her brilliant eyes at that boy; and that was what he was—a boy. He doubted whether Chris was old enough to be served alcohol.

Damn! Talk about bad luck. If he didn't have bad luck, then he wouldn't have any luck!

The woman he had wanted to carry his name and bear his children slept or had been sleeping with his best friend, while the woman with whom he was to share a house for the summer batted her lashes at men who weren't old enough to buy her a beer.

Caryn was seated in the Wrangler with Domino in her

arms. His tiny pink tongue darted out as he tried licking her chin. Logan warned her about spoiling his dog. He wanted Domino as a companion. Give her a week and she would turn the puppy into a mush.

Staring straight ahead, Caryn's eyes narrowed behind the lenses of her sunglasses. Her rage had ebbed slowly, and only now had she regained control of her temper. All Logan had to do was say a word—a single word—and she would let him have it. They had been thrown together for less than two hours, and he was doing to her what had taken Thomas Duff two years to do—make her decisions for her.

Logan noticed the set of Caryn's jaw and decided it best they discuss what needed to be discussed behind closed doors. He loaded the back of the Jeep with her purchases and returned the cart to its proper place, then slipped into the four-wheel-drive vehicle beside her. Their return to the house was accomplished in complete silence.

He parked along the side of the house and wasn't surprised when she didn't wait for him to help her down as she cradled Domino carefully in her arms. Sitting down on the top step of the porch, she sat and watched the waves wash up on the stretch of beach as he unloaded the car and took everything into the house.

Domino whined and wiggled, trying to free himself of her protective hold. She put him down on the porch, and he sniffed along the boards, his tiny black nose examining his new world.

The screen door opened and closed slowly with a soft click, and Caryn knew without turning around that Logan stood behind her.

"Don't ever do that to me again," she warned him softly.

"Did you get a sick thrill out of teasing that boy?"

She went completely rigid, then rose slowly to her feet. Standing this close to Logan made her realize that he towered over her by at least six or seven inches. She was five-five and he had to be at least six-one or two.

"For your information, I wasn't teasing him. I was just being polite."

Logan's sweeping black eyebrows nearly met as he frowned at her. "Polite!" he drawled. "The boy wanted to show you some *real* action, Caryn. Do I have to spell out what kind of action he was talking about?"

Sweeping off her sunglasses, Caryn turned her back. "It would never come to that."

"You tell Chris the Golden Lover that. He was salivating every time you leaned over to take something out of your shopping cart."

Glancing down at the front of her sundress, she realized quite a bit of cleavage *was* visible if she leaned over. And that meant Logan had also gotten an eyeful as he stood over her.

Spinning around, she rose on tiptoe. "Jealous, Mr. Logan?"

His gaze fixed on her mouth. He shifted an eyebrow. "Not of a boy, Miss Edwards."

A smile crinkled her eyes. "You could've fooled me."

Throwing back his head, Logan let loose with a deep peal of laughter. He was still laughing when a young couple in an ancient Volkswagen Beetle pulled up in front of the house. He dropped an arm over Caryn's shoulders and waited until the two college students climbed out of the car.

A tall, lanky man extended his hand as he climbed the half dozen steps to the porch. "Mr. Logan, I'm Steven Shelton and this is my twin sister, Stephanie. My grandfather said you needed someone to clean up for you for the summer."

Logan shook Steven's hand and nodded to his sister. "Forget about the mister and call me Logan." His arm slipped from Caryn's shoulder to her waist. "And this is Caryn."

"Mrs. Logan," Steven and Stephanie chorused in unison.

"I'm not—" she protested quickly, not wanting them to believe she was Logan's wife, but he interrupted her.

"Caryn and I would like you to come at least three times a week to dust, clean the bathrooms, and keep everything in order. I don't care how long it takes you to get everything done as long as it's done well. The pay will be the same whether it takes you an hour or four hours."

Stephanie, as tall and lanky as her red-haired, green-eyed brother, said, "When do you want us to start?"

"How about now?"

"Good!" they said in unison.

Caryn waited until they returned to their battered car before she rounded on Logan. "What do you think you're doing?"

"I'm making certain you won't have to clean up after me."

"You didn't have to go and hire help," she argued.

"That's where you're wrong, Caryn." His strong fingers tightened slightly on her waist before he released her. "I've never cleaned up after myself. And now that I'm thirty-five, I think it's a little too late to learn."

The admission told Caryn more than she needed to know about the man she would spend the summer with. There was no doubt Logan was privileged.

Her curiosity piqued, she wanted to know exactly who he was, where he had come from, and why his wedding was canceled a week before he was to be married.

The Shelton twins returned to the house carrying mops, brooms, and a box filled with cleaning supplies.

Logan dropped a kiss on the top of Caryn's head. "Come, sweetheart, tell the kids what you want them to do first."

She glared at him before making her way into the house to direct the brother and sister team to the kitchen.

Stephanie made quick work of cleaning the refrigerator

while Caryn rinsed fruits and vegetables before storing them in their respective bins.

Stephanie removed the dust covers from the furniture and wiped away layers of dust from the highly polished pine floors. The odor of wax mingled with the tangy smell of salt water as French doors were opened to take advantage of a rising ocean breeze.

Logan and Steven carried a gas grill from the second-level storage room and set it up at the rear of the house. Logan took the empty tanks into town to fill them with propane while Steven carried the white wicker porch furniture down the staircase and set them where Caryn directed him to place each piece.

Logan returned with the filled tanks, and he and Steve set up the grill, making certain it was operable. The smell of hot charcoal wafted in the evening air as Steven and Stephanie completed their chores. They thanked Logan effusively when he paid them, promising to return again in two days.

Caryn sat on a cushioned love seat on the porch, her bare feet cradled on a matching cushioned wicker ottoman. The whirling blades of the overhead fans managed to cool her moist face. It was almost seven o'clock, and she hadn't realized how tired she was until she sat down. She'd been up before five, on the road at six, and the twelve hours had blurred into one. She had planned to take her time settling into the house, but with Logan's intervention it was accomplished in less than six hours. Her stomach rumbled, but she was too tired to get up and prepare something to eat.

Logan made his way slowly up the porch steps, his gaze fixed on Caryn as she lay sprawled on the love seat. He knew by the slight drooping of her eyelids that she was exhausted.

He had fed Domino, walked him, and put him in his cage for the evening. It would take another couple of weeks before he trusted the puppy enough to have the run of the house.

Taking a chair opposite Caryn, he stretched out his legs, crossing his feet at the ankles. "What are you doing for dinner?" he asked quietly.

"Nothing," she replied, not opening her eyes.

"Aren't you hungry?"

She smiled. "I'm starved, but I'm too tired to even attempt to get up."

"What would you say to eating out tonight?"

She opened her eyes and stared at him. The sun was behind his back, making it impossible for her to see his expression. The rules she had set up were falling away quickly. She didn't want to see Logan any more than she had to; and there was certainly no need to share her meals with him. She needed to be alone to sort out the uncertainties in her life, and she couldn't do that if he intruded at every turn.

"I'll pass," she replied. "Thanks for the offer."

Logan rose to his feet and walked around to the rear of the house. Moments later she heard the sound of his Jeep as he sped away. She waited until the sound faded completely, then stood up and went into the house.

Pulling her weary body up the staircase, she made her way down the hall and into her bedroom. Somehow she managed to go through the motions of brushing her teeth and showering before she collapsed, facedown, on her bed. A cool breeze swept over her naked body as the sun set and a full moon rose, silvering the room with an eerie light.

She didn't hear Logan return or Domino's excited barking as he was released from his cage for his final walk for the evening.

And she didn't hear or see Logan as he walked into her room to check on her, stopping short when he saw her bare form sprawled out across the bed.

Retreating quickly, Logan closed the door, gasping painfully as his body reacted violently to the scene inexorably branded in his head.

Even after he stood under the icy spray of a shower, he

still could see the perfection of Caryn's long, slim legs, rounded hips, and the lush fullness of her breasts against a floral sheet. Her unbound hair flowed down her back like curls of black ribbon, and it took all of his willpower not to lie down beside her.

His mind said no while his body had betrayed him. It took more than an hour for the heaviness to leave his lower body and with it came sleep. A deep, dreamless sleep.

Chapter Four

Logan awoke as he did every morning, before dawn pierced the black cover of night, ready to run two miles before he went through his routine of preparing to go to the offices of J. Prescott and Associates.

This morning, he lay in bed, eyes closed, thinking of how different this day would begin. He planned to run the two miles, but his only contact with J. Prescott and Associates would be through the beeper, cellular telephone, laptop computer, and fax machine he brought with him when he left Raleigh.

His mouth tightened in a grim, hard line. This week was to have been the beginning of his ten-day honeymoon at a private villa on the French-Caribbean island of Martinique. All of that had changed because instead of sharing a villa with Nina in Martinique, he was waking up on a small island off the coast of North Carolina, sharing an exact replica of a Louisiana low-country house with a woman who was as different from Nina Smith as night was from day.

Nina's mahogany-brown skin, stylized short-cut hair, slanting black eyes, and her tall, thin body had earned her the sobriquet as the Black Ice Princess, while Caryn's black curly hair and lush, slim body made her ripely seductive and dangerously tempting as an enchantress.

However, Nina's unapproachable image was shattered completely once she shared his bed. And it had taken two years, a proposal of marriage, and direct proof of Nina's infidelity for Logan to realize that he hadn't loved the woman as much as he loved her passion. Nina was the first woman he had met whose passions were as strong as his own in their intensity.

Thinking of passions reminded him of his body's reaction to seeing Caryn nude. The reaction was just as unexpected as it was violent. It was so powerful and violent that a cold shower failed to relieve the heaviness in his groin, and it angered him because he did not want to want her. He didn't want to want *any woman.*

Swinging his long legs over the side of the bed, he slipped into an athletic supporter, a pair of shorts, and his running shoes and made his way to the bathroom at the head of the staircase.

Less than five minutes later, he released Domino from the large cage he had placed in an alcove near the door leading to the rear of the house.

Domino jumped up and down, whining excitedly. There was no doubt he was pleased that his master had released him from his overnight captivity.

Tucking the Dalmatian puppy under his arm, Logan opened the back door and walked down the steps of the double stairway. The air was warm, signaling it would be another day of near-ninety-degree temperatures.

He lowered Domino to the sand-littered ground and began a series of stretching motions as the dog sniffed every blade of sparsely growing grass before marking his territory. Logan whistled sharply and his spotted head lifted alertly. It was the signal that he was to chase his master.

Man and dog ran leisurely along the beach, Logan slowing periodically so that Domino could catch up. He discovered jogging on the beach was very different and much more exhilarating than jogging around the indoor track at the housing complex where he occupied a two-bedroom apartment in a self-contained private community. The housing development was one of the more successful ventures of J. Prescott and Associates.

Logan's father, Jace, had made a name for himself in Raleigh as an astute businessman who secretly and quietly bought large tracts of commercial properties in the capital city. And as a trained architect and urban planner, Logan directed the building of malls, affordable housing developments for low- and middle-income families, and a business complex that housed not only office buildings but also a hotel, convention center, upscale shops and restaurants, a multiplex movie theater, and an entertainment center.

He couldn't think of J. Prescott and Associates without thinking of the Smiths. Nina's father had provided his father's company with their financing for years. Nothing had been said, but he doubted whether the Smiths would continue to invest in any future Prescott projects. What Logan had to do was find additional financial backing for J. Prescott and Associates' upcoming project. Staying at the house on Marble Island was the perfect setting for him to develop proposals for potential investors.

Pinpoints of sun broke through the dawning sky, and he felt the buildup of heat on his bare back as he glanced down at the puppy who managed to keep pace with him.

He estimated that he had jogged about a half mile before he turned back. Domino was more than content to rest in his master's arms for the return trip.

Logan reentered the house the way he had left. He cleaned Domino's cage and filled his bowl with fresh water. It wasn't quite six-fifteen, but he wanted to be showered and dressed before seven. Even though he wouldn't go into his traditional office, he did not want to break his routine. His workday always began at seven.

He placed his foot on the first step of the staircase leading to the upper level at the same time Caryn began her descent.

For the second time in two days, Caryn stood at the top of the staircase staring down at Logan. He hadn't made an attempt to ascend the stairs, and she tried curbing the dizzying waves of excitement coursing through her as she placed one foot in front of the other.

She had slept soundly, but upon waking her thoughts were those of Logan. She tried recalling the sound of his rich drawling voice, the midnight pitch of his penetrating eyes, and the coarse texture of his raven-black hair—hair that now glistened with droplets of moisture.

Her gaze inched lower to his bare chest. What she glimpsed the day before was manifested tenfold. Natural and unabashed vital masculine power radiated from his beautifully proportioned body. The developed muscles in his smooth, broad chest and wide shoulders appeared to be from a regimen of exercise which did not include lifting heavy weights; and her gaze lingered on his chest, not attempting to risk shifting below the waistband of his shorts.

She didn't want him to see her doing what he had accused Chris Barnett of doing—salivating.

And Caryn was practically salivating as she forced an open smile. Coming abreast him on the last stair, she said, "Good morning."

Tilting his head at an angle she had come to recognize whenever he studied her intently, Logan returned her warm greeting. "Good morning to you."

He was surprised his voice sounded so natural as his pulse quickened with desire. The hauntingly feminine scent he associated solely with Caryn Edwards wafted in his sensitive nostrils. Her natural body fragrance and the perfume she had chosen to wear reminded him of a newly opened flower dotted with early morning dew. She smelled good. Clean. Sweet.

A pair of shorts and an oversized T-shirt failed to conceal

the unbidden image of her long legs and full breasts as he'd watched her descend the staircase. And seeing her unbound curly hair cascading down her back within inches of her waist conjured up the image he'd happened upon the night before.

Again, his body betrayed him. The rush of blood to his groin almost embarrassed him. Why, at thirty-five, was he unable to control what he'd taken years to acquire? From the first time he confessed to his father that he had slept with a woman, Jace Prescott lectured him sternly about self-control. Jace's warning that he never let his hormones do his thinking for him was something he never forgot; however, it wasn't until he discovered Nina's infidelity that he admitted to himself that his hormones had significantly overshadowed his gray matter when it came to her.

But right now what he wanted to do was get away from Caryn before she noticed his aroused state. Not lingering, he brushed past her, taking the stairs two at a time.

He walked into the bathroom, stripped off his clothes and stood under the icy spray of the shower until his teeth chattered and his lips lost their natural color, taking on a bluish hue that matched the undertones in his dark skin, before he adjusted the water temperature, shampooed his hair, and washed his body.

Caryn filled the automatic coffeemaker with the specially blended coffee she had bought in an Asheville gourmet shop. The cold water filtered through the well, heating up and releasing the aromatic aroma of finely ground beans.

Humming to herself, she withdrew a large peach, an orange, cantaloupe, several strawberries, and kiwi from the refrigerator. Her weekday breakfast consisted of coffee and a fruit salad, while she set aside the weekends for pancakes or french toast with bacon or ham.

She hadn't decided on a routine, but she intended to walk from the house into town at least three times a week.

She had clocked the mileage, and it was only a mile and half each way.

Swimming, reading, listening to the many cassettes and CDs she had packed, were also top priorities.

She also planned to do a few things she had neglected since her marriage ended: keep a daily journal, bake her own bread, knit or crochet a wearable garment, and she had exactly seven weeks to complete the tasks before she returned to Asheville and another year of teaching.

Working quickly and skillfully, Caryn peeled and sectioned the fruit in a large colorful plastic container. She had just filled a large mug with the brewed Irish Creme coffee and a small bowl with fruit when the sound of the doorbell shattered the quiet stillness.

She glanced at an overhead wall clock. It registered six fifty-five and she wondered who would come visiting at the early hour. Making her way to the front door, she opened it and stared through the screened door at a tiny gray-haired woman with bright blue eyes holding a basket covered with a pristine white linen towel to her chest.

"Good morning," Caryn said, her voice cheerful and friendly.

"Good morning, Mrs. Logan. I'm Elaine Shelton. Your husband hired my grandchildren to take care of this place for the summer," the elderly woman explained quickly.

A slight frown furrowed Caryn's smooth forehead. What husband? Who was Mrs. Shelton talking about? Logan wasn't her husband. Then she realized that the twins also thought Logan was her husband. Had he told them they were married?

Mrs. Shelton shifted the basket uncomfortably, and Caryn felt a wave of heat suffuse her face. She had forgotten her manners.

Opening the screen door, she smiled. "Please come in."

Mrs. Shelton stepped into the entry, her intelligent bright blue gaze darting around the space. "The Crawfords have such a lovely home. It seems odd not to see them this summer." Something caught her attention, and she flashed the practiced smile that helped her win the title of Miss North Carolina for the 1945 Miss America pageant.

Caryn glanced over her shoulder to find Logan returning Mrs. Shelton's winning smile. She felt the restless, leashed power in his tall body as he neared her and the older woman. His blatant masculinity screamed silently through his white T-shirt and faded jeans.

He's a panther, she thought, then quickly changed her mind. Logan's black hair, ebony-hued skin and sharp, piercing black eyes were more like a bird's—a raven. And he's also a *fraud,* she mused, telling people they were married. Well, it wasn't as if two couldn't play the same game.

She walked over to Logan, looping her bare arm through his and registered a momentary tightening of his muscles before they eased.

"Darling," she crooned, smiling up at his impassive expression. "Steven and Stephanie are Mrs. Shelton's grandchildren."

Logan extended his free hand. "My pleasure, Mrs. Shelton. Caryn and I are quite pleased with their work."

Elaine Shelton shook the proffered hand. "That's wonderful. They don't mind spending the summer here on the island, but earning some extra pocket money will probably be the highlight of their stay."

Logan disengaged his arm and curved it around Caryn's narrow waist. Tightening his grip, he molded her slim curves against his length and it was her turn to tense up. He smiled down at her seconds before dropping a kiss on her sweet-smelling curly hair. The gesture shocked Caryn and she inhaled sharply. It was the second time he had kissed her hair.

She was confused by her unexpected response to his touch and wondered whether she had gone too far. The solid hardness of his thigh pressing against hers, the fragrance of his freshly showered body and sensual aftershave, and his overt virility shocked her senses, reminding her how sterile her life had become. Her marriage ended legally two years before, but her role as a wife did not survive the first of their four-year union.

Her heart thumping uncomfortably, Caryn smiled at Elaine Shelton. "Logan and I were just going to sit down for breakfast. Won't you join us, Mrs. Shelton?"

"Please call me Elaine." She handed the basket to Logan, who was forced to release his hold on Caryn. "Perhaps another time. I had my breakfast when I sampled a couple of blueberry muffins this morning. I decided to make a bit more than my usual batch after my grandchildren sang your praises. Think of it as a small welcoming gift to Marble Island."

Lifting the napkin, Logan inhaled the sweet smell of warm muffins. "Caryn and I thank you." He flashed his devastatingly sensual smile. "When can we return the favor?"

"Come to our island-wide Fourth of July picnic celebration the day after tomorrow. The entire island shuts down while everyone gathers in the large field behind the church at noon. The only requisite is that you bring something to eat. It doesn't matter what you decide to bring because whatever it is you can rest assure that it will be eaten. There's a short pause for everyone to digest their food before the dancing begins. The older folks usually leave around eight or nine, but the younger folks go on until midnight."

"We'll be there," Logan replied, answering for himself and Caryn.

"Well, if that's the case, then I'd better be getting back so I can help Jack open up the store. We have to close down for the Fourth because we house the post office, and people around here always seem to act a little strange when they can't get to pick up their mail. You'd think we weren't a part of the United States the way they come in checking on mail. They talk about coming down here to get away from all of the rush and stress, then look for mail from people they came here to get away from." Shaking her snow-white head, she walked to the door.

"Thank you for the muffins, Elaine," Caryn called out.

"You're most welcome. Hope to see you soon."

Logan took several long strides and opened the door for Elaine. "We'll see you on the Fourth," he promised.

She patted his forearm. "Caryn's such a pretty girl," she whispered, winking at him. "Once the men on the island get a glimpse of her, there's going to be a lot of tucked-in bellies."

He managed a tight smile. That was what he was afraid of. Once the single men on Marble Island discovered that Caryn was available, then the privacy he coveted would dissipate like a puff of smoke. And he intended to protect his privacy—at all costs.

Caryn joined Logan as he stood on the porch, watching as Elaine Shelton drove away. For the second time in two days, she found it difficult to control her temper.

"What do you think you're doing?" she said slowly between clenched teeth.

Turning his head, he stared down at her. "What are you talking about?"

"Why does everyone on Marble Island think that we're married?"

Confusion crossed Logan's features before rage twisted his mobile mouth and, if possible, darkened his midnight eyes.

"Married!" The single word exploded from his mouth.

"Yes, married, Logan."

"Where did you get that preposterous idea?"

"It wasn't my idea," Caryn shot back, her own temper rising to the explosive point. "Mrs. Shelton and her grandchildren called me Mrs. Logan. The last time I checked I was Miss Edwards, not Mrs. Logan."

"Even if they do call you Mrs. Logan, it still wouldn't make you my wife." What he didn't want to do was reveal his last name. If anyone connected him to Nina, then his quest for anonymity would vanish abruptly. And knowing Nina as well as he did, he was certain she would follow him to Marble Island for what was certain to become a knock-down, drag-out confrontation.

"Don't play word games with me, Logan," Caryn warned hotly.

"It doesn't matter what they call you, Caryn, because the fact remains that we are not married and I would *never* marry you." What he didn't say was that he would never marry any woman.

She went completely still, her gaze widening. "That suits me just fine. One husband in one lifetime is more than enough for me." She averted her head but not before he saw the pain in her eyes.

Turning, she walked back into the house leaving Logan staring at the space were she'd been. A chill swept over his body as he bit down hard on his lower lip. He hadn't known; there was no way he could've known that she had been married. He didn't know why, but it bothered him. He had been called a lot of things in his life but not cruel, and what he'd said to her was cruel.

He would not marry her, but he could be her friend.

Logan found Caryn in the kitchen sitting at the cooktop counter, sipping lukewarm coffee from a decorative mug. He placed the basket filled with the blueberry muffins on the counter before approaching her.

He swallowed several times, hoping to relieve the dryness in his throat. Seeing her there, her expression impassive, the pain in her gold-green eyes, made him want to comfort her. He wanted to take her in his arms and hold her until her anguish subsided. But he didn't; he couldn't. To offer her comfort would make him too vulnerable, and he didn't want to become vulnerable—not with Caryn Edwards.

He'd been raised to cherish and protect women, not insult them; and that is what he had done to Caryn. His caustic statement had gone deep, cutting through her defenses.

"I'm sorry," he said, apologizing. His voice was low and

controlled. "I didn't mean it the way it came out. He saw her back stiffen as her fingers tightened around the smooth surface of the coffee mug.

"You said it because you meant it," she retorted, staring into the depths of the coffee. "And I said what I said because I meant every word. I don't want nor do I need a husband."

Her gaze lifted, meeting his dark eyes. This time there was no pain, only determination. Caryn was determined not to fall under the spell Logan emanated without his being aware of it.

He shrugged a broad shoulder. "You don't need a husband and I don't want a wife." There was just a hint of a smile at the corners of his attractive masculine mouth. "At last we seem to agree on something."

She returned his smile, her luminous eyes enchanting and appealing. "You're right about that."

Exhaling audibly, he extended his right hand. "Friends?"

Caryn stared at his long, beautifully tapered fingers for several heartbeats before slipping her smaller delicate hand into his. Both of them jumped at the contact of her flesh touching his, but recovered quickly.

"Friends," she returned, flashing a warm, sensuous smile.

Logan reluctantly withdrew his hand, still savoring the warm velvet texture of Caryn's touch. "Well, friend, how about we sample Elaine Shelton's blueberry muffins?"

Their recent acerbity forgotten, she took down two small bowls and plates, handing them to Logan. "Where would you prefer to eat, in the kitchen or out on the porch?"

"Outside," he replied quickly.

She directed him to cover the round wicker table with a colorful cotton tablecloth while she brewed another carafe of flavorful Irish Creme coffee.

Fifteen minutes later they sat on the porch, watching the early morning surf sweep over the pale, sun-bleached sand, while sipping coffee, eating the fresh fruit medley and the moist, berry-filled muffins which appeared to melt on the tongue.

Caryn peered into the basket which had contained a dozen muffins. They had eaten half. She had eaten two and Logan had quickly devoured four. Draining the remains of the coffee in her mug, she smiled at him over the rim. He returned her smile, the tiny lines around his piercing dark eyes deepening.

"Never have I appreciated a more enjoyable breakfast, setting, or breakfast partner," he said in a quiet tone.

And Logan hadn't lied. It was only now, after having spent a day in Caryn Edwards's presence, he realized that she was the most exotically sensual woman he had ever seen. The sight of her with her black curly hair flowing down her back and the brilliance of her jeweled eyes touched a chord within him that reached a depth he wasn't aware existed. Her delicate beauty was so understated that he had to take a second look before he realized what he was looking at was real and not something he had imagined. She claimed a dark, sultry beauty that reminded him of slow-burning coal with its deceptive lingering white ash. It appeared cold until one touched its core.

Caryn could not stop the flare of heat in her cheeks; however, her gaze was steady as she held Logan's. "I thank you and return the compliment, Mr. Logan."

Shaking his head and wagging a finger, Logan lowered his eyebrows and glared at her. "None of that Mr. Logan business, Caryn. Remember, we're friends."

She rose to her feet, smiling. "If that is the case, *friend,* then I'm going to leave you to clear the table while I go for a walk."

He stood up, towering above her and resisting the urge to reach out and thread his fingers through the mane of hair lifting softly around her finely boned face in the warm morning wind.

"Would you like company?"

"Not this morning, thank you." Raising her chin, Caryn

stared up at him. She registered his stern-faced expression. "Perhaps tomorrow."

Logan's expression did not change. "Tomorrow it is."

He stood on the porch and watched Caryn as she made her way down to the beach and begin her leisurely stroll as the waves washed over her bare feet, rinsing them clean of particles of sand before the soft oozing grains settled between her toes once again.

He watched until she became a small speck against the brilliant expanse between the sea and sky before he reclaimed his chair. He sat, staring at the spot where Caryn disappeared beyond his line of vision, seeing and not seeing.

Closing his eyes, he inhaled the salt-filled sea air, felt the breath of moisture on his face and smiled. For the first time since he had made the decision to spend time on Marble Island, Logan Prescott felt the fragile fingers of healing feather throughout his being.

He had made the right decision to leave Raleigh; he had made the right decision to accept Michael's offer to stay at his sister and brother-in-law's summer home to escape the gossip, and he was pleased that he would share the house with Caryn for the month he intended to spend on Marble Island.

Caryn Edwards was who he needed to help him keep his perspective with regard to the opposite sex. Nina Smith was not representative of the entire female species, but of those who could not nor would not become or remain faithful wives.

Opening his eyes, he wondered about Caryn. She claimed to have been married, and he wondered what it was that ended the union where she decided that she did not want or need to marry again.

Who was he, this faceless man, who had put the undeniable pain in her eyes, and what had he done to her to turn her off on men?

* * *

Caryn returned from her walk along the beach completely relaxed. The leisurely stroll permitted her to feel stress-free for the first time in a very long time. The sound of the surf was hypnotic, lulling her with its rhythmic rising and falling. She had enjoyed the caress of the warm sun on her bare legs and feet and the salty droplets of water dotting her exposed flesh.

She neared the house and spied Logan. He had not left the porch. He sat at the table, his fingers racing quickly over the keyboard of a laptop computer. A thickly bound report also lay on the table. It was apparent he had come to Marble Island to work.

His fingers stilled, and he glanced at Caryn as she walked slowly up the stairs, his black gaze sweeping over her flushed face. A sprinkling of freckles dotted her short rounded nose. The hot sun was taking its toll on her delicate skin.

Rising to his feet, he arched a sweeping black eyebrow as a smile parted his lips. "How was your walk?"

Caryn could not help but respond to his sensual smile. "Wonderful."

His smile faded, and a slight frown added vertical slashes between his eyes. "Are you putting sunblock on your face?"

She stared at him for several seconds, then said, "No. Why?"

"You're beginning to look like a cooked lobster."

She laughed and his frown deepened. "Give me a couple of days, and it'll go away." What she didn't say was that the hot sun brought out an array of freckles on her nose which quickly blended into an attractive deep umber-brown that remained until late fall.

"You're going to ruin your face." He thought of Nina and how she protected her face at any cost. She never ventured out without layers of sunscreen or block and had affected a style for wearing hats with wide brims to shade her face during the hot summer season.

"I'll worry about my face when I'm seventy-five." There was no mistaking the humor in her voice.

Logan realized that there was no false vanity in Caryn Edwards. She was a natural beauty, and, unlike Nina, she affected her beauty without primping and preening.

He laughed, the sound deep and vibrant. "I'd like to see you at seventy-five."

Resting her hands on her slim hips, Caryn tilted her chin. "I'd rather see you at seventy-five, *old man.* I'm willing to bet that you'll live alone in some monstrosity of a house with stacks of old newspapers cluttering every room while two dozen dogs snap and snarl at one another to garner the privilege of sleeping in the bed with you."

Crossing his arms over his chest, Logan wagged his head. "That's where you're wrong, *kid.* Before I get to that state, I'd advertise for a seventy-five-year-old woman to share my bed." He gave her a quizzical look. "Thinking about applying?"

She forced back a smile. "I don't think so."

"Why not?"

"I'd be too young for you. I'd only be sixty-eight."

The sparkle in Caryn's brilliant eyes enchanted him, and at that moment he wished the memory of his ex-fiancée's infidelity wasn't so vivid because he found his housemate not only beautiful, but charming and bewitching. She possessed a little-girl quality along with a womanly seductiveness.

"Isn't that a pity," he drawled.

"Yes, it is." She gave him a smile of teasing merriment. "I'll let you get back to your work." Opening the screen door, she walked into the house.

Logan wanted to tell her that he hadn't been able to concentrate on anything that resembled work because his thoughts kept drifting back to her, her hauntingly hypnotic eyes; her lush, full mouth; and a petite, compact body that was perfect—with or without her clothes.

And every time he saw her, the images were reinforced and imprinted on his brain. What he had to do was stay away from Caryn. He would have to find a way to work away from the house, coming back only to take care of Domino, shower, and sleep.

But where was the question that nagged him as he headed down the porch and around the side of the house where he had parked his Jeep.

Where on Marble Island?

Chapter Five

Caryn retreated to her bedroom, picked up a small canvas case containing a portion of her collection of CDs, the clothbound journal from the bedside table, and made her way down the staircase to the family room. It was her second day on Marble Island, and she had yet to establish a routine. The fact that she was to share the house with Logan had thwarted her plans—but only temporarily. What she wanted to do was pretend he wasn't there, he didn't exist. A wry smile touched her mouth, and she shook her head. Even if she managed not to get another glimpse of Logan for the remainder of her stay, she would always be aware of his existence.

The scent of his distinctive aftershave lingered long after he left a room. It wasn't an overpowering fragrance, but quiet, subtle, and hypnotic. Much like the man.

She turned on the stereo component, slipped a half-dozen discs on the carousel of the CD player, then pushed the button. Within seconds the smooth, sexy sounds of a saxophone filled the space. She let out her breath in a long, shuddering sigh of relief. Now she was ready for total relaxation. Sitting down on an overstuffed wing chair with a cushioned footstool, she opened her journal and read the last entry. Wincing, she noticed the date: May second. It had been exactly two months since she had made an entry. She removed the top from a fine-point pen and wrote the date:

July second—

I arrived on Marble Island, N.C., yesterday. It is as enchanting as Marcia described it, and the house even more beautiful. I feel as if I've come to a magical, mythical place that can only be entered using a special key.

I had somewhat of a temporary shock when I realized I wouldn't have the house to myself. I will have to share the house with a man and his dog. He says his name is Logan—that's the man's name—and his very cute Dalmatian puppy is Domino. I don't know whether Logan is his first or last name. He hasn't been forthcoming with this information. He's hiding out on Marble Island because he called off his wedding a week before he was supposed to exchange vows. The bride's family is upset—probably pissed would be a better word—and Mister-I-almost-got-hitched-Logan is cooling his heels here.

Punk!

It's hard to believe he'd run away from a woman, judging from his appearance and borderline dictatorial manner. However, I must admit the brother is quite kind on the vision: very tall, very dark, and very beautiful.

Caryn's gaze raced quickly over what she'd written, wincing as she read and reread the last sentence. *How could you?* a silent voice berated. "But he is," she whispered. And she couldn't deny it. Logan was gorgeous. Closing her eyes, she composed her thoughts, opened them, then continued writing.

There is an island-wide Fourth of July celebration, and I have to decide what I'm going to prepare for the festivities. I don't want to bring the usual: pies, cakes, fried chicken, potato salad, or watermelon. I don't intend to ask Logan what he's going to contribute because I don't want him to think this is a "couple" thing, although several people are under the impression that we are married. Isn't that a kick in the head? Marrying once was enough for me, and it appears that Logan has no intention of marrying—if judging by his recent flight from matrimony. The only thing we have in common is sharing a house for a few weeks. I don't see him staying more than a few weeks because it appears as if he's here to work. The man brought an office away from the office: cell phone, fax, laptop computer. All that's missing is the private secretary.

What I intend to do is relax, relax, and relax some more for the next month and a half.

She replaced the top to the pen and slipped it between the pages of the journal. Closing her eyes, she let her mind drift and within seconds was swept away by the sensual sounds of the sax player seducing her with the carefully chosen music notes.

The lingering note on the last selection on the third CD faded. Caryn opened her eyes, reached for the remote, and turned off the component. She had spent the better part of two hours writing and meditating. It had been a long time, too long since she'd enjoyed doing *nothing.*

Whenever she returned home hours after classes were dismissed to the small house she rented, she usually was close to emotional exhaustion. She was aware that many of her colleagues mocked her discipline because it wasn't one of the academics. But she knew teaching and preparing young adults to survive was just as important, and most often more important than the academics they were required to take. The academics prepared them to communicate effectively, while her career skills prepared them for Life 101. She'd earned an undergraduate degree in English and American literature; however, her professional degree prepared her to teach what had been known as home economics and was now referred to as life and career skills.

She enjoyed the give-and-take of the students' dialogue whenever they challenged her, but she also saw results. Within weeks she noticed changes in attitude, an increase in confidence and self-esteem, and a mature approach in trying to solve their life problems. And the problems were many for some of the high school students. Problems that fifteen-, sixteen-, seventeen-, and eighteen-year-olds should not have had to encounter until they were much older.

It was a myriad of problems affecting her students that sometimes kept her beyond dismissal time. Problems they did not want to discuss with their parents or their guidance counselors. They related to her on a teacher-student basis while confiding in her as if she were a peer. After a few of the after-school sessions with several students, she seriously contemplated whether she should return to teaching Literature. She usually dismissed the notion as soon as it entered her head, because she had to admit she enjoyed the less formal method of group discussion to lecturing to a class of less-than-interested students who could care less about who wrote what and for what reason.

Her career skills students learned to manage predetermined levels of income; shop and prepare wholesome, inexpensive meals; purchase or make their own clothes; and were made aware of alternatives to emergency situations.

Her own life skills expertise had come from her parents, who had planned their finances carefully and retired in their midfifties. Her parents had owned more than a half-dozen bed-and-breakfast retreats throughout the South. The elder Edwards's established a reputation of offering exquisite lodging accommodations in conjunction with gourmet meals. They had acquired the practice of soliciting culinary schools for their most promising and innovative students. The combination was a winning and profitable success for thirty years before they finally sold off the chain of eight B&Bs.

Pushing off the chair, she reached for her journal. She would put it away and go for a swim before it got too hot. Then she would plan what she wanted to do for the rest of the day.

Logan parked his vehicle behind Caryn's and strode purposely into the house. He had been gone longer than he'd intended. He had driven southward, marveling at the beauty of the North Carolina seacoast. Living in a suburb of the capital city in the middle of the state was a sobering departure from opening one's front door to the sight of pounding ocean surf and the smell of tangy, salty ocean breezes.

His professional eye had noted the design of the homes along Pamlico Sound, and he'd admired the clean lines of most of the beachfront properties. He'd acknowledged the authentic replication of the Crawfords' Louisiana low-country plantation-style home; however, he much preferred large open spaces with glass walls and towering ceilings. And seeing these homes prompted him to contemplate designing an ocean-view vacation house for himself.

The last time he'd sat down to design a structure had been five years ago. Now that task was left to the architects employed by J. Prescott and Associates because Logan much preferred his role as an urban planner.

From the moment he'd proposed to Nina, she nagged constantly that she wanted him to design their "dream house." He had balked, telling her he wanted to wait until they were married for several years. His two-bedroom apartment was spacious enough for a couple with a child for an easy and comfortable style for living and entertaining.

The disturbing image of Nina with his best friend surfaced, and his hands tightened into fists at the same time as he knelt at the cage to release Domino from his captivity.

"Hey, fella," he crooned softly as the puppy yipped and scrambled for escape. Logan's frown faded the moment he noted the absence of stains on the paper lining at the bottom of the cage. "Good boy," he continued. It had taken the puppy only a week to control his bladder for a period of four hours.

Cradling Domino in his arms, he took him outside and waited patiently as the dog sniffed and scratched before he marked his territory. Retrieving the leash from his Jeep, Logan attached it to the collar circling the Dalmatian's neck, then looped the leather strap around a pole supporting a line for the telephone in an area shaded from the brilliant rays of the hot sun by a lone tree.

He patted his pet's spotted head. "I'll bring you some food and water before I brush you." Domino responded with two excited yelps, then lay down with his muzzle between his front paws, waiting patiently.

Returning with a small dish filled with a portion of dog food with an equal portion of biscuit, he placed it in front of the puppy. Domino attacked the food as if he hadn't eaten in days, then daintily lapped up a second bowl filled with fresh cool water. Knowing the drill, he promptly lay down on his side and waited for his master to begin a grooming ritual.

Logan did not disappoint his pet as he sat on the ground and gently drew a specialty brush over the dog's spotted coat. Daily grooming was necessary to keep the animal from depositing white hairs on furniture or carpeted surfaces. Domino was asleep before the grooming session ended and lay peacefully in the shade.

An uncomfortable emotion of restlessness assailed Logan as he returned to the house. He had wasted away half a day. If he'd been in Raleigh, he probably would've had several meetings—one a luncheon meeting—with bankers or anyone contemplating investing in J. Prescott and Associates' latest project. But he wasn't in Raleigh but on Marble Island, hiding out like a common criminal.

Another surge of rage gripped him, and he cursed softly under his breath. He damned Nina Smith for her adultery and Wayne Singleton for his deceit.

She's not an adulterer, a silent voice reminded him. Nina was not his wife and therefore not an adulterer. He shook his head. It didn't matter if she had been unfaithful, because from the time he and Nina had first shared a bed, he *had been* faithful to her. Not once had he looked at or thought about another woman. He had pledged his future to the woman who had joyously and tearfully accepted his offer to share her life with his.

He felt tight, on edge. Making his way up the staircase, he noticed the door to Caryn's bedroom stood open. Slowing, he saw the T-shirt and shorts she'd worn earlier that morning on the foot of her bed; his brow furrowed and he wondered where she was. Her car was parked at the house, and that meant she couldn't have gone far.

Shrugging his broad shoulders under his own T-shirt, he headed for his bedroom, closed the door behind him, and stripped off his clothes. Ten minutes later he descended the staircase, clad only in a pair of swim trunks. He would use the healing power of the water to assuage his restlessness.

Caryn cradled the large hand holding a fork filled with a creamy portion of sweet cole slaw, guiding it to her mouth. Chewing slowly, her eyes widened in shock. It was incredibly delicious.

"Did I lie to you?" asked the velvet-sounding male voice.

Shaking her head, she closed her eyes and savored the taste of shredded cabbage flavored with familiar and some not-so-familiar ingredients. "What's in it?"

The man sitting beside her shook his handsome head. "Can't tell. It's a family secret."

She gave Randy a bright smile. Flecks of green darkened her clear gold eyes, drawing Randy's gaze to linger on them. "Okay. Be like that."

Randy Bell lowered the fork at the same time he lowered his head. "I really can't tell you. My grandmother would disown me."

Caryn laughed, the low, husky sound floating over Randy and pulling him under her sensual spell. He had just relieved the daytime hostess at Addie's for the second of her three ten-minute breaks when Caryn Edwards walked into the family owned establishment. The season had just begun, and because of this he hadn't had the opportunity to meet everyone who would spend the summer on the island. There were many vacationers who prepared their own meals, but the Bell family knew instinctively that everyone would eventually come to Addie's for at least one meal before departing.

Marble Island was small, the permanent residents a warm, friendly, and closely knit group. They all awaited the arrival of the *summies,* welcoming them as if they were long-lost family members. The Bell family had owned and operated Addie's for nearly sixty years, and for the past three years Randy had come to Marble Island to help his family with the swell of customers patronizing the restaurant. This was the first time he did not mind leaving his own restaurant in the capable hands of his two partners to help out his grandparents. He'd changed his mind the moment Caryn Edwards walked through the door and asked for a table for one.

"I suppose you'll go with the cole slaw?" he asked.

Caryn nodded. "I'll have the slaw, crab cakes, sweet potato fries, and an iced tea."

Randy continued to stare at her, his gaze moving down to the shiny copper color on her lips. "Do you want corn bread or biscuits?"

She studied the menu in front of her, wrinkling her nose. "I think I'll pass on the bread."

Lowering his voice and his head, Randy patted her hand. "I'll give you a small sample of each. I do want you to come back again."

Her head came up, and she looked at the classically handsome young man sitting next to her. Randy Bell was cute—almost too cute for a man because his delicate features were better suited on a woman. His coloring was a rich shade of chestnut brown. It was the perfect contrast for his large dark eyes, silky black sweeping eyebrows, and his close-cut curly hair. What surprised her on close examination was that Randy's hair wasn't black or dark brown, but a deep auburn. At first she wondered if he lightened it, but dismissed that notion when she saw the short red hair on the backs of his hands. And like herself he also claimed a light sprinkling of freckles over the bridge of his narrow nose.

She arched a delicate eyebrow. "I'll be back."

Randy smiled. "I'll be looking for you." He patted her hand again, then stood up and walked back to the kitchen to place her luncheon order.

Caryn smiled at his retreating figure before she turned to gaze out the floor-to-ceiling windows. She stared, shocked, at Logan standing on the other side of the glass, glaring back at her. She missed the ice-blue, short-sleeve, linen shirt he'd paired with a tailored pair of navy-blue linen slacks when her gaze rested on his stoic face. The seconds lengthened until she raised her right hand and beckoned him in. She waited less than two minutes for the hostess to show him to her table.

The hostess placed a plastic-covered menu on the table as she gave Logan a seductive smile. "Enjoy."

Logan thanked the young woman with an infectious smile, then sat down on the chair Randy had vacated. His expression revealed none of what he was feeling at that moment. He angry—no, it was more like annoyed with Caryn. She was at it again: batting her lashes at a man. And with Addie Bell's very single, very flirtatious grandson no less. He had eaten at Addie's the night before and had watched Randy Bell work the room. He'd noticed the chef lingering at the table of single women, while he barely nodded at those dining with a male escort.

His obsidian gaze lingered on her evenly tanned face. Her quiet beauty shouted out to him as he visually admired the woman sharing the house with him. She'd brushed her hair off her face and secured it in a chignon at the back of her head. And with her hair up and off her neck, he noticed the brilliance of a pair of diamond studs in her delicate ears for the first time.

Cocking his head at an angle, he continued to stare at her. "Thank you for sharing your table."

"You're welcome. I eat alone a lot, so having company is a treat for me." The moment the revelation was out of her mouth, she knew she had said too much.

Logan picked up on the cue. "You're not seeing anyone?"

She shook her head. "Not at the present time."

His gaze dropped to the menu in front of him. "That makes two of us."

"I'd suppose not, if you just called off your wedding."

His head snapped up, and the lethal calmness in his gaze pinned Caryn to the back of her seat. He sucked in his breath, then let it out slowly as he swallowed back the virulent words poised on the tip of his tongue. He had to remind himself Caryn wasn't Nina. Only Nina was Nina.

He forced a smile. "You're right about that. I'd really be a dog if I dropped one woman and picked up another within a span of two weeks."

"I didn't say you were a dog, Logan."

"Enough sisters call brothers dogs and—"

"This sister's not calling you a dog unless . . ." She had interrupted him, but didn't finish her statement.

He cocked his head at the angle she found so attractive. "Unless what?" he asked when she didn't finish her statement.

Running her tongue over her lower lip, she formed a pout. "Unless you show me otherwise," she teased.

Leaning over the table, he pursed his lips and let out a low howl. "How's that for a start?" Caryn threw back her head and laughed, the sensual sound bubbling up from her silken throat. He stared at her animated features before his gaze moved down to her delicately crocheted, bright orange cropped cardigan. He could discern the lace of a matching bra through the open-work garment. His features tightened along with a familiar tightening between his thighs as the image of her naked body flashed in his mind.

What he wanted to do at that moment was reach across the table and pull Caryn onto his lap. He wanted her to feel what he was feeling—his uncontrollable desire whenever they were together. He was also angry because he couldn't control his mind or his body whenever he came within six feet of Caryn Edwards. And he wanted to take her—without the tenderness he was capable of offering a woman. The deep-seated anger made him want to punish her for Nina's infidelity. He wanted to punish her because he didn't want to want her.

What was he to do? He'd stayed away from the house all morning, putting some distance between them. It had worked, but only temporarily. He had come to Marble Island to escape one woman, but found himself trapped by his unbidden desire for another woman.

He was faced with a perilous dilemma. He planned to spend no more than a month on Marble Island, which meant he had two choices. He could return to Raleigh and face whatever negative publicity ensued, or he could remain on Marble Island and let fate determine his destiny.

His gaze returned to Caryn's face, drinking in her natural beauty. Within seconds he made his decision. It would be the latter. He would remain on Marble Island and let his life unfold.

Chapter Six

A slow smile spread over Logan's face, softening his features and transfixing Caryn with the sensual expression. His dark gaze lingered on her face, bringing with it a rush of mounting heat.

"What is it about me that you find so amusing?" she asked after an uncomfortable silence.

Propping an elbow on the table, he rested his chin on the heel of his left hand. A sober expression replaced the smile as he chose his words carefully. "I find you not at all amusing. What I find is that I like you, Caryn Edwards. You're nothing like the women I usually find myself attracted to, yet I like you."

She sat still, very, very still, and only the shifting of one eyebrow indicating any reaction to his declaration. Who did he think he was? What did he expect her to say? Because he liked her she should genuflect?

"Should I feel honored because you *like* me?"

A thread of annoyance quickly replaced Logan's feeling of well-being. "Not at all. I was just hoping that you'd like me."

"Like you how, Logan? Like a friend?"

He nodded. "Yes. Like a friend."

He'd lied. He didn't know why, but he wanted more than friendship from her. After only two days he wanted to run his fingers over the silken skin of her face, committing her features to memory; he wanted to sculpt her form with his fingertips until he knew every curve of her body; and he wanted to lie with Caryn, while easing his hardness inside her until she felt what he felt anytime they shared the same space.

Letting out her breath slowly, Caryn offered him a gentle smile. "I suppose I could get to like you if you'd stopped acting like my older brother whenever you see me with a man."

"Your brother chased away your boyfriends?"

She laughed. "They all weren't my boyfriends. Most were just friends."

"How many boyfriends did you have?"

Her expression grew serious, and she berated herself for steering the conversation where she could not avoid bringing up her ex-husband. "One." The single word was layered with heavy sarcasm.

This time his eyebrow shifted upward. "The one you married and divorced?"

Lowering her head, she stared at the tabletop. "Yes, Logan. The one I married and divorced."

He stared at her lowered head, not knowing how, but he felt her pain. "At least you got out of it when you realized it wouldn't work."

Her head came up quickly. "I wish I could've been smart enough to end it before it began."

"If you hadn't married, then chances are you would've always second-guessed yourself, wondering whether it could've worked out."

"Are you second-guessing yourself?" she asked in a quiet voice. "Do you regret not following through with your wedding plans?"

His eyes widened until she thought she would drown in the obsidian pools. The pain and bitterness Logan struggled to erase after he saw Nina with his best friend surfaced quickly, but somehow he found the strength to repress most of it before Caryn registered the weakness he would never permit anyone to see.

"Never."

"You say never, Logan, while I see pain and regret."

His eyebrows met in an angry frown. "You don't see a damn thing!" His voice, though low, quivered with rage.

Her temper rose, matching his. "Don't you dare bark at me, Mister—"

"Prescott," he finished before he had a chance to think. Caryn's jaw dropped, and he knew she'd recognized the name. She now knew who he was. Leaning back, he crossed his arms over his chest. "I suppose you'll tell everyone that I'm the low-down, dirty bastard who walked out on Nina Smith a week before her wedding?"

Caryn lowered her gaze, remembering the veiled, titillating rumors in the gossip columns about the man who'd jilted Nina Smith. She hadn't paid much attention to her fiancé's name; however, most African-Americans in North Carolina were directly or indirectly aware of who the Smiths were. The name was synonymous with insurance and banking.

Her downcast eyes lifted slightly as she observed Logan through lowered lashes. "What went on between you and Nina Smith is your business, and only your business. And if anyone on Marble Island uncovers who you are, then I want you to know that it won't come from me."

A slight smile tugged at the corners of his wide mouth before it blossomed into a full grin. The expression held her rapt attention, and she couldn't help but return it. She marveled how stern and solemn his unsmiling face was, while on the other hand a smile softened his features wherein he looked like a different person.

"Thanks for helping me out, friend."

She nodded demurely. "You're welcome, friend."

Now that Caryn knew who Logan Prescott was, she also wondered what could've happened to make him walk away from Nina Smith. She had read enough about Nina's father in *Ebony* and *Black Enterprise* to know the man ran his companies like a tyrant, while offering his employees excellent salaries and generous bonuses to abide his sometimes questionable workplace policies.

She recalled Marcia's telephone message: *He's gotten a lot of flack from her family, so I offered the house because there are not too many places he can go where people won't recognize him. His photograph and the story made all of the major dailies.*

Well, she hadn't recognized his face, and she hoped not too many others on Marble Island would recognize him. Yes, she concluded, it would be healthier for Logan Prescott if he stayed on Marble Island for as long as he could.

"What were your parents' reaction to you calling off the wedding?" Her voice was low, barely a whisper.

Logan shifted a sweeping eyebrow, his gaze fused with Caryn's. "I suppose they were disappointed."

"You suppose they were?"

He registered her incredulous tone. "My mother said whatever my decision, she supported me."

"You didn't tell her why?"

"I didn't have to."

"What about your brothers, sisters, or your friends in the wedding party? They had to be as shocked as your fiancée."

"My friends also accepted my decision without elaboration. As to brothers or sisters, I have none. I'm an only child."

He's spoiled, Caryn mused. It was no wonder he did not know how to clean up after himself. And that also explained his sometime dictatorial manner. There was no doubt his parents, his mother in particular, indulged him, and at age thirty-five it had continued.

"I'm not the unfeeling ogre you think I am," Logan said quietly.

A slight smile curved her full mouth. "How do you know what I'm feeling?"

A smile crinkled his eyes, softening his stern features. "Your eyes give you away. They are truly the window to your soul, Caryn Edwards."

"What are they saying?"

"I'm a monster."

Her expression sobered. She didn't think him a monster.

What she thought was that Logan Prescott was used to having things his way. If not his way, then no way.

"I have no right to judge you. After all, I'm not the aggrieved party." What she wanted to say was that she wasn't the jilted fiancée.

"How did your parents come to name you Logan?" she questioned, deciding to change the subject. She did not want to probe too deeply into Logan's love life because she did not want to have to reciprocate in kind.

"Logan is my mother's maiden name. Her first name is Maeve."

"Maeve Logan. It sounds so beautiful. So Irish."

"And that she is."

Caryn sat, unblinking for several seconds. "Your mother is Irish?" He nodded slowly. "And your father?"

"As WASP as he can get."

Her searching gaze moved slowly over his face, registering everything. She examined his wide mouth with a full lower lip, straight nose with a narrow bridge, the large black eyes with a hint of an upward slant at the corners, *and* the inky darkness of his skin. A smooth sable brown over layers of blue undertones. There were no obvious indications that Logan Prescott was anything but a descendant of African heritage.

"I was adopted," he explained as Caryn's delicate jaw dropped slightly. A knowing grin tipped the corners of Logan's generous mouth. Her reaction was similar to most who saw him with his parents for the first time.

She recovered, squaring her shoulders and pressing her back against the cushioned chair. "I would've thought many things about you, but I don't think I'd ever considered you being adopted."

Folding his arms over his crisply laundered blue shirt, Logan regarded her with a narrowed look. "You think about me?"

"Don't flatter yourself."

"Answer my question, Caryn. Do you think about me?"

Their gazes met and fused across the small expanse of the

table. There was no hint of teasing or challenge, but there was a glimmer of an awaiting interest and expectation. In two days their initial annoyance with the other had slipped away, replaced by a dawning realization of a wanting to know more and wanting to see more of the other.

"Yes, Logan," she replied truthfully, "I do think of you."

He didn't move, blink. "How?"

"You're arrogant." He flinched noticeably. "And you're also dictatorial, spoiled, chauvinistic . . ."

"Enough," he said softly.

Caryn successfully concealed a smile when she saw his pained expression. "Oh, I have a few more adjectives."

He waved a hand. "Forget I asked."

"Have I not been truthful?"

"Partially."

"Explain."

"I admit to being a little spoiled. That's comes from upbringing, but I won't admit to being chauvinistic or dictatorial."

She arched an eyebrow. "Are you the boss or a manager of a company?"

"I work with my father."

"Does he own the company?"

"Yes. What does that have to do with anything?"

"You're the boss's son. You're dictatorial. Case closed."

Logan affected a woeful expression. "You're judging me unfairly."

"No, I'm not. Can't you see yourself, Logan? There is nothing going on between us, yet every man I either talk to or smile at starts you glowering at them. Living with you will certainly not help my love life this summer."

Lowering his arms, he placed both hands, palms down, on the table. The smoldering flame in his coal-black eyes startled Caryn, eliciting a dizzying current of awareness of the tall, dark, handsome man with whom she would share the same space for at least a month. He angled his head, staring at her parted lips.

"Are you looking for a summer dalliance?" His rich, deep voice lowered to a sensual whisper.

She wanted to shout out a resounding *no,* or *that's none of your business,* but decided against it. Shrugging a shoulder under her orange crocheted top, she smiled. "I wouldn't put it that way. I'm more apt to say that I haven't put it on my *Do Not* list."

Logan's expression hardened. "Which means you are looking?"

Caryn nodded slowly. "Somewhat." She had half-lied. She actually wasn't looking for someone to fall in love with because the pain of her failed marriage had not faded completely.

Vertical lines furrowed his smooth forehead. She was looking and he wasn't. And there was no doubt that she was looking. There probably wasn't a man on Marble Island who hadn't caught the hypnotic sparkle of her luminous eyes or her brilliant smile.

The frown faded as soon as it formed. She hadn't smiled at him the way she'd done with the store clerk or Randy Bell, leaving him to believe he was certain not to become one of her hapless victims. He pitied any man Caryn Edwards purposefully set out to seduce.

"What are you going to order?" she asked, pulling him out of his reverie.

He hadn't glanced at the menu. "What did you order?" She told him and he nodded. "I'll probably have the same."

The words were barely out of his mouth when Randy appeared, expertly balancing several plates and dishes along the length of his arm. His bright smile faded the moment he spied Caryn sitting with the tall, dark man who had come into Addie's the night before.

Randy's professional smile was back in place as he neared the table. "Here we are. I hope you'll enjoy."

Caryn was delighted with the beautiful presentation of the food. "It looks delicious." Glancing up, she rewarded Randy with a sensual smile. "Logan has decided to order the same."

Logan rose from his chair, extending his right hand. "It's nice seeing you again."

Randy shook the proffered hand. "Same here, Logan." His gaze shifted from Logan to Caryn. "You two know each other?"

"We should," Logan replied. "We're living together."

Randy was momentarily speechless in his surprise, but he recovered quickly. "I suppose you *would* know each other." He flashed another professional smile. "I'll be right back with your order."

Caryn waited for Logan to retake his seat, then reached for his left wrist, her fingernails biting into his flesh and leaving small half-moons. "How dare you tell him we're living together."

Covering her smaller hand with his larger one, Logan held her captive. "We *are* living together. Would you have preferred if I said we were *sleeping* together?"

"We're not living together or sleeping together," she hissed through clenched teeth.

"Then what the hell are we, Caryn?"

"We are *sharing* a house, Logan." There was no mistaking the facetiousness in her voice. "Sharing a house is *very* different from living together."

He tightened his grip on her delicate hand. "Semantics."

Her eyes flashed sparks of green fire. "That's bull!"

Logan released her hand, then extracted her fingers from his wrist with a minimum of effort. "Eat, Caryn," he ordered in a bored tone, waving a hand. She opened her mouth to come back at him, but he stopped her. "Let's not quarrel in public. I don't want everyone to think we're having a lover's spat."

Her gaze narrowed at the same time her fingers tightened on her fork. "You're right. Let's not quarrel."

Turning her attention to the dishes in front of her, she smiled. Eating would give her something to concentrate on rather than the man sitting less than three feet away. Spearing a small piece of crab cake, she bit into it, watching Logan observe her as she ate. The succulently prepared flaky crab meat literally melted on her tongue. Each time she brought a portion of food to her mouth, his eyes followed the motion. She did not know why, but it was the first time she felt uncomfortable having a man watch her eat.

Placing the fork on the napkin beside her plate, she stared back at him. "Do I have food on my face?"

Logan shook his head. "No." What he did not want to tell Caryn was that her mouth transfixed him. Picking up his own fork, he reached for a small portion of the untouched crab cake and popped it into his mouth. Arching his eyebrows, he chewed thoughtfully before reaching for a second piece. "Delicious."

Caryn folded her hands on her hips. "What are you doing?"

"Sampling your food."

"Did I give you permission to sample my food?"

"Have pity on me. I'm starved."

Leaning closer, she whispered, "Whose fault is that? Why didn't you eat earlier?"

He pilfered another portion of the crab cake along with several sweet potato fries. "I didn't want to eat before I went swimming."

Chewing slowly, he watched Caryn watching him as an expression of annoyance narrowed her gaze. She reminded him of a cat with her large, expressive gold-green eyes. And he could tell her mood by their color. Gold indicated she was relaxed, happy, while pinpoints of green revealed anger. He didn't know why, but he wondered what color they would be if she were aroused by passion.

And he knew she was a passionate woman. He had seen her flirt openly and deliberately with several men, while her full lower lip was a positive clue to her voluptuous nature.

"You don't clean and you wait until you're nearly starving to eat because you can't cook—"

"I never said I couldn't cook," he interrupted defensively.

A low, sultry laugh bubbled in her throat as she gave him a disbelieving stare. "No! *You* cook?"

"Yes, I do. And very well, too."

Caryn registered his annoyance at her implication of his ineptness along with a hint of cockiness. "What can you prepare?"

"Everything. You name it and I can prepare it."

"If that's the case, then what are you going to prepare for the Fourth of July celebration?"

A wide grin revealed the perfection of his straight white teeth. "My lip-smacking baby back ribs."

His fork dipped again, this time in the creamy cole slaw, but Caryn was too astounded by Logan's claim that he could cook to protest. "Where did you learn to cook?"

"Miss Nettie. She's my family's cook. She came to work for my parents several years after they'd adopted me. And when I was old enough to differentiate that I looked nothing like the man and woman whom I called Mama and Daddy, I instinctively gravitated to Miss Nettie."

"I take it Miss Nettie is African-American?" He nodded, smiling. Wrinkling her delicate nose, she gave him an expectant look. "Will you allow me to sample a few of your lip-smacking ribs before you take them to the celebration?"

"Of course," he replied quickly. "But only if you'd let me sample your contribution."

"I haven't decided what I want to make."

"You have only a day to make a decision."

Caryn picked up a fry with her fingers. "I'll probably bake several loaves of homemade bread, but I can't decide whether I want to make an antipasto platter or a seafood salad."

Logan took the wedge of sweet potato from her limp grasp and popped it into his mouth. "It probably would be easier to get the ingredients for the seafood salad than the antipasto."

"You're right." She slapped at his hand when he reached for another potato. "Logan, stop. You're eating all of my food."

"I promise I'll let you have some of mine when it comes."

And he kept his promise, spooning a portion of everything on his plate onto hers. They ate in silence, their gazes meeting across the small space of the table and surreptitiously measuring the other's reaction.

Logan reluctantly admitted that he was more than physically attracted to Caryn Edwards, and he now felt comfortable with her despite their initial acerbic encounter. She was beautiful, feminine, and appeared quite at ease with her femininity. And because she was, it was expected that men would be attracted to her. He had not been exempt.

"Where are you going after you leave here?" he questioned Caryn as she touched the corners of her mouth with a paper napkin.

"I'm going back to the house to pick up my car."

"You need a ride somewhere?"

She nodded. "I want to go to a larger supermarket." Marble Island's minimarket did not stock the items she needed to prepare a dish for the Fourth of July celebration.

I'll drive you. There are a few things I also have to pick up."

"You don't mind?"

"Not at all." And he didn't mind. Driving Caryn around would allow him more time with her. They'd shared breakfast and now lunch. And the more time he spent with his housemate, the more he wanted to spend with her. He didn't think he would've openly acknowledged it when he first stepped foot onto Marble Island, but now he had to admit to himself that he looked forward to sharing the house with a woman—especially if that woman was Miss Caryn Edwards.

Logan reached for the check at the same time Caryn withdrew her wallet from her oversized summer bag. "I'll get it. Consider it my treat. Besides, I ate most of the food."

Rising to her feet, she smiled as he rose with her. "The next one is on me."

He pulled out her chair and stood aside for her to precede him. The fingers of his right hand went to the small of her back, burning her sensitive flesh through the lacy cardigan top. Her spine stiffened as she fought the impulse to give in to the strength of his long, slender fingers.

Instead of waiting for him to pay the cashier, she walked

out of Addie's and into the brilliant summer sun, blinking furiously while she groped in the bottom of her bag for her sunglasses. She found them and perched them on the end of her nose, spying Logan's Wrangler in the parking lot.

"Ready?"

She jumped at the soft sound of his voice close to her ear. His approach had been so silent that she hadn't heard him come up behind her. Smiling up at him through the darkened lenses, she nodded.

For the second time within the span of minutes, Logan's hand went to her waist as he led her to his parked automobile. The gesture was so natural and anyone glancing their way could assume they were a "couple."

He opened the passenger side door. His hands circled her waist, and he lifted her effortlessly off the ground and settled her onto the seat. His ebony gaze bored into hers, he visually measuring her reaction.

"I thought you would have a problem trying to climb up with your *little* skirt," he explained when she lifted an eyebrow.

"It's not little."

He shrugged a broad shoulder. "Well—it is kind of tight."

Her sand-colored denim skirt was neither. It was slim, ending just at her knee, and therefore it would not have been difficult for her to raise it slightly to step up into the four-wheel-drive Jeep.

Giving him a dubious look, Caryn pulled the seat belt over her chest. A hint of a smile played at the corners of her mouth. Logan Prescott was either staid or very conservative. She'd packed one dress which she was certain to raise his eyebrows or make him stop in his tracks, and she made a mental note to model the garment at least once before he left Marble Island.

Logan started up the Jeep, slipped on his sunglasses, then maneuvered out of the parking lot, heading southward. The overhead sun beat down on his exposed flesh, and he mentally berated Caryn for refusing to wear a hat to protect her face. *She's not Nina,* a small voice reminded him. And she was nothing like Nina. Not in looks and not in temperament.

They rode in silence for twenty minutes, each lost in their private thoughts as a warm breeze caressed their faces and the distinctive smell of salt-filled air stung their nostrils. Seagulls sailed wind currents on a constant prowl for food, while the sun played hide-and-seek with white puffy clouds in a brilliant blue sky.

Caryn felt alive, physically and spiritually alive for the first time in years. She forgot the bitter words she'd traded with Tom before their idyllic marriage ended, and the months of loneliness she encountered since she'd walked away from the only man she'd ever loved. She forgot the shrouded fear that had controlled her life once she discovered she was being stalked by a student who unknowingly had become obsessed with her. The stalking began a month after she left Tom; a time when she was most vulnerable; a time when she needed the protection of her husband.

Inhaling, she savored the scent of the salt-filled air and marveled at the crashing waves washing the face of the beach with its incoming tide in the same way she felt cleansed and healed. She turned slightly, glancing at the sharp, distinctive, clear-cut lines of Logan Prescott's profile. He stared straight ahead, his regal head held high with pride. *He's a magnificent African prince,* she mused as her gaze kissed the length of his long, strong neck and wide shoulders. Her gaze inched down to his hands, admiring their shape and strength. When he'd lifted her effortlessly onto the seat of the Jeep, she'd registered the strength of his fingers, the power in his upper arms, and the haunting subtle scent of aftershave clinging to his smooth, dark cheek.

Logan felt the heat of the sun and also that of Caryn's gaze behind the lenses of her sunglasses on his face. He wondered what she was thinking, and for an instant he turned his head and stared back at her. Shrouded glass concealed the depths of their gazes from the other, yet both were aware of the deliberate interest in the other.

Returning his attention to the road in front of him, he turned off the local road and maneuvered into the strip mall containing a Winn-Dixie supermarket. "I'll help you down," he announced softly, turning the key in the ignition and shutting off the engine.

Caryn unbuckled her seat belt and waited for Logan to come around to her side of the car. He opened the door, extending his arms. Her slender arms circled his neck, and she felt the unyielding hardness in his powerful body for the first time as he molded her body to the length of his before slowly lowering her until her espadrille-covered feet touched the concrete surface of the parking lot.

They stood motionless, gazes fused. Caryn felt the heat sweep from her face, rush to her breasts, and still lower, and she was certain Logan felt the swell of her breasts against his chest as her nipples exploded against the lace of her bra and crocheted cardigan.

Closing her eyes, she prayed silently. It had been a long time, a very, very long time since she had acknowledged the absence of intimacy in her life. She could not begin to count the number of days, weeks, and now years since she had lain beside a man or taken him into her body.

Damn Logan for reminding her of what she'd missed and had been missing since she walked away from her husband. Why did he have to be so attractive, so male, and so very virile?

Pulling away from him, she turned and reached for her handbag off the floor of the Jeep. Then she straightened her shoulders and walked across the parking lot, heading for the supermarket and feeling the heat all over again as Logan's penetrating gaze followed her retreat.

Chapter Seven

Logan caught up with her before she could make her way through the automatic doors. The fingers of his right hand caught her left one, and he held it protectively as the sliding doors opened silently. They were met with a wave of cool air which feathered over their bare flesh, eliciting a noticeable shiver from Caryn.

"Are you cold?" he questioned. He released her hand and curved an arm around her shoulders, offering his body's heat. "I have a sweater in the car if you need it."

Rubbing her hands up and down her arms, she gave him a gentle smile. "Thanks for the offer, but I'll survive."

"Let's see how quickly we can shop so I can get you out of this igloo."

She nodded, still rubbing her arms. "You won't get an argument out of me."

Logan pushed a shopping cart up and down spacious aisles, following closely behind Caryn as she selected items from shelves, and refrigerator cases, and it wasn't until an elderly woman whispered to her husband that they looked like a "lovely young couple" did she realize the picture they presented.

Waiting until the older couple passed them, Logan pulled alongside Caryn, smiling. "Do you want to be Mrs. Prescott or would you prefer I become Mr. Edwards?"

"Behave," she whispered, returning his smile.

"You heard what they said, didn't you?"

"They said we look like a couple. That doesn't have to mean we're married."

"What do you think—"

"Raven!"

The words died on Logan's tongue when he turned around and spied a man whom he hadn't seen in years. "Ham!"

Caryn stood motionless, watching a tall, slender, tanned man with long, sun-streaked golden hair pull Logan against him in a rough embrace.

"Hamilton, you old dog. How long has it been?" Logan asked.

"Too long, Raven."

Draping an arm over his friend's shoulder, Logan extended a hand to Caryn. She took the proffered hand, and he pulled her close to his side. "Caryn, I want you to meet an old college buddy. H. Hamilton Wheaton. Ham, Miss Caryn Edwards."

Hamilton placed his left hand over his heart, extended his right, and bowed from the waist. "My pleasure, Caryn."

Logan slapped his back with a resounding thud. "Still the ham, aren't you?"

Hamilton straightened, his dark blue eyes twinkling with merriment. "I must live up to the nickname." His gaze swept appreciably over Caryn before it returned to Logan. "What are you doing this far south? Last I heard you had put down permanent roots in Raleigh. Leo Griffin told me you'd gone into business with your father."

Logan nodded as he studied the patrician features of the man who had been one of the more popular students on the Yale campus. "I do work with my father, but I'm taking a month off for some R&R."

"Where are you staying?"

"Marble Island. What about yourself?"

"We're practically neighbors. Cynthia and I are renting a little bungalow at Gooseneck."

Logan nodded at this news. Hamilton had married his college sweetheart during their senior year. "How long are you guys staying?"

"Until the end of July. Look, Raven, why don't we get together? You and Caryn and can hang out at our place for a few days."

Logan saw Caryn's warning glance. "Better yet, why don't the two of you come up to Marble Island, then we'll reciprocate," he suggested.

"Sounds good," Ham agreed. "How about this weekend?"

Logan arched a questioning eyebrow at Caryn. "Would you mind having company this weekend, sweetheart?"

Her gaze narrowed even though her mouth was smiling. "Of course not, *darling.*"

Hamilton combed his fingers through his tousled hair, pushing it off his forehead. Light caught the glow of a wide gold band on the third finger of his left hand. "Great. We'll come up Saturday afternoon and stay over until Sunday. How do I find the house?"

Caryn counted to ten—very, very slowly as Logan gave his friend directions to the house on Watermelon Patch Lane. She had left Asheville for Marble Island with the intent of spending two months alone. However, she hadn't been on the island for two full days, and within that time she was living with a man who had invited another man and his wife to stay with them. And the problem was she couldn't complain about it. Marcia and Terrence had given Logan permission to use the house, which meant he had just as much right to the property as she did.

One month, she told herself. She only had to put up with him for a month, then the house and the privacy she sought would be hers.

Hamilton embraced Logan again, smiling around his shoulder at Caryn. "I'll see you Saturday."

She returned his friendly smile and found some of her agitation slipping away. "I'm looking forward to it." Ham, as Logan called him, and his wife would be staying for only a day. After all, they were Logan's guests, not hers.

Logan waited until Hamilton walked away, then turned to Caryn. "Thanks for agreeing to share the house with my friends. They'll be my responsibility. I'll do the cooking and cleaning—"

"But you don't clean," she cut in.

He winked at her. "The twins will clean up." His expression sobered. "I'd like to ask a favor of you."

Her gaze fused with his. "What?"

"Will you be my hostess this weekend?"

He looked at her as if he were photographing her with his eyes. Something potent radiated from the depths of the dark pools, and Caryn felt like he'd reached inside of her and extracted what she'd withheld from any man—a recklessness, a need to let go of her iron-willed control. Tom had complained that she wasn't spontaneous enough and was at times quite boring.

There was something unknown, intangible, about Logan Prescott that made her want to throw off her mantle of feigned perfection. Everything in her life was orderly. She planned her days and weeks by a calendar, rarely deviating from her assigned tasks, and now and only now did she realize how banal her existence was. She had come to Marble Island to reflect and relax. She hadn't expected to share the house or her existence with another person—especially a man. She wasn't consciously looking for a summer romance or a relationship; but there was something about Logan that shattered her resolve, and within that second she decided to let her life play out. After all, Logan Prescott was going to share the house for only a month, and she was realistic enough to know not much could happen within that period of time.

"Yes, Logan. I'll be your hostess for the weekend."

He reached for her and cradled her head to his shoulder. His warmth swept over her cool body, bringing with it a sensual heat that threatened to scorch her bare flesh. Raising her chin, she smiled up at him.

"Thank you," he whispered, seconds before his head came down and his mouth covered hers in a soft, tender, healing kiss.

The healing was as much for him as it was for her. Both had loved and lost, both were carrying pain, and both sought healing from the other.

The kiss ended, the contact of flesh meeting flesh lasting only seconds, but it could have been longer, much longer, while a throbbing, lingering awareness remained.

Caryn was certain Logan felt her trembling under his touch, and what she did not want to acknowledge surged through her. He disturbed her; everything about him disturbed her sense of order and balance. There was no way she could ignore his blatant masculinity or her own voluntary celibacy.

Squaring her shoulders, she glanced up, a secretive smile softening her lips. "I'll be your hostess, but what I want you to try and remember is that we are *not* a couple."

Releasing her shoulders, he took a step backward. "You don't have to worry about that, because one thing I do have is an excellent memory."

"Now that we've settled that, let's finish up here. My teeth are beginning to chatter again."

They finished their shopping, and Logan suggested she wait outside in the Jeep while he paid for their purchases. She gave him a whispered thanks and made her way out of the supermarket and into the warmth of the summer sun. The contrast was startling as she reveled in the heat penetrating her chilled flesh.

Logan emerged through the automatic sliding doors, pushing a cart brimming with their purchases. Within minutes, he filled the cargo area and the backseats with a dozen paper sacks. He returned the cart to an area in the parking lot where others were lined up in neat rows.

Caryn watched his return as he walked toward the Jeep, her gaze measuring him behind the dark lenses of her sunglasses. His purposeful stride indicated confidence. He'd admitted to being spoiled, yet it hadn't overshadowed what she had come to recognize as his generous nature. She knew he had come to Marble Island to hide out and to work. However, he was willing to take time out to entertain his college friends while she wanted to covet every minute of her time on the island for her own purpose.

She smiled with his approach. The month she would spend with Logan Prescott would be good for her. Unknowingly he would teach her to share and help her to relax.

He swung himself up and behind the wheel with a minimum of motion, taking his sunglasses off the dashboard. "Is there anyplace else you'd like to stop before we go home?"

"I'd like to stop at that vegetable stand we passed on the way."

He slipped the key in the ignition and turned on the engine. "Your wish is my command."

She smiled at his profile. "I didn't know you were into granting wishes."

"Only one per day," he teased, flashing a wide grin.

Caryn affected a pout. "If I would've known that, then I'd really have thought of something good."

"There's always tomorrow."

She nodded, holding on to the roll bar as he swerved quickly to avoid hitting another Jeep Wrangler filled with at least a half-dozen adolescent boys and girls coming at them at more than forty miles an hour.

"Buttheads! I hope they survive the summer," Logan mumbled under his breath.

"They're just kids, Logan."

"They're fools."

She chuckled. "I can see you're not used to dealing with teenagers."

"And I suppose you like them?"

"In fact I do. That's why I decided to teach seven through twelve. They're not quite adults, but I find it easier to reason with them than the ones in the lower grades. I try not to interact with them as if they're children, because they aren't. They are exactly what they are—young adults."

"Don't the boys try to hit on you?"

"Not usually."

He gave her a quick glance. "I take it there was an exception?"

"Once."

"What happened, Caryn?"

Closing her eyes, she relived the terror she experienced whenever she saw the boy watching her when she stepped out of her house or glanced over her shoulder.

"A student stalked me for about two months."

A frown furrowed Logan's smooth forehead. "What did your husband do to protect you?"

"He couldn't protect me because we were separated at the time."

"You were still his wife, which meant he should've protected you."

"I finally went to the police, and they handled it."

"He stopped?"

She nodded. "His parents transferred him to another school."

"And that ended it?"

"I have to assume his father being warden of a state prison had something to do with it." She smiled when Logan whistled under his breath. "Why did your friend call you Raven?" she questioned, quickly changing the topic of conversation.

"I was captain of Yale's rowing team, and everyone said I resembled a bird flying across the water. Given my race and my coloring, the name was quite fitting."

That explained his developed upper body, she mused. "So, you're a Yale man. Somehow I had you pegged as a Howard or Morehouse brother."

"Before graduating high school, I applied to Howard, Yale, Morehouse, and Harvard. They all accepted me, but I decided on Yale because my father was a Yale man and his father before him. Every American Prescott man has been a Yale man except for one."

"What happened to break the tradition?"

"The Civil War. Johnston Edicott Prescott went to William and Mary instead. What college did you go to?"

"Vanderbilt."

"Very nice. What was your major?"

"Literature. And yours?"

"Architecture."

"Why architecture?"

"My father is an architect."

She remembered him saying he worked for his father. "Did you become an architect because you wanted to, or did your father insist on it?"

"My father never insisted I do anything I didn't want to do. It wasn't until years later, that I understood why I always got a rush when Dad unrolled his blueprints. The first time I completed a set of plans, my hands shook so hard, I had a problem signing them. My father stood at my side, nodding his head slowly, while his eyes filled with tears. The emotion of seeing your final creation on paper is inexplicable."

"Do you experience the same emotion after seeing the actual structure completed?"

He was silent for a moment, shaking his head. "The feelings are not the same. It's like writing a symphony, then having someone else play what you've created. You sit back, detached, and hold your breath, while listening for mistakes. Once I saw the first house I designed constructed, I became very critical, telling myself I should've done this or that."

"Are you good, Logan?"

He heard the velvet softness of her voice; he turned, and took a quick glance at her profile. "I was. Some of my designs have won awards."

Her eyebrows shifted. "Was?"

"I haven't personally designed anything in years. I'm now what is called an urban planner."

"Do you like it better?"

He shrugged a broad shoulder. "It's satisfying."

Caryn exhaled audibly. He was satisfied with his work, while she wasn't certain whether she would continue classroom teaching. The notion of returning to college to enroll in courses for school administration had nagged at her for more than a year, but her indecisiveness would not permit to give up the classroom. Not yet.

"Have you ever met your birth mother?"

Logan registered the soft hesitancy in her question. It was as if she didn't want to pry, but needed to know what others had openly expressed once they realized he did not share the same physical characteristics as his adopted parents.

He shook his head slowly. "No." And it was not as if he didn't know who she was. "She was the daughter of a very prominent educator who found herself pregnant at fourteen.

"Meanwhile Maeve Prescott had tried unsuccessfully for years to adopt a white infant after she discovered she would never have children. But when she unwittingly discovered that the college president's daughter was pregnant, she approached him and asked to adopt the baby. At first he balked because of her race, then agreed and everything was arranged beforehand.

"He sent his daughter up North to live with a relative to escape what was certain to become a scandalous scenario for his family. I was delivered at a small, private hospital. My biological mother never saw me, and when the doctor filed the papers recording my birth, the entry for my mother's name read Maeve Logan. Jace Prescott was listed as the father. Maeve and Jace Prescott returned to Raleigh with a son whom they'd named Logan."

"Was that legal?"

"As legal as if Maeve had given birth herself."

"Is your birth mother still alive?"

Exhaling audibly, Logan nodded slowly. "Yes. She married an elected official and is the mother of two teenage daughters. Whenever I see photographs of her, she appears very happy, and there is nothing I would do to destroy that happiness. Even though her parents forced her to give up her first child, I believe everyone came out a winner."

What he didn't tell Caryn was that his birth mother never knew the man and woman who claimed her firstborn for their own.

"You were very fortunate."

"I've been blessed, Caryn. I love my parents very much, and there isn't anything I would do to hurt them."

But he had hurt them. He remembered about how disappointed his father was when he told him that he wasn't going to marry Nina. Jace merely nodded, saying he would abide with his decision. Maeve's navy-blue eyes had filled with tears, overflowed, and stained her pale cheeks. There was no way she could hide the pain when he'd held her and whispered that it was best he end the relationship now rather than have it end years later in a divorce. Maeve had forced a smile after he reminded her that when Prescott men married, they married for life.

The vegetable stand came into view alongside the road, and Logan maneuvered behind a battered pickup truck loaded with watermelons. He applied the parking brake, but did not turn off the engine. Hopping down nimbly, he came around and swung Caryn to the sand-littered grass.

He waited while she selected a watermelon and several containers filled with fresh berries. A middle-aged couple totaled her purchases, and he paid for them. He cradled the large watermelon under his arm, while Caryn carried a carton with the berries back to the automobile.

He placed the watermelon on the floor behind the front seats, then adjusted a sack of groceries on the backseat to make room for the berries.

"Do you need anything else?" he asked.

"If I did, where would we put it?"

"You're right about that."

Lifting her skirt, she attempted to climb up into the

four-wheel-drive vehicle, but was thwarted when Logan's fingers circled her waist and lifted her effortlessly.

She smiled down at him, the gesture causing his breathing to falter. "Thank you again."

He nodded. She'd flashed the smile he'd seen her give the young store clerk and Randy Bell. Whether she was aware of it or not, she was seducing him. But what surprised him was that he wanted to be seduced. There was something about Caryn Edwards that said if they did have a summer affair she would be as mature about it as he was certain he would be. They would enjoy each other's company, and when it ended it would end smoothly without guilt or emotional entanglements. Maybe, just maybe he would let down his guard and let himself succumb to her seductive wiles.

Chapter Eight

The remainder of the afternoon passed quickly for Caryn. She and Logan returned to Marble Island, put away their purchases, then retreated to what had become their sanctuaries. For her it was the family room and for him the front porch. After changing into a pair of shorts with an oversized T-shirt, she picked up her journal and concluded her entries for the day:

I must admit it has been a very interesting day. I hadn't planned to spend it with Logan Prescott—he finally revealed his last name, but I wasn't given much of a choice. Now that I know who he is, I understand why he's hiding out on Marble Island. He's the one who jilted the very beautiful and very wealthy Nina Smith. And there's no doubt her father is gunning for him, so if I were Mr. Prescott, I would seriously consider changing my zip code—to another state.

Lunch was very interesting and what followed equally interesting. We drove down the coast to a larger supermarket where Logan ran into a college friend who is vacationing on Gooseneck with his wife. They were Yale men, and Logan was captain of their rowing team. His friend Hamilton—

Logan calls him Ham—invited us to stay over with him and his wife. but thankfully Logan convinced him to stay with us. I much prefer to be the host rather than a guest, especially if sleeping accommodations become questionable. There is no way I could share a bed with Logan and remain celibate.

I'm certain of this because of his kiss—not a deep, soul kiss, but still a kiss which left me wanting more. I try rationalizing my wanting more is due to a lack of intimacy for more years than I want to remember, but I must be honest with myself. Logan "Raven" Prescott can turn me on with just a glance. There's something so mysteriously sensual about him that my insides quiver with an awareness of my femininity that no man—and that includes Tom—could elicit. It is exciting as well as frightening. I don't know what will happen between us—there's no guarantee anything will—however, a secret voice is telling me to just enjoy it, while the voice of reason says "don't go there." I suppose I'm going to have to let it all play out.

Raven—the nickname is quite fitting—is a trained architect who now prefers urban planning—lives in Raleigh and works for his father. Speaking of his parents—he's adopted. There's no doubt he's been spoiled and is quite privileged. But I must admit that he appears very well adjusted emotionally, considering his parents are caucasian. And if I had one word to sum up Logan Prescott, it would be unique.

Caryn read her small, neat slanting script, smiling. Logan admitted he liked her, and she also had to admit to herself that she was beginning to like him. She was still smiling when she stood up, and her bare feet were silent as she made her way up the staircase to her bedroom and placed her journal on the bedside table. Standing at the window, she was aware of how quickly dusk had descended as the setting sun resembled a large orange basketball suspended in midair.

Watching nature prepare for nightfall was awesome. The

sky darkened to a soft gray, then a deeper blue to reveal a spray of stars dotting its surface. The sun was now a blood red as it sank slowly beyond the horizon until it disappeared from view. A full moon lit up the summer sky, and she tried making out some of the constellations visible to the naked eye.

She wasn't certain how long she'd stood at the window when she heard Domino's excited barking. A tender smile softened her mouth at the same time she spied the spotted puppy frolicking on the sand. She watched him make his way toward the incoming tide, then retreat whenever the breaking waves washed over his paws. The dog repeated his game of tag with the ocean until a high-pitched whistle garnered his attention. Standing completely still, he turned his head, then bounded back to the house.

She wanted to go downstairs and sit on the porch, but did not want to intrude on Logan and his pet. It was only nine-fifteen, but she decided to go to bed early again. Making her way across the bedroom, she closed the door.

Logan took Domino for his last walk, then returned to the porch. He'd managed to get some work done, not much, but at least he'd made an attempt. The architects at J. Prescott and Associates had designed the structures for a private community he'd projected to be as self-sufficient as a small city. The scheme was modeled to accommodate close to a thousand residents, who if they purchased units would live less than an hour's drive from downtown Raleigh.

He recalled his excitement when he'd first revealed the idea to Nina and her reaction. She did what she always did whenever he told her of his visions—she listened intently. And not once had she ever given him any feedback other than, "That sounds wonderful."

And he thought she had been wonderful. He'd told himself that she would make a wonderful wife and a wonderful mother. His mouth tightened. How wrong he'd been.

The distinctive sound of a telephone interrupted his tortured thoughts. It rang three times before he attempted to go into the house to answer it. He made it to the kitchen and picked up the receiver on the fifth ring.

"Hello."

There was a noticeable pause before a strong, masculine voice came through the wire. "May I please speak to Caryn Edwards."

Logan hesitated. "Hold on and I'll get her." His tone was polite, but he was feeling anything but polite. It had taken only two days for the men to begin their pursuit of his beautiful housemate. The family room was dark, so he knew Caryn had to be upstairs.

Taking the stairs two at a time, he walked down the hallway and knocked on her door. "Caryn. You have a phone call." He waited, then knocked again. His hand was poised to knock a third time when the door swung open.

Caryn stood in front of him, her damp hair falling over her shoulders. His penetrating gaze moved slowly and seductively from her face to her chest. It was apparent that she'd hastily thrown on a silky, peach-colored kimono to conceal her nakedness.

"You have a telephone call," he repeated as she secured a matching belt around her narrow waist.

The smoldering flame she saw in his bold stare startled Caryn. She couldn't move. It was as if he'd hypnotized her, rendering her motionless. She forced herself to take a step, but he blocked her means of egress.

She heard the runaway beating of her heart outside of her body, and she was certain he also heard it. "Logan." His name was a whispery breathless sigh.

He was motionless, rooted to the spot. Nothing moved, not even his eyes. "Yes." The single word came out like a long, drawn-out shudder.

The sound of his voice broke the spell as Caryn took another step, bringing her only inches from the man who had invaded her space, her existence. "I have to answer the phone."

Turning to his right, the motion so fluid and quick she thought she'd imagined it, he stepped out of the doorway. His gaze followed her as she brushed past him and made her way down the hallway to the room the Crawfords used for their library.

Closing his eyes, he luxuriated in the haunting fragrance of her perfume-scented flesh. Even with his eyes closed, he still could recall the vision of her damp black hair curling over her forehead, the sun-browned darkness of her fragile face, the brilliance of her large gold-green eyes, and the softly rounded curves of her very feminine body.

It was difficult, and becoming even more difficult with each passing hour to dismiss Miss Caryn Edwards. Unknowingly he had run away from one woman to find another who enchanted him as no other had before.

He'd tried not succumbing to the bewitching aura surrounding Caryn and had failed miserably. And it was only now he realized his attraction to his housemate had nothing to do with a physical temptation. Opening his eyes, he stared down the hall, a slight smile softening his mouth. It was about Caryn—the woman. Sharing his afternoon with her had been totally relaxing and comfortable. An invisible bond had surrounded him when he strolled up and down the wide aisles of the supermarket when they shopped for groceries. He'd felt a warm glow after the older woman had referred to them as a "lovely young couple."

And he wanted to be a couple. At thirty-five he wanted to settle down, marry, and father children. He'd become a successful architect and urban planner, but his personal life was not as tidy and orderly as his career. However, he had believed he would achieve the elusive personal success the moment he'd proposed sharing his life with Nina Smith.

Inhaling and letting out his breath slowly, he walked down the hallway and returned to the lower level. Entering the kitchen, he replaced the receiver of the wall telephone on its cradle, and in the few seconds it took to complete the motion he heard the soft laughter of Caryn's voice mingling with that of the man who'd called her.

"What are you hiding from me, baby sister?"

Caryn settled herself on a rattan rocker and raised her bare feet to a matching cushioned ottoman. "I'm not hiding anything, Kyle." There was just a hint of laughter in her voice.

"You tell me that I won't see you this summer because you need to spend some time alone to *find yourself.* Does finding yourself include living with a man?"

"Don't be such a stuffed shirt, Kyle Edwards," she admonished her brother. "I'm not living with a man. I'm sharing the house with him." There was a noticeable pause. "And you'd better not start in on me. Even if I *were* living with a man, there's nothing wrong with—"

"Hold up, Caryn," Kyle interrupted. "I'm not judging you. You should know me better than that. If you are living with a man, then I applaud it. You have to know all of us were worried about you when you broke up with Thomas."

She winced. "Please don't ever mention his name again."

Kyle chuckled. "You have my word on that. What I'm trying to say is you managed to convince me that you were pretty much turned off of men."

"I'm not turned off of men. I just don't want to go out with your partner."

"You know Larry still asks about you."

"That's nice, but I still won't date him." Lawrence Mackie was her brother's business associate. The two men had formed a partnership and had established the largest Black-owned foreign car dealership in Philadelphia. And what Kyle failed to realize was what she recognized immediately in Larry's personality was something she failed to realize in Tom's until it was too late. Both men unconsciously regarded females as inferiors and therefore felt the need to control, dominate, and subjugate a woman. It had happened once, and she would never permit it to happen again. Not with *any* man.

"The kids have been asking for you," Kyle continued. "They miss you."

"Tell them I'll come up in the fall."

"You'll hardly recognize them by then. Both are growing like weeds."

Her nine-year-old niece and seven-year-old nephew had inherited their father's rawboned lankiness.

"We don't get to see you enough, Caryn."

"The past few years haven't been the best," she admitted.

"That's why you need your family."

"What I need is to get my head together. And for that I need time alone."

She and Kyle talked for another ten minutes, laughing at the latest escapades his children had managed to get into. She ended the conversation confirming her visit to Philadelphia in the fall, then hung up.

Hearing her brother's voice elicited a feeling of loneliness and detachment. Kyle missed her and she missed him. She missed his wife, their children, and her parents, but she would endure the sacrifice in order to put her life in order.

She returned to her bedroom, closed the door, slipped out of her robe, and got into bed. Picking up the paperback novel on a stack of a half dozen, she opened to the first page of Ralph Ellison's *Invisible Man.* She had promised herself she would try to reread as many of her favorite novels as she could over the next two months.

She managed to finish thirty pages before reaching over to turn off the bedside lamp, plunging the room into darkness. Closing her eyes, she slept without any dreams to disturb her restful slumber.

* * *

Caryn awoke early, an hour before sunrise, refreshed, and to the sound of rain tapping softly against the windows. Rain always made her want to remain in bed and snuggle under the blankets, but she decided to forego the luxury when she remembered she had to put up several batches of dough. Her donation to the Fourth of July celebration would be a cheese and chive braided loaf, several dozen leek and bacon garlic knots, and a watermelon boat filled with fresh melon balls and berries.

Slipping out of bed, she reached for her bathrobe, shivering slightly against the dampness seeping into the room from the open window. How quickly the weather had changed from sunny and hot to cloudy and wet.

Within half an hour she'd made her bed, showered, and was dressed in a pair of faded jeans with an equally faded college sweatshirt, and a pair of thick white socks. She brushed and braided her hair in a single plait, securing the curling end with an elastic band.

Staring at her reflection in the full-length mirror on the back of the bathroom door, she realized she looked no older than some of her students with her face free of makeup and her hair pulled back in the braid. However, she did notice the slight puffiness under her eyes that had been a constant reminder of her stress was no longer visible. Going to bed early the past two nights and sleeping undisturbed throughout the night had taken care of most of her physical fatigue.

She walked out of her bedroom and noted the door to Logan's was closed. It wasn't quite five o'clock, and it was apparent that he was still asleep. The house was dark, quiet, and she turned on several table lamps, hoping to dispel the gloominess.

Logan walked into the kitchen at exactly six o'clock and found it filled with the enticing smell of brewing coffee and the sight of Caryn kneading dough on a floured countertop. The overhead light shone down on her jet-black shiny hair and highlighted the rich burnished gold undertones in her bronzed face.

He found himself studying her, trying to discover what it was that drew him to her. It couldn't have been the way she looked physically because he'd always found himself attracted to taller, darker women. And although there was a seven-year difference in their ages, he usually dated women who were no more than a year or two younger than he was, but there were times when he did date those who were older. He had made it a practice to stay away from the ones who'd elected to act like girls, because he detested playing head games or public histrionics. Several had accused him of being too serious, but he was quite comfortable with who he had become. He smiled. Caryn Edwards was different. She may look young, but she was no girl.

"Good morning."

Caryn's head came up quickly, and she smiled at Logan leaning against the entrance to the kitchen, muscular arms crossed over his navy-blue T-shirt. Like herself, he also wore a pair of jeans.

"Good morning," she returned, giving him the sensual smile he'd come to look for. "Coffee's on if you'd like a cup."

He returned her smile. "As soon as I let Domino out, I'll take you up on your offer."

"I'm also offering breakfast this morning."

Logan stared, complete surprise on his face. Nina had never offered to prepare breakfast or any meal for him, even though he had made it a practice to cook for her whenever she spent time at his place.

"Why, thank you."

Caryn nodded, then turned her attention back to the dough. Giving Logan breakfast was the least she could do. After all, he had paid for all of the groceries.

She turned a large ball of dough mixed with shredded cheddar cheese, fresh chives, and green onions into an oiled bowl and covered it with a clean towel. She then repeated the process with a dough mixture of sauteed leeks and crisp broiled crumbled bacon. Both would double in bulk before she rolled them out into ropes for a large braided bread loaf and dozens of smaller leek and bacon knots.

She chopped green and red peppers and added it to a reserve of finely chopped sauteed leeks and a small portion of shredded cheese. Working quickly and efficiently, she then rolled out biscuits with a hint of cinnamon and brown sugar.

Logan returned, sans his wet running shoes, drying his hands before he wiped a sheen of moisture from his hair and face with a towel.

"How is it outside?" she asked at the same time as she leaned over and placed the pan of biscuits in the heated oven.

"Damp. It looks as if it's going to rain all day."

Straightening, she stared at him. Suddenly the space seemed smaller with his presence, and she found it difficult to draw a normal breath with him standing less than five feet away. Her gaze was fixed on the breadth of his wide shoulders and powerfully developed upper body. She recalled the sight of his half-naked body when he'd left to go jogging the day before, and the heat in her face had nothing to do with the increasing warmth from the oven.

Tilting his head at an angle, he regarded her with silent expectation. "Do you need any help?"

She nodded quickly. She needed him to do something, anything, except stand around and stare at her. "You can set the table."

He returned the towel to the half-bath off the kitchen, then busied himself taking down plates, cups, and saucers from the overhead cabinets.

"Do you want to eat in the dining room or in the kitchen?"

"The kitchen," Caryn replied. And she always preferred eating breakfast in the kitchen with the lingering smells of brewing coffee, broiling bacon, and baking breads. Dining rooms were better suited for lunch or dinner.

Logan set the round oaken table situated where they would have a view of the outside porch with serviceable tableware and cutlery before Caryn directed him to remove a bowl of fresh fruit from the refrigerator. She broiled strips of bacon on the stovetop griddle, then added beaten eggs filled with the pepper, leek, and cheddar mixture.

The rising wind swirled the falling rain in a slanting pattern, and Logan quickly checked all of the windows to make certain they were shut. He returned to the kitchen and to the enticing sight of the table filled with platters of hot biscuits, fluffy omelets, and cups of fragrant coffee and a fresh fruit medley.

"Don't be shy. Sit down and eat, Logan."

He circled the table and pulled out a chair for her. She sat down and he lingered over her head, the cloying fragrance of his hauntingly sensual aftershave wafting in her nostrils.

She smiled up at him. "Thank you."

Leaning over, he kissed the tip of her nose. "I'm thanking you in advance for breakfast," he explained, as she gave him a puzzled look.

He flipped on the radio and turned the dial until he found a station that featured soft jazz, then rejoined Caryn at the table. Picking up a fork, he speared a portion of blackberries and cantaloupe. "Where did you learn to cook like this?" he questioned after biting into a fluffy biscuit.

"My dad taught me. He's a retired chef."

"And your mother?"

"She's a retired interior designer."

Logan swallowed a piece of crisp bacon, staring across the table at his dining partner. Caryn was only twenty-eight, and he wondered how old her parents could be. "I assume they retired young?"

She nodded. "They retired two years ago. Daddy was fifty-eight and Mama was fifty-five."

"That's young."

"They worked steadily for thirty years without taking a vacation."

Logan's coffee cup was poised in midair. "What did they do?"

"They owned a string of bed-and-breakfasts along the East Coast. They started out with one in western Pennsylvania, then managed to add one every three years. They usually bought a large house that was in foreclosure and renovated it. Mama decorated all of the rooms while Daddy hired the staff. He made it a practice to recruit the best students from culinary schools all over the country, offering them starting salaries they couldn't refuse. Each B&B was set up with the same menu with one exception."

"What was that?"

"Each chef was allowed to create one special dish. And the dish always bore their name."

"Who runs them now?"

"A consortium of restauranteurs."

"Why didn't your brother take over?"

"Kyle is a salesman, not a chef. My very smooth, silver-tongued brother can convince someone to buy a Lamborghini or a Ferrari in less than two hours, yet he can't boil an egg."

A bright smile crossed Logan's face. "A Lamborghini. Now, that's a beautiful machine."

Caryn put down her fork. "Don't tell me you're also into outrageously overpriced vehicles?"

"I happen to like Ferraris."

She wrinkled her nose. "You men and your toys."

"Either it's cars or women. And I much prefer to collect cars."

"Why must men always collect something?"

Leaning back on his chair, Logan gave her a penetrating stare. "And you women don't?"

"Not like men."

"How about material things?"

"Not in the least."

"I've known women who make it a practice to collect

engagement rings. Others collect husbands, while some lovers."

"And some men find it necessary to keep a count of their conquests," she shot back.

"I'm not one of those who do," he admitted softly.

Caryn noticed Logan watching her intently. It was as if he were waiting—for what she didn't know.

"What do you collect, Caryn Edwards? First-edition books? Or perhaps love letters?"

She dropped her gaze, staring at his well-formed hands. "I collect journals."

"Medical journals?"

She shook her head. "Personal journals." Tilting her chin, she met his unwavering midnight gaze. "My mother gave me a beautiful tapestry-covered journal for my sixteenth birthday. She told me to write down my dreams and aspirations, and then one day read the entries to find out whether any of them had come true."

Reaching across the table, Logan caught her hand, his fingers tightening as she attempted to free herself. "Have any of them come true?"

Biting down on her lower lip, she closed her eyes. "Some of them."

He saw the quivering muscle in her delicate jaw. "You wanted to marry and you did," he said perceptively. She nodded, not opening her eyes. "And you wanted children?" Again she nodded. "It can happen, Caryn. Just because it didn't work out the first time, that doesn't mean you can't try again."

Her eyes opened and she glared at him. "It can't happen again."

"Why not?" he shot back.

"Because I'll never allow a man to control my life again."

"Marriage is not about control. It's about loving, sharing, and give and take. No one person is right all of the time, and no one person is wrong all of the time."

The bitterness she'd always directed at Tom was transferred to Logan, and at that moment Logan Prescott became Thomas Duff. "You're a fine one to talk. If you know so much, then why did you call off your wedding a week before you were to be married?"

Without warning, he released her fingers and stood up. His chair clattered noisily to the floor behind him. "Wouldn't you if you caught your future husband in bed with your maid-of-honor?"

She gasped loudly, covering her mouth with her hand. "Oh no, Logan," she mumbled through her fingers.

"Oh yes, Caryn," he countered angrily, picking up the chair and stalking out of the kitchen.

Chapter Nine

Caryn stared at the place where Logan had sat, debating whether to go after him. She knew he was entitled to his privacy, but it wasn't as if he hadn't told her what she knew he hadn't told anyone else—not even his parents.

Rising from her chair, she walked out of the kitchen to the place where she was certain to find him. He stood on the porch, hands at his sides, fingers curled into tight fists, staring out at the falling rain.

Wouldn't you if you caught your future husband in bed with your maid-of-honor? She replayed Logan's query, feeling his pain as surely as if it were her own; and whatever she thought of her ex-husband, there was one thing she knew Tom hadn't been and that was unfaithful.

Pushing open the screen door, Caryn stepped out onto the porch and stood behind Logan. She was less than a foot away, and she knew he had to know she was there even though he hadn't moved. Taking another tentative step, she curved her arms around his waist, offering comfort and understanding.

"You did the right thing, calling off the wedding," she

whispered. She felt him stiffen slightly before he relaxed enough to unclench his fingers.

Logan drew in a deep breath, holding it until he felt his lungs burn. He wanted to punish himself for not acknowledging what he should've known sooner. How could he have been so blinded by beauty and sophistication that he was unable to see the real Nina Smith? There were times when he second-guessed himself and said it wasn't her beauty that blinded him as much as it was her passion—a passion that always left him wanting more. She offered herself to him, but he never got enough of her, and that was when he surmised he couldn't exist without her. But he had survived and would continue to exist without her in his life. The past two weeks had verified that.

Logan grasped the slender arms circling his waist, feeding on their delicate softness. He had yet to figure out what it was about Caryn Edwards that prompted him to bare the secret he hadn't revealed to anyone, not even his parents. Jace and Maeve Prescott deserved more than the explanation he'd offered. He owed them more than *I've decided not to marry Nina.*

Caryn moved closer, the pressure of her firm breasts burned his flesh through the T-shirt. He held his breath again, this time not to punish himself but to counter the shock of his body's response to her womanly heat. Closing his eyes, he felt her relax as she laid her cheek against his back. They held the position a full minute before he unclasped her hands and turned to face her.

Holding her hands, his penetrating gaze searched her face, lingering on her tempting mouth. Lowering his head, he brushed his mouth over hers repeatedly with soft, nibbling kisses. Her moist breath mingled with his, her lips parting slightly.

He gathered her closer and buried his face in her fragrant-smelling hair. "Thank you for helping me unburden myself," he whispered against her ear. "Just saying the words has helped me let go of some of my anger and guilt."

Caryn snuggled closer, unconsciously seeking Logan's protection. It had been a long time, too long, since she'd experienced a man's protection. "Why should you feel guilty about ending a relationship based on infidelity?"

"It's not about Nina, but my parents. I don't know whether it was the first time Nina and Wayne slept together or the hundredth. The fact remains, he's a lifelong friend and she was to become my wife. I don't owe either of them an explanation. But on the other hand, my mother and father deserve more than my trite statement that I was calling off the wedding."

Pulling back, Caryn smiled up at him. "It's not too late to explain, Logan. Call and tell them what happened." He hesitated, giving no indication whether he would follow through on her suggestion. "Do it," she urged in a quiet tone. "It's time you put some of your demons to rest."

His hands fell away and he took a step backward. "You think I have demons tormenting me?"

She detected a hint of censure in his tone. "Yes, I do. Otherwise why would someone as young as you be, as my students would say, 'such a tight-ass.' "

Logan stared at Caryn with complete surprise on his face. "Is that how you see me? You think I'm uptight?"

"Very."

Crossing his arms over his chest, he regarded her with a disapproving look. "I suppose I'll have to prove you wrong, won't I?"

"Don't challenge me, Mr. Prescott, because you'll only come up a loser."

"We'll have to see about that." His frown vanished, replaced by a bright smile.

Caryn returned his smile. "Yes, we will." Turning, she opened the screen door and walked back into the house, leaving him on the porch staring at her retreating figure.

Logan's smile was still in place as he folded his long frame down to a cushioned chair. The wind had died down, and the rain had slacked off to a steady drizzle. A little scrap of a woman with near-waist-length hair and gold-green eyes had challenged him. He had to admit he was a bit too serious at times, but certainly not a tight-ass, as Caryn had referred to him. She was wrong, and he would prove her wrong, but first he would call his mother and explain why she would never claim Nina Smith as her daughter-in-law.

He went into the house and up the stairs to his bedroom. He retrieved the cellular phone and dialed his parents' residence.

"Good morning."

Logan smiled when he heard the soft, drawling greeting of Maeve Prescott's. "Good morning, Mama."

"Oh! My baby!"

"Mama," he said softly, "I stopped being your baby years ago."

"Don't you dare lecture me, Logan Prescott. As your mother I can call you anything I please."

Rolling his eyes upward, he shook his head. He'd always thought of Maeve as a motherhood zealot.

"Yes, ma'am."

"That's better. How are you, sweetheart?

"Wonderful. I just settled in, and I must say the house and Marble Island are the perfect places for an impromptu vacation."

"Have you decided how long you'll be down there?"

"Probably until the end of the month." He paused. "I'm calling because I have to tell you something."

"And what is that?"

"You deserve to know why I decided not to marry Nina."

"You don't have to tell me if you don't want to, Logan."

"I *need* to tell you." He paused, closing his eyes and reliving the scene in Nina's bedroom. "I walked in on Nina and found her in bed with Wayne Singleton."

A gasp came through the line before Maeve responded. "Oh, sweet heaven, no!"

He opened his eyes. "They didn't know I saw them."

"Oh, baby, I'm sorry."

"So am I, Mama."

"I never thought she would be such a—a trollop. And with your best friend, no less." Logan forced back a smile at Maeve's description of Nina's morals. "And she has the nerve to come here every day asking for you," Maeve continued. "Of course, Jace and I haven't told her where you are. But don't worry your heart, baby. I know you'll find someone who'll be faithful to you. And I'm certain she'll love you as much as you deserve to be loved."

"I'm not looking for anyone right now. I need a lot of time to unload some emotional baggage."

"Don't take too long. I'd like to claim grandmother status before I turn eighty."

"You're only sixty-six. What's the rush?"

"The rush is that all of the women in my social club are grandmothers. Some of the more catty ladies always manage to give me pitying looks when they pull out updated pictures of their grandchildren."

Logan shook his head. "If that's the case, then why do you socialize with them?"

"Why? Because they're my *friends.*"

He wanted to suggest that she select a new set of friends, but didn't. "Tell Dad I should complete the preliminary draft for the zoning board on the Fairview project next week." J. Prescott and Associates had to have the zoning board's approval before they could secure the necessary financing for construction.

"I'll tell him to call you."

"Remind him not to give out this phone number for any reason. I promise to call you in a couple of days."

"Thank you, sweetheart. I love you, Logan."

"And I love you."

He rang off, feeling as if most of his problems had vanished like a puff of smoke. Caryn was right. His confession made him feel less uptight. "But I'm still not a tight-ass," he mumbled as he made his way down the staircase.

He found Caryn in the kitchen, stacking dishes in the dishwasher. Moving behind her, he pulled her back against his chest. "Thanks, friend," he whispered close to her ear.

Turning in his loose embrace, she smiled up at him. "Anytime, friend."

"I want to thank you twice: for the advice and for a wonderful breakfast." He kissed the right side of her mouth, then the left, feeling her stiffen in his arms. "Relax."

"I am," she countered, wiggling and trying to free herself. "Please let me go, Logan. I have work to do."

Instead of releasing her, he tightened his hold on her waist. "Now, who's uptight?"

She frowned up at him. "I'm not uptight."

"Then relax. I'm not going to bite you."

He increased his grip on her body, pulling her closer and allowing her to feel the hard planes of his muscular physique. Caryn ceased struggling, realizing it was useless against his superior strength. Her arms moved tentatively up and around his waist as she laid her cheek against his chest, listening to the calm, steady pumping of his heart. Closing her eyes, she counted the beats of his heart and was amazed when her own slowed to a matching rhythm.

He emitted a low sigh of satisfaction when she went completely pliant in his embrace. Now that she was in his arms, she had no desire to pull away. The crush of his body was so warm, so male. Her mind told her to resist and reject Logan Prescott, but her body refused to follow the dictates of her head. *This is not supposed to happen,* a secret voice whispered to her.

Caryn lost track of time as they offered each other healing, she floating to another dimension and marveling at the sense of fulfillment she felt in Logan's arms. When she'd first arrived on Marble Island, she thought she wanted to be totally alone. But with him holding her, she knew she'd lied to herself.

"What did he do to you to make you leave him?"

She jumped, the sound of his voice startling her more than his question. She gave him a questioning look. He'd bared his soul and his innermost secrets, and he expected her to do the same. He'd had secrets, and so did she; secrets she would never tell anyone.

Composing her thoughts, she began very quietly, "Thomas Duff did everything for me except breathe. He planned our lives by the clock. At first I welcomed it because I'm also pedantic, but he took it to an extreme. We ate dinner every night at the same time, not a minute before or a minute after. We went to the supermarket every second and fourth Saturday at exactly 10:00 A.M. And he washed our cars every Sunday morning at nine, rain or shine. He claimed the car wash didn't clean them the way he wanted them cleaned. I finally realized no one could meet his standards.

"His dogmatic behavior didn't begin to bother me until he began complaining about my style of dress, how I wore my hair or my makeup. We'd make a date to have dinner at a restaurant, but if I showed up wearing something he didn't approve of, he would cancel the reservation and walk out.

"Then we began arguing about everything: which movies to see, where to go on vacation, who to invite for dinner parties, when to make love, when I should get pregnant, and on and on.

"The final straw came when he wanted me to give up my teaching position to become a full-time housewife. He claimed I couldn't handle working outside the home and tend to his needs at the same time. What he actually believed was that I was having an affair with one of the male teachers. One day I woke up and decided it was over. I moved out of my perfect little house, left my very perfect husband with only my personal possessions, and filed for a divorce. The divorce proceedings were less than amicable because Tom contested everything. My leaving him indicated that he'd failed as a husband.

"I wanted nothing from the union except my maiden name, while he missed court appearances because of undocumented catastrophic illnesses. What helped Tom was that as a very popular attorney he knew all of the judges in Asheville, who occasionally overlooked his blatant attempt to postpone the final decree."

Logan shifted an eyebrow. "The man sounds as if he needs professional counseling."

"Tell that to his second wife."

"He remarried?"

She nodded slowly. "There was no reason for him to remain single for any appreciable length of time. He presents a very attractive package: intellect, good looks, and excellent resources."

Lowering his head, Logan pressed a comforting kiss on her forehead. "You're lucky you got out without becoming a basket case yourself."

Caryn nodded again, but what she didn't say was that she hadn't escaped unscathed. She had scars. Invisible scars.

Loathing to leave the protective warmth of Logan's arms, she pushed gently against his chest. "I really have work to do."

He released her, a frown creasing his smooth forehead. "I hope that work doesn't include house cleaning because the Sheltons are due back today. And they'll have their work cut out for them because I'm going to make my barbecue sauce."

"You make it from scratch?"

"Yes. Do you want to help me?"

"You don't mind giving away the secret ingredients?"

"That depends on who's on the receiving end." He winked at her. "Consider yourself one of the privileged few."

She wondered if Nina Smith had also been one of the privileged few, but didn't voice her thoughts aloud.

They spent the entire morning in the kitchen. Caryn's yeast dough had doubled in size, and she punched one down and rolled strips into six long ropes, using three of each for two loaves of cheese and chive bread; she then rolled another thirty-six ropes from the other mixture for three dozen leek and bacon knots. She showed Logan how to form the knots, and with his assistance she completed everything in half the time it normally would have taken her. The bread and knots rose a second time. She placed everything in plastic bags, storing them in the freezer.

He stopped to feed and walk Domino before he returned to the house to begin the preparation of his celebrated sauce. Caryn sat on a tall stool and watched carefully as he pureed several cans of crushed tomatoes in a blender before transferring them to a large Dutch oven. He added precisely measured portions of cider vinegar, firmly packed brown sugar, molasses, dried mustard, cloves of garlic, onion, ginger, and Worcestershire sauce. Hours later, the aroma of the simmering sauce still lingered when Steven and Stephanie Shelton arrived with their cleaning supplies, both commenting about how wonderful the kitchen smelled.

Caryn and Logan shared a late lunch of a mixed green salad and a fruit platter before she retreated to the family room to read and Logan to the second-floor library to begin his preliminary proposal for the Raleigh zoning board. It was after eight when he walked into the family room and asked if she was willing to watch several videos he had found in the Crawfords' library.

"I will if it's not blood and gore."

"I suppose that means no Rambo," he teased.

"And no war films, please."

"How about Schwarzenegger?"

Her eyes brightened. *"The Terminator?"*

He nodded, visually admiring the delicate dewiness of her skin under the flattering glow of a table lamp. "I found both *Terminators, True Lies,* and *Eraser.* It appears either Marcia or Terrence really like Arnold."

Unfolding her legs, Caryn closed the book and stood up. "It's Marcia," she confirmed.

He gave her the smile she'd come to look for. She hadn't meant to call him a tight-ass, but she had to admit that their initial meeting was anything but amicable. It was now their third day together, and she found the more time she spent with him the more time she wanted to spend with him.

He was easy to talk to and a remarkable listener. She was beginning to feel comfortable sharing the house with him because his presence offered her a sense of security she would not have had if she'd been alone.

Logan placed the videos on a side table. "You make the selection while I make the popcorn."

She picked up one and read the jacket cover. "This one."

He took the video from her, smiling. "Good. *True Lies* would have been my choice."

Caryn placed the video atop the VCR, turned on the television, then sat down and waited for Logan to return with the promised popcorn. She tried imagining sitting at home on a rainy night watching a movie with Tom and failed miserably. Their home had been professionally decorated expressly for entertaining purposes. Tom always seemed to grow an extra inch whenever someone commented on the elegance of the carefully chosen furnishings. And she had walked away from it all—the opulence and her very successful husband. She hadn't realized she was a prized, caged bird until after she'd attained her freedom.

Logan returned, cradling a large bowl of hot buttered popcorn and a couple of bottles of chilled seltzer. He handed her the bowl of popcorn and sat the seltzers down on matching coasters on the coffee table. He popped the video in the VCR, dimmed a lamp, then sat down on the love seat next to her.

He sat close, too close, and despite the heat coming from his large body Caryn shivered slightly. The setting was very intimate—a darkened space, both sitting close enough where their shoulders and thighs touched; and every time Logan reached over to pick up kernels of popcorn his left hand grazed her breast. She smoothly placed the bowl on his lap, eliminating the need for him to touch her upper body.

Forty-five minutes into the film, she shifted, tucked her legs under her body, and rested her head on Logan's solid shoulder. He placed the bowl of popcorn on the table with the half-empty bottles of seltzer, curved an arm around her shoulders, and pulled her closer.

Logan glanced down at Caryn when he felt her head slide off his shoulder, coming to rest on his chest. He moved slightly, and her head jerked up before sliding back down again in his cushioning embrace.

His gaze was fixed on her face instead of the images on the television screen. He wanted to push her away because her presence brought back memories, memories he wanted to forget. He didn't want to want her; all he wanted was to share the house, a platonic relationship with Caryn Edwards, and nothing else, but he knew that was impossible.

He'd enjoyed spending the day with her and sharing in their cooking tasks. He'd found her beautiful, charming, and intelligent. And he was aware of the wall she'd erected to keep him at a distance whenever he attempted to touch or kiss her. He had tasted her mouth, and despite his silent denouncement wanted much more than a kiss. Pressing his lips to her hair, he closed his eyes and reveled in the sweet warmth emanating from her body.

His mind was a jumble of confusion as he tried assessing his emotions. For the first time in his adult life, he felt a soothing, gentle peace. With Caryn he could be who he was—Logan Prescott. He wasn't the adopted son of Jace and Maeve; he wasn't an equal partner with his father in J. Prescott and Associates; he wasn't the only African-American who captained the Yale Rowing Team to a national championship; and he wasn't the man who was cuckolded by his fiancée and best man a week before his impending marriage. With Caryn Edwards all he had to be was *himself!*

He picked up the remote, stopped the video, and turned

off the television. Caryn groaned softly when he gathered her in his arms to pick her up. She stirred once, then settled back to sleep as he carried her up the staircase to her bedroom. A smile creased his face when he realized how light she felt in his arms. There was even less of her than he'd first imagined.

Walking into her bedroom, he placed her gently on the bed and covered her with a lightweight blanket folded at the foot. Leaning over, he kissed her mouth, careful not to apply too much pressure. He stood, motionless, staring down at her until he forced himself to turn off the bedside lamp, leave the room, and close the door behind him.

It had taken only seconds for him to realize spending the entire day with Caryn had changed him forever. She may not have looked anything like the women he usually found himself attracted to, but she was the woman he wanted.

Chapter Ten

Caryn woke up totally disoriented, her body layered with moisture. Pushing herself into a sitting position, she rested her back against the headboard. The diffused light coming in through the windows offered no indication of the hour. She reached for her watch on the bedside table and peered closely at the numbers on the face. It wasn't quite five o'clock.

Running a hand over her damp hair, she closed her eyes, trying to remember why she had gone to bed fully dressed. An image of Arnold Schwarzenegger riding a horse into an elevator while a frightened couple clung to each other in a corner crowded her blurry memory. Moaning softly, she massaged her temples. She had fallen asleep while viewing the movie, and Logan had carried her up to bed.

Biting down on her lower lip, she halted a curving smile, recalling the solid hardness of his body when she'd snuggled against him. Logan was the complete opposite of Tom. Her ex-husband tended to admonish her whenever she offered him any affection out of bed.

A quick frown formed between her eyes when she

thought of Tom. He'd been in her thoughts more times in the past three days than he had been in a long time. She'd told Logan about him, but only what she wanted him to know. There were details about her married life she would never disclose to anyone.

She straightened, turned on the lamp, and reached for her journal. The only way she could exorcise Thomas Duff was to write down her troubling thoughts. Uncapping the pen, she wrote the date:

July fourth—Independence Day . . .

It's been a while since I've written an entry about Tom. His name came up yesterday when Logan asked why I'd left him. I told him the truth—what I've told everyone about his need to control my life. But what I really wanted to do was reveal all of the sordid little details about my marriage that I've never disclosed to anyone. How could I tell about his constant verbal abuse?

About how he belittled me when he claimed I could never satisfy him sexually. What I failed to understand was that he managed to satisfy me while I never could satisfy him.

I still find it hard to believe that the first year of our marriage was truly wonderful. Tom was the first man I'd fallen in love with and the first man who had taken my innocence. I will continue to ask myself over and over—what happened to change him? Us?

I can still recall the day he walked into the B&B in Arlington, requested a room, and his presence literally took my breath away. At seventeen I thought he was the most handsome, brilliant man to walk the earth. It hadn't mattered he was ten years older than I—all I knew was I'd found my Prince Charming.

But Prince Charming turned into a monster. In my naiveté and blinded by an all-consuming need to please him, I set myself up to become a willing victim to all the abuse he heaped upon me. After a while I realized I could retaliate verbally, but readily acknowledged I would never survive the physical abuse.

The day he pushed me and I fell headfirst down the staircase and lay bleeding I knew it was over. If only I had left him the day before, I wouldn't be writing these words, because I hadn't known at the time a new life was growing inside my womb. I'd made the ultimate sacrifice—my baby's life for my own survival.

Closing her eyes, she blinked back hot tears. She held her breath, hoping not to break down. She was unsuccessful. The tears fell and she cried without making a sound. She lay on the bed, waiting for the calm which always followed the sobbing.

She was getting better. It had been long time since she'd cried. She knew she had healed, even though the invisible scars would never fade completely.

Gripping the pen, she continued:

Today is Independence Day, and I claim my independence. This will be the last time I'll write Tom's name in my journal. I am free of him and will only remain free if I don't allow him in my consciousness. I have divorced him not once but twice.

I'm looking forward to this Fourth of July. There are plans for big doings on Marble Island, and I intend to enjoy every event.

Caryn met Logan coming up the stairs, carrying a tray as she was descending.

He frowned at her. "You ruined my surprise, Sleeping Beauty. I was going to bring you breakfast in bed."

She flashed him a smile that spoke volumes. It said she was pleased to see him. "I can always go back to bed if you want me to."

"That's all right. Now that you're up, we can eat on the porch together." She lifted the white towel covering the tray, trying to see what he had prepared for her, but he pulled it out of her reach. "No cheating."

"You're a tease, Logan."

He went completely still, staring down at her upturned face. *No, you're the tease, Caryn,* he shouted back silently. He hadn't slept more than two hours throughout the night because everything about her excited him until all he wanted was to spend every minute with her. He wanted to lie down beside her and hold her until her soothing, quiet spirit fused with his, offering him the peace he'd sought since fleeing Raleigh.

His gaze telegraphed her damp curly hair floating around her face, over her shoulders, down her back, then shifted to her eyes. They were slightly swollen, yet appeared lighter and more luminous with the added color to her face. His eyes widened at the same time as he felt a familiar stirring in his groin. Caryn was clothed in a T-shirt and a pair of shorts, but she could've been totally nude as the first night he'd observed her sleeping on her bed in the full moonlight. The same hot, rushing surge of desire gripped him until he couldn't move.

The realization hit him hard. He wanted her! Not just for a slaking of his passions, but for more. He wanted to protect and take care of her. He wanted to erase the bitter memories of the man who felt the need to dominate her instead of worshipping her. He didn't know why, but he wanted to take her to his bed and love her until both dissolved in a renewal baptism of reverent trust.

He wanted all of that and more, even though he'd continued to tell himself that he didn't want to fall in love with her. Not because he did not want to, but because he could not. Not yet. It had been only two weeks since Nina's deception, and he knew it would take a lot more time for him to learn to trust a woman again.

He flashed a half-smile. "Aren't you going to let me surprise you?"

Caryn wrinkled her pert nose. "I'm not much for surprises."

She didn't like surprises, but she would have been shocked if she'd known the thoughts swirling in his head and not permitting him a restful night's sleep.

Turning, Logan made his way down the staircase, she followed, and the scent of her clean, scented body cloaked him in a cloud of silent seduction. She pushed open the screen door, holding it while he placed the tray on the round wicker table.

Leaning over, he kissed the top of her damp head. "Wait for me. I'll be right back."

Instead of sitting, Caryn walked over to a corner of the porch and stared out at the panoramic scene before her. The healing beauty of Marble Island was bewitching. It was as if she had come to a mystical place accessible only to a privileged few who knew the magic word to gain entrance. The rain had passed over the island, leaving in its wake a shockingly blue cloudless sky, a brilliant sun, and a calm ocean breeze. Occasional shrieks from circling gulls competed with the lulling sound of the incoming tide. The weather had cooperated, setting the stage for what was sure to become a spirited Fourth of July celebration.

After breakfast she planned to cut up the fresh fruits she'd purchased and make a watermelon fruit boat, then bake the breads she'd prepared the day before. Her lips parted in a smile when she anticipated sampling Logan's barbecued spareribs. He'd dropped a minute portion of the thick red sauce on her forefinger for her to taste. She'd savored the sweet, piquant sensation of mild spices lingering on her palate, wanting more.

The distinctive sound of the screen door opening garnered her attention, and she turned to find Logan balancing another tray. She strolled forward and watched him set the table with a carafe of steaming coffee, a platter of hot waffles covered with a mixture of fresh berries and toasted pecans, links of broiled sausage, and a pitcher of squeezed orange juice.

"How wonderful. It's looks delicious, Logan."

He nodded. "Thanks. Please sit down and eat before the waffles get cold." Pulling out a chair, he seated her, then shifted another chair and sat down beside her.

They ate in silence, staring out at the beach as a gentle breeze cooled the air and countered the buildup of heat from the hot summer sun. The silence was comfortable, neither seeking to initiate conversation, each enjoying the food, companionship, and the setting.

Logan drained his second cup of coffee, his gaze fixed on Caryn's delicate profile as she touched the corners of her mouth with a napkin. "Are you going for a walk?"

Her head came around slowly, a smile crinkling her eyes. "Yes."

He leaned closer. "Would you mind company?"

Caryn went completely still, her gaze fused with his. Their faces were only inches apart, close enough for her to feel the warmth of his moist breath on her cheek. She photographed his face with the large jet-black eyes, high cheekbones, lean shaven jaw, strong chin, narrow bridge of his straight nose, and the fullness of his masculine lower lip. The sable-brown flesh covering his face was smooth, appearing almost poreless, and radiated excellent health. Her gaze lingered on his face because she didn't trust herself to venture lower and examine his broad chest covered with a tank top or his long, strong legs revealed by a pair of walking shorts.

Her smooth forehead furrowed. What was it about Logan Prescott that drew her to him against her will? What had he done to elicit a desire she hadn't felt in years?

Could she afford to take a chance and lower the barriers she'd erected not to permit a man in her life? Could she have a summer dalliance with this man and walk away unscathed?

Why not? the silent voice reminded her. It wasn't as if she was looking for anything beyond a physical liaison. She was old enough and certainly mature enough to offer a man her body for sexual gratification without demanding or wanting more. And she doubted whether Logan would want more.

"I'd love company." Her voice was soft and hauntingly

hypnotic. She rose to her feet at the same time Logan pulled her chair away from the table.

Reaching for her hand, he led her down the steps and several hundred feet to the beach. They walked hand-in-hand without talking. They met other couples, young and old, who were also walking leisurely along the beach. Everyone nodded, exchanging smiles before continuing their journey.

Caryn and Logan walked the mile and a half to the center of the business district, then turned and retraced their steps. He waited for the return trip to release her hand and curve his arm around her waist, prompting her to do likewise. She smiled up at him, he returning it, and she was astonished at the sense of fulfillment settling into her being.

They would complete a three-mile walk in a little more than an hour without exchanging a single word, and both realized what they felt and were beginning to feel for the other did not necessitate conversation, because words could not begin to explain the invisible thread binding them together.

They returned to the house, cleared the table of the remains of their breakfast, then retreated to the kitchen to complete the preparation of their dishes for the afternoon festivities.

The smell of food and the sound of voices raised in merriment was apparent even before the large tent set up in an open field behind the small white steepled church came into view.

Logan maneuvered into an area set aside for parking alongside an assortment of vehicles ranging in style from four-wheel-drive, minivans, luxury sedans, to racy two-seater models.

Circling the Wrangler, he reached up and swung Caryn down to the grassy area. "I'll carry all of the food into the tent."

She opened her mouth to tell him she wasn't helpless, but decided against it. It had taken her all of three days to come to the realization that Logan Prescott was raised in the true sense of old-fashioned Southern manners. Men took care of women, protected them, and saw to their every need. It had been a long time since she'd been pampered, not since she was a little girl and her father granted her every wish. She had nothing to lose and everything to gain for the month he remained on Marble Island. It wouldn't make up for the abuse she had endured during her marriage, but it would help erase some of the scars.

Elaine Shelton saw her and waved. Crossing the field, Caryn stepped into the coolness of the large tent. A loudspeaker attached to a flagpole blared out patriotic songs, and she recognized a Sousa march.

Elaine smiled, extending both hands. "I'm so glad you and your young man decided to attend."

Caryn grasped her hands, returning the smile. "We wouldn't have have missed this for anything."

Glancing around the large tent, she noticed a half-dozen long tables and benches set with disposable plates, cups, and utensils with decorative red, white, and blue logos. At the far end of the tent were several tables crowded with foodstuffs contributed by the residents and visitors on Marble Island.

"The men have set up three or four gas grills to keep meats warm, and there are a few portable freezer chests for the perishable dishes," Elaine explained.

"I just took my breads out of the oven so they'll stay warm for a while. But I think my watermelon fruit boat should be refrigerated. Logan will need the grill for his contribution."

Elaine's blue gaze shifted when she spotted Logan carrying a large aluminum tray with his spareribs. "You're a lucky woman."

Caryn stared at Elaine Shelton, a perplexed expression on her face. "Pardon me."

"Your husband. He's breathtaking," Elaine whispered.

"I should tell you first before you hear from some other woman. He's the talk of the island. I'm certain you know he ate at Addie's the first night you arrived, and a few of the single women just about shamed themselves when they began flirting with him. I can assure you that he was very polite and refused to sit with them."

Caryn's gaze measured Logan with his approach. She had to agree with Elaine. Logan was breathtaking. He claimed a dark masculine beauty which afforded him a potent sensual quality. This winning combination made it a certainity women would try to come on to him with his arresting face and exquisitely proportioned powerful body. He had elected to wear white: jeans, deck shoes, and a V-neck cotton pullover with a narrow red and navy-blue border along the neckline, cuffs, and hem.

She compressed her lips. And he was a fine one to talk. He'd accused her of flirting with men while he had to fight off women who saw nothing wrong with trying to pick him up in a restaurant. Well, an outdoor island-wide celebration was very different from a restaurant setting, and only time would tell how successful he would be at this venue or if he would require her assistance.

Elaine gave Logan a sensual smile. "Something smells very good under that cover."

"Spareribs," he replied.

"Hmm-mm. One of my favorite." Leaning over a table, she wrote down SPARERIBS above the printed words DONATED BY on a small place card. "What are your full names?"

"Logan and Caryn Edwards," she answered smoothly. Without moving, Logan lowered his eyelids slowly in a gesture of gratitude and flashed a sly wink.

"What else are you two donating?"

Caryn gave Elaine the information while Logan took his tray to where an elderly bearded man directed him outside the tent.

At exactly twelve noon all of Marble Island gathered under the large tent and bowed their head as the minister of the nondemoninational church led the assembled in a benediction, followed by the Pledge of Allegiance and the national anthem.

The Shelton twins, Chris Barnett, and Randy Bell had volunteered to serve the attendees, and Caryn smiled and exchanged words with each of them as she filled her plate with Logan's spareribs, small portions of potato salad, Addie's cole slaw, one of her own leek and bacon knots, and a thin slice of her cheese and chive braided bread.

Tables groaned under platters of fried chicken, whole honey-roasted hams, flaky crab cakes, tender corn on the cob, relishes, salsa, fluffy biscuits, rich buttered corn bread, gumbo, varieties of fish including golden-fried catfish, black-eyed peas, and appetizers offering egg rolls, spicy chicken strips, deep-fried dill pickle chips, and okra. A table set up only for desserts elicited everyone's attention, but would remain untouched for several hours.

A knowing smile curved Caryn's mouth as she sat beside Logan and watched two young women sit down opposite them. It was apparent these were the two who had approached him at Addie's. Both were young and extremely attractive African-American women. The taller had affected a short natural hairdo which showed off the perfection of her balanced features and flawless brown skin, while the other claimed a profusion of gray-streaked hair she had styled in a becoming wedge-cut.

The shorter woman extended her hand, smiling. "Shevonne Wilson."

Logan shook the proffered hand. "Logan." He withdrew his hand, at the same time curving an arm around Caryn's shoulders. "I'd like to introduce my wife, Caryn Edwards."

The introduction was accomplished so smoothly, Caryn's shock mirrored the startled expressions on the faces of the two women. It was one thing to let people assume they were married, but another to openly lie about it.

Recovering quickly, the other woman glanced down at their ringless fingers. "Mandisa Leonard," she said around a forced grin.

"Are you two from around here?" Caryn questioned, picking up a glass of ice-cold lemonade.

"No. We're from New York City," Shevonne replied. "Do you guys live on Marble Island?"

Logan shook his head. "Not year-round. We're here on vacation."

"Do you intend to spend the entire summer here?" Mandisa's gaze was fixed on Logan even though she had addressed Caryn.

"Yes," Logan answered. "How about yourselves?"

"We only have another week," Shevonne said, scowling.

Caryn flashed a knowing smile. "Try to enjoy every minute."

Shevonne nodded. "That's what we've been trying to do."

Sure you have, Caryn thought. *And with my housemate, no less.* But what the two women did not know was that Logan Prescott was not interested in becoming involved with any woman, no matter how attractive she was.

Logan stood up, the fingers of his left hand curving around Caryn's neck. "Can I get you anything else, sweetheart?"

Smiling up at him, she shook her head. "No, darling."

He smiled at Shevonne and Mandisa. "Ladies?"

Mandisa shook her head while Shevonne handed Logan her plate. "If there are any more ribs left, I'll take a few."

Logan's spareribs were the talk of the afternoon. His special sauce was sweet and spicy, while the meat was so tender it literally fell off the bone. She had sampled a few after he'd finished grilling them and requested he hold back half a rack. He'd wiped away smudges of sauce from her cheeks, grinning broadly, then showed her a full rack he'd placed in the freezer.

Randy Bell joined them at their table, along with the others who had volunteered to serve, and the energy level escalated considerably. Everyone was given the opportunity to tell a joke, and Caryn had to search her memory to tell one successfully without giving away the punch line.

She and Logan found themselves at different tables every hour throughout the afternoon, as it was a mandated Marble Island Independence Day ritual to acquaint themselves with all of the permanent and vacationing residents.

Around seven many of the younger parents left, taking their youngsters and toddlers home as the sun began its slow descent. A DJ arrived and set up his equipment under the tent, while a clean-up committee made quick work of removing discarded food and other debris, while Caryn marveled at how quickly the time had passed.

Glancing down at her blue and white striped cotton slacks, she winced. They were stained with a variety of foodstuffs, while her white blouse was covered with smudges of chocolate from a brownie held by a toddler who had crawled onto her lap. Shrugging a shoulder, she realized it was too late to go back to the house and change.

The familiar strands of a popular ballad came through the powerful speakers, followed by the distinctive mellifluent voice of Frank Sinatra singing "Witchcraft."

Caryn felt heat behind her, and she inhaled the now familiar fragrance of the aftershave belonging to the man with whom she was sharing a house. Closing her eyes, she leaned back against his chest, humming softly. His arm circled her waist, holding her firmly.

"You're a very smooth liar, Logan." Her soft voice feathered around him like a cloaking fog.

"And so are you, Caryn," he countered. "Logan Edwards?"

She chuckled softly. "And I suppose that makes us even?"

"For me it does. Now, may I have this dance, *wife?*"

Turning slowly, she studied his smiling face. "Yes, you may, *husband.*"

Taking her hand, he led her out of the tent and onto the grassy lawn. He pulled her against his body, molding her to his length. She closed her eyes, melting into his strength. Other couples joined in the dancing as a magical curtain descended on Marble Island and all who inhabited it.

"Thank you for not revealing who I am," he whispered close to her ear.

"You're welcome," she whispered back. "I'm usually not such an accomplished liar, but I didn't know what else to say when Elaine asked your full name. And I suppose perpetuating the lie came in handy because you were about to be plucked royally by two Big Apple divas."

Pulling back, he squinted down at her. "What are you talking about?"

"Shevonne and Mandisa. They want you."

He snorted, shaking his head. "They don't want me."

"Don't they, Logan?"

"No, they don't."

"Are you blind? Didn't you see Miss Mandisa Leonard eat you up with her eyes?"

Tightening his grip on her waist, he pulled her closer. "No," he repeated in a quiet tone. "I can't even remember what she looks like."

He'd told her the truth. In fact, he hadn't paid much attention to any of the women on the island except the one in his arms. Introducing her as his wife had come as natural as breathing. And it was after the words were out, he'd wondered if his life would've taken a different turn if he'd been engaged to Caryn instead of Nina. Would she also have proven herself unfaithful?

And for the first time he questioned his own behavior and what he had done or not done to elicit fidelity from a woman. Had he been too involved in his work? Had she blamed him for not seeing her more often? Or had he not offered her what she needed for total sexual gratification?

A switch was flipped, and the string of bulbs ringing the open field illuminated the entire area with a soft glow as the Sinatra ballad segued into another one featuring the velvet voice of Nat King Cole.

Caryn lost track of time as she and Logan danced to a continuous string of ballads, she following his expert lead.

The tempo of the music changed, becoming more upbeat the later the hour, and both agreed it was time they headed back to the house.

Yawning delicately behind her hand, she leaned back on the seat in the Jeep and closed her eyes. The night air was warm and humid as it feathered over her face in the open vehicle.

Logan drove slowly and turned off the main road onto Watermelon Patch Lane, pulling into the driveway of the last house on the dead-end street alongside Caryn's parked car. He shut off the engine, then came around to help her out.

Her arms circled his neck as he lifted her gently and carried her up to the house. He loathed putting her down, but was forced to when he had to retrieve the key.

The porch lights shadowed her features as she turned to him. "Thank you for a wonderful day, Logan."

He turned the key in the lock. "I should be the one thanking you." Pushing open the door, he reached for a button on the wall and flooded the second-story hallway with light.

Caryn felt a foreign urgency to escape the man standing a few feet away from her. She'd spent the past sixteen hours with him, eating together, dancing together, and pretending to be his wife. Now, they were behind closed doors and there was no need for the pretense. She could be who she was and he who he was—Caryn Edwards and Logan Prescott.

"Good night," she mumbled softly as she made her way toward the stairs.

Taking three long strides, Logan was beside her. His fingers closed around her upper arm, tightening slightly when she tried freeing herself.

Holding her and making her his prisoner, he pulled her to his chest, his head lowering with a deliberate slowness. "Good night," he whispered, his hot mouth covering hers and robbing her of her breath and her will.

This kiss was different from the others they'd shared. It

was slow, unhurried, gentle, and persuasive. He applied a steady pressure until her lips parted, allowing him total access.

The caress of Logan's lips on hers ignited the flame that had been extinguished years before. The heat spread from her mouth to her chest, and still lower to the secret place between her thighs.

Caryn did not know when it happened, but without warning she was returning the kiss, her tongue meeting Logan's, she succumbing to the forceful domination of his mouth. Her fingers tightened on the soft fabric of his sweater as she tried getting even closer.

It was as if Logan Prescott's presence had teased her for days, and now she was able to commune and partake of everything he was offering. Caught up in the rapture of his mouth and the hardness of his body melding with hers, she surrendered to the healing passion and the realization that she wanted Logan—not just his kiss, but all of him.

Logan pulled her closer, wanting to absorb Caryn into himself. His right hand moved down her back and cupped her hips. He wanted her to feel his rising passion, his hardness. He wanted her to know he wanted her, wanted to be inside her. His left hand was as busy as his right, pulling the hem of her blouse up, baring flesh before his fingers closed over the sheer lace covering her breast.

Her breast swelled, the nipple hardening against his palm. Caryn moaned against his lips, seeking to escape. She thought she was ready for Logan and mature enough to engage in a sexual liaison with him, but she wasn't. She needed time, a lot more time than just three days.

"Logan, no," she mumbled, anchoring her hands between their bodies and pushing against his hard chest.

Without warning, he released her and she turned and walked determinedly up the stairs, her body trembling uncontrollably from the force of the passion pulsing at the juncture of her thighs.

Logan watched her retreat, his hands tightening into fists. He was angry, angry with himself. He'd made a mistake and moved too quickly, when all he wanted was for her to want him as much as he wanted her. One thing he was, was a quick study. It would not happen again.

A slight smile transformed his stoic expression. "Good night, Sleeping Beauty," he whispered.

He stared at the staircase for a full minute, then turned and made his way to the rear of the house. He'd left Domino in his cage for more than eight hours. He would walk his pet, clean the cage, then sit with the puppy until he fell asleep.

Chapter Eleven

July fifth—

He kissed my soul!

Even now, hours later I can still recall the taste of his mouth, the texture of his tongue, the smell of his body.

His friends may call him Raven, but I call him Warlock!

He is a powerful magician who has lured me into a sensual trap. A trap from which there is no escape.

But I'm not certain whether I want to escape—not yet.

Caryn put away her journal, picked up her handbag, and quietly made her way down the staircase and out of the house. She'd gotten up early, deciding to spend the day away from Marble Island. She wanted to drive up the coast and shop—for what she was uncertain. Perhaps she would stop in a small, quaint town and pick up a few craft items.

Muted shades of color in gray and mauve crisscrossed the sky as she started up her car and backed out of the driveway, and by the time she'd left Marble Island behind a watery sun shimmered over the ocean.

* * *

Logan had not realized it was the sound of a car's engine that woke him until he rose and looked for Caryn and discovered her and her car missing.

He felt oddly disappointed not seeing her, while refusing to acknowledge he missed her or that she had become an integral part of his existence while on Marble Island. He saw to Domino's needs before jogging the mile and a half along the beach to the island's business center and returning to the house to begin a day of work.

He shaved, showered, pulled on a pair of well-worn jeans, a T-shirt, and covered his bare feet with a pair of tattered leather moccasins. Releasing an excited, whining Domino from his cage, he rewarded the obedient puppy with an outing of the run of the front porch when he looped an extended leash around a column. Fortified with a large mug and a carafe of strong coffee, Logan retrieved his power notebook and sat on the porch with the intent to complete the draft of a proposal for Raleigh's zoning board.

Time passed quickly, and hunger pangs forced him to stop and glance at his watch. It was nearing noon, and all he had consumed had been three cups of black coffee. A noticeable frown furrowed his smooth forehead. If Caryn had been home, he probably would've eaten breakfast, and if not breakfast then brunch.

The frown vanished as a realization washed over him. He didn't like eating alone. Why hadn't he been aware of that before meeting Caryn Edwards? He smiled. He liked Caryn. In fact he liked her a lot, and found her to be more sexy than any woman he had ever met. And he suspected she was unaware of how very sexy she actually was.

Closing his eyes, he relived kissing her and how she had fitted so perfectly against his body. When he had taken her into his arms, she resisted slightly before going pliant and returning his kiss. The feel and taste of her tongue was imprinted on his brain, along with the soft crush of her breasts against his chest.

A soft moan escaped him as he recalled the size and weight of her breast and the hardening nipple against his palm. He had aroused her in the same manner she had aroused him. And again, he wanted her. He wanted her naked, in his bed, his body joined with hers. And he wanted her writhing uncontrollably in his embrace while both soared with a passion taking them beyond themselves and exploding into a lingering satisfaction that would last a lifetime.

Lifetime! His eyes opened and his chest heaved heavily as if he had run a grueling race. What was wrong with him? He had walked away from one woman, and within two weeks he found himself caught in the spell of another who barely tolerated his presence.

Saving what he had typed, he turned off the computer and went into the house to find something to eat. He hadn't eaten anything in eighteen hours, and maybe, just maybe he was confused because of food deprivation.

By late afternoon the sky darkened with fast-moving angry clouds, and Logan pushed a button on the Wrangler and put up the soft top to keep out the impending rainfall. A strong, rising wind caused the ocean to stir restlessly in its bed and pound the shore with dull gray, white-tipped waves. Standing on the porch, he watched the waves break higher and higher over the beach, while Domino stood at his side shivering.

"It looks like a storm, fella," he said softly, leaning down and scratching behind the spotted head. The wind gusts increased, moaning like someone in pain.

A rumble of thunder shook the earth, followed by an ear-crashing clap of lightning, and Domino whined while at the same time tried to hide between his master's denim-covered legs.

A second roll of thunder followed, and when the lightning struck, it bounced off the water and exploded like a bomb. As an experienced boatman, Logan knew the impending storm was a dangerous one, and his thoughts turned to Caryn. Where was she? And, would she know enough to seek shelter until the storm was over?

Logan continued to ask himself the same questions three hours later, as he sat in the family room with a sleeping Domino at his feet. The puppy had yelped and whined incessantly until he released him from his cage. It was apparent the sound of the howling wind frightened the dog so much, he refused to relax.

The light from a table lamp flickered twice, but managed not to go out. An all-news radio station offered a storm update every fifteen minutes, warning all residents along the coast to seek shelter. A police bulletin followed with reports of flooding and power outages up and down the Carolina coast.

All of the windows were closed, yet he still could hear the roar of the ocean over the sound of the howling, screaming wind.

"Caryn, where are you?" he whispered angrily. The words spewed out because he needed to hear another sound, other than that of the wind, rain, and the powerful roar of the ocean.

Pulling the toe of his moccasin from under Domino's limp head, he stood up and walked over to the window. It was only seven-fifteen, but it could have been midnight. His gaze met blackness, as a sliver of fear wound its way into him.

What if something had happened to her? What if she was trapped in her car by the rising waters? What if she lay injured somewhere along the road?

His apprehension swelled into a paralyzing, pregnant fear. He cared about her. No—it was more than concern or caring, and in an instant, Logan had to admit to himself that he was falling in love with Caryn Edwards. And, the love he felt for her was so different from the one for Nina Smith.

This love was soothing, gentle. It made him want to protect her from all, or any harm. He wanted to love her, but only on his terms.

He debated whether to go out into the storm and look for her, or remain at the house in case she telephoned. The lights flickered again, then went out, quickly solving his dilemma. The island was completely dark, making it impossible to see anything.

Moving slowly, he inched his way out of the family room and into the kitchen, hoping he would not step on Domino. Holding his hands in front of him, he felt along a wall until he encountered the gas-burning cooking range and turned a knob for a burner. Bright blue flames lit up the kitchen once all of the burners were lit. They provided enough light in the space for him to locate a supply of candles stored in a drawer under a countertop. He lit a candle and placed it on a small ceramic dish, then another. Using the flickering candle as a beacon, he returned to the family room and picked up the dozing puppy and placed him back in his cage. He didn't want the dog to wake up and race around frantically in the dark.

Shielding the candle with one hand, he crossed the dining room and stood in the entry. A wave of fear and panic settled in his chest with each passing second as terrifying images flooded his mind. He shook off the picture of her trapped in her car while rushing flood waters filled its interior.

"She's safe," he whispered as he paced back and forth. *She's just waiting out the storm.* He stopped pacing. "Then why hasn't she called?" he continued in his monologue.

He stared into the flame, mentally willing her to come to him. *Caryn, sweetheart. Come to me. I'll take care of you.*

He jumped, nearly dropping the candle, when he heard a wailing sound before it was snatched away by the howling wind. At first he thought he'd imagined it, but he heard it again, followed by a drumming sound on the door.

Logan took two steps, opened the door, and it was torn from his grasp by the wind which slammed it against its frame and quickly extinguished the candle. He could barely discern the churning foam of the waves cresting more than six feet in height in the unnatural darkness. Reaching out, he attempted to close the door when he glanced down and saw her.

Caryn lay facedown on the porch, her arms covering her head in a protective gesture. "Fool!" he spat out seconds before he gathered her up in his arms. The scrappy little fool had challenged the violent fury of a tropical storm with winds blowing more than forty miles an hour and rising tides sweeping away anything in its path.

Placing her over his shoulder, he held her legs as he pulled the screen door closed and locked it securely, then closed and bolted the inner door, shutting out the violent sound of nature's fury.

Caryn felt the warmth of Logan's body seeping into her chilled limbs. "Lo-Lo-gan." His name came out in a raspy whisper at the same time her teeth chattered like rolling dice.

He felt the unnatural iciness of her body through her soggy clothes, and his irritation quickly turned to alarm. He had to get her out of the wet clothes and warm her before she went into shock.

Returning to the kitchen, he placed her on the table and ripped off her blouse when he couldn't push the buttons through their openings. Her running shoes, slacks, underpants, and bra quickly followed. He left her long enough to light three more candles and place them strategically around the kitchen. The flickering flames highlighted her face and he stared numbly at her, not recognizing the woman he had spent the past four days with. She had cut her hair, the shortened strands clinging to her scalp like a black cap.

His shock was short-lived as he removed his T-shirt and rubbed her naked body vigorously until she moaned softly under the ministration.

"Stop," she pleaded. "No more."

He ignored her plea. "I have to warm you."

Her right hand flailed out, catching him under his chin. His head snapped back, and quicker than the eye could follow he caught her hand, holding it firmly. "Don't fight me, Caryn. I'm not going to hurt you," he hissed between clenched teeth

All of her fight vanished, and she did what she had wanted to do from the moment she realized a bridge she had driven across only seconds before had been washed away by a wall of rushing water—she cried. Turning, she rested her forehead against Logan's bare arm and cried.

"I—I thought I wasn't going to make it," she whispered between sobs. "The water was rising—everywhere. It came—came into the car, and I thought I was going to drown. All I thought of was being trapped in the car while the water rose around me, and—"

"It's okay," Logan crooned, stopping her. Pulling her gently to him, he picked her up and held her as if she were a small child, placing tender kisses all over her face. "It's all right, baby. It's over and you're safe. I'll take care of you."

He held her effortlessly, offering his warmth and his protection in the candlelit space. A slight smile touched his mouth as she quieted, then went still in his embrace. Closing his eyes briefly, he offered a silent prayer of gratitude for her safe return.

Picking up a candle, he held it at an angle so he wouldn't drip wax on Caryn's exposed flesh. Moving slowly, he made his way out of the kitchen and up the staircase to the second floor. He needed to get her into bed, then prepare something warm for her to drink.

Logan entered her bedroom, placing her on her bed, and covered her with a sheet and a lightweight blanket. Leaning over, he brushed his mouth over hers. "Relax, baby."

Nodding, she closed her eyes, and when she reopened them ten minutes later Logan sat on the side of the bed, holding a cup. She could barely make out his features in the soft glow of candlelight.

"Try to sit up," he urged in a quiet voice.

Pushing herself into a sitting position, Caryn clutched the sheet over her bare breasts, taking small sips of overly sweetened tea as Logan held the cup to her lips. Her gaze met his, fusing over the rim of the cup seconds before her lids lowered slowly.

He placed the cup on the bedside table as she lay back against the pillows cradling her shoulders. Within minutes she fell into a deep sleep, shutting out all of her fears and nature's wrath running amuck.

Logan sat on the side of the bed, staring at her composed features in the wavering candlelight. He tried and failed to analyze why he'd found himself drawn to Caryn Edwards. Why did he find it so easy to pretend she was his wife. Why he was willing to think of her as his wife. And what was it about her that melted his distrust where he was willing to permit himself to fall in love with her?

Caryn awoke to total darkness and to the lingering sound of the moaning wind. She sat up, disoriented, not knowing whether it was day or night.

The image of her car filling with water as she drove through what had become swollen, rushing currents flooded her memory, eliciting a violent shaking. She'd thought she was going to drown, the car becoming her watery tomb. But she had made it. She had driven over the bridge connecting Marble Island with the mainland minutes before it was swept away, leaving a surging waterway instead of a concrete structure.

Once she realized she had escaped death by drowning, she had vividly recalled the images of her parents, her brother, sister-in-law, and her niece and nephew. And she did not know why, but Logan's face had also appeared, and she'd wondered whether she would ever see him, touch him, or kiss him again.

She hadn't understood what had propelled her back to Marble Island during the storm until she found herself in his arms. She had challenged the tempest because she knew she had to see him one more time.

She remembered him calling her a fool, and that she was. She was a fool for falling in love with Logan Prescott, and even more of a fool for wanting him.

Pushing aside the sheet, she swung her legs over the side of the bed and reached for the lamp. She turned the switch, but the bulb remained unlit. The power was still out on the island. Slowly and tentatively, she felt her way across the room and down the hallway, her fingertips maintaining contact with the wall.

Counting doorways, she came to Logan's bedroom, pushed open the door and walked in. She heard movement, then his voice. "Caryn?"

She went completely still, unable to see in front of her hand. There was only the sound of her breathing, it sounding unnaturally loud in her ears. She wanted to tell him she wanted him, she needed him, and that she did not want to be alone.

"Are you all right?"

Inhaling deeply, she held her breath then let it out slowly. "Yes."

She remained in the same spot as she heard him move off the bed. Then he was beside her, the heat from his body nearly suffocating her when he pulled her naked body against his.

Holding her gently in his strong embrace, Logan lowered his head and dropped a kiss over her ear. "I'm going to take you back to your bed."

She shook her head. "I don't want to go back to my bed." Her voice was a tremulous whisper.

Logan sucked in his breath, holding it until he was forced to exhale and praying he could control the rush of blood to his groin. He stood in a darkened space, holding a woman to his nude body—a woman who had managed to weave her way into his heart without trying. A woman who made him want her, although he continued to tell himself that he did not want or need any woman.

"I'm going back to bed," he said softly. "And if you come with me, then I can't promise you I won't make love to you."

Her fingertips inched up his bare chest to his lips. Rising on tiptoe, her mouth replaced her fingers and answered his challenge. "Then don't promise," she whispered.

Bending slightly, Logan swung her up in his arms and backed up until his calves hit the side of the bed. He sat down, holding Caryn protectively in his embrace. He registered her slight intake of breath as his rising hardness pressed up against her derriere, searching for the heat of her moist opening.

The passion rushing headlong throughout his body told him to take her quickly to ease the throbbing ache, but he ignored it. Caryn deserved more, because he loved her. He would make certain she would find fulfillment before he took his own.

Easing her off his lap, he placed her on the center of the bed and covered her body with his, supporting his weight on his arms. His fingers swept through her hair, pushing the short curls off her forehead and over her ears. He felt the warmth of her quickened moist breath on his throat before he captured it in a explosive kiss that sucked the very air from her lungs.

Caryn arched, her arms curving around Logan's strong neck. Kissing him, holding him, feeling his hardness rising up against her belly verified she was truly alive; that her passion had been asleep. It had a long time, too long, since she'd lain with a man while acknowledging that her own passions ran strong and deep.

Her legs curled around his, making him her willing prisoner. His tongue moved in and out of her open mouth in a slow, measured rhythm, precipitating a matching throbbing between her thighs.

Reaching between their bodies, the fingers of his right hand lingered on her thigh as it inched up and found the source of her feminine heat. Raising his hips to permit him access, one finger slipped between the moist folds hiding her femininity. She gasped at the invasion as he pushed into her and prepared her for his total possession. His thumb covered the tight, distended bud of flesh at the apex of her thighs. He increased the pressure, massaging gently until her moans escalated along with her rising desire.

Logan measured the contractions of her flesh opening and closing around his finger, feeling them coming stronger and faster. Angling his hips, he pushed his sex into her body at the same time her body arched in her first soaring climax. Her pulsing flesh pulled him in until he found himself drowning in the ecstasy hurtling him beyond himself.

Caryn gasped in sweet agony as Logan's hardness aroused her to heights she hadn't thought possible. Explosive sensations buffeted her again and again, over and over until she thought she would surely die from the pleasure. Her breathing quickened, she writhing against his hard, damp body, wanting to get closer, wanting to become one with him.

Then she heard it, his long, shuddering groan of surrendering ecstasy overlapping her soft moans as they soared together in an awesome, shattering, explosive shower of liquid passion.

They lay together, breathing heavily, his sated body pressing her down to the mattress. Smiling, she welcomed the pleasurable, protective heaviness.

Loathing to withdraw from the scorching heat of her body, Logan held her tightly and reversed their position. He smiled in the darkness and placed soft, tender kisses on her silken, scented throat. Caryn moaned softly, rested her cheek on his shoulder, and slept.

Logan reached down and pulled the sheet up over their moist bodies, and within minutes he joined her in the sleep reserved for sated lovers.

Chapter Twelve

The rising sun clearly revealed the devastating aftermath of the storm that bore down along the Carolina coast with abandoned vehicles and flooded structures. Logan turned over and stared at Caryn, wondering what secrets she kept as she lay sleeping. The silken crush of her firm breasts against his chest elicited a knowing smile as he recalled her unrestrained passion. Their coming together had been intense, but all too brief. He'd wanted it to last longer, but it was not to be. At the moment he entered her body, he knew she had been celibate for some time, and any prolonged bout of lovemaking would have left her tender for days. And he did not want anything to interfere with his sharing her body.

Resting his head on a folded arm, his smile vanished. He'd slept with her without using protection, and something told him Caryn was not practicing contraception. He shuddered to think if he'd gotten her pregnant. And if she was, there was no doubt he would take full responsibility for his actions. Unlike his sixteen-year-old biological Native-American father, who hadn't been told he'd fathered a child, he would care for Caryn, as well as his own child.

His free hand touched the soft curls clinging to her scalp, lifting them gently. Caryn stirred under his light touch, her eyelids fluttering until they opened. They widened in shock, and she appeared startled to find herself waking up in his bed.

"Good morning," she said shyly, dropping her gaze.

"Good morning," he returned, his smile back in place. Last night, with the darkness and in concert with the storm, she had come to him, offering up all she had. Now, in the full sunlight she was visibly embarrassed by what had occurred between them.

He decided to make it easy for her. He would not mention their lovemaking unless she brought it up. "Why did you cut your hair?"

Her hand came up, and she threaded her fingers through the shortened black curls. "I decided I wanted a different look."

Logan's penetrating gaze registered everything about her lovely face. The shorter hair was flattering, making her appear older and more sophisticated. "Why would you want a different look?"

Her gaze met his, all traces of gold missing and leaving them a deep verdant green. "Because I'm not the same person I was when I decided to let it grow long."

Curving an arm around her bare waist, he pulled her closer. "Is that a good thing?"

Nodding, she gave him a half-smile. "A very good thing." What she wouldn't say is that she was a different person since meeting him. Knowing she was falling in love again had changed her—forever.

"I like the new and different Caryn Edwards."

She searched his features for a hint of guile, but found none. "Thank you."

"You're quite welcome." Pressing a kiss to her forehead, he whispered, "You pack a mean wallop, Miss Edwards."

She remembered hitting him the night before. "I'm

sorry I hit you," she apologized, staring at the hard muscles under his powerful shoulders. "I didn't mean it."

He nodded slowly. "I realized that after you nearly broke my neck. You hit me with an open hand. Have you been trained in the martial arts?"

She hadn't meant to hit him that hard. "Yes. I took a self-defense course after the stalking. I never wanted to become that vulnerable again."

Logan whistled softly. "I'm willing to bet you can kick some serious butt."

"I will if I have to."

"You're a scrappy little thing, aren't you?"

The heat in her face intensified. "I'm not scrappy."

Raising his chin, he pointed to the spot where she'd struck him. "Look at my jaw. I'm willing to bet it's swollen."

Her gaze visually traced his stubbled jaw. "No, it's not."

"Touch it."

Reaching out, she ran her fingers along his jawline, encountering a small lump under his chin. Caryn bit down on her lower lip. "I said I was sorry."

Logan held her hand firmly. "Kiss it and make it better," he crooned in a coaxing tone.

Her eyes widened. "No." It was enough she had come to him the night before seeking comfort and protection. But the storm was over and so were her fears. And she knew her wanton behavior was the result of her falling in love with him, but that love for him would remain her secret.

"I kissed you and made you better," he countered.

"When?"

"When you were shaking so hard from the cold that you couldn't stand up or talk."

Caryn watched him warily as he stared at her. She lay on his bed, naked. There may have been a teasing quality in Logan's challenge; however, she knew instinctively what had passed between them was far from teasing.

Her fingers splayed over his jaw as she leaned in closer and pressed her mouth to his at the same time he caught her head, increasing the pressure. The heat from his large body reignited the flame in hers, his mouth searing hers with an uncontrollable heat which spread to her chest and still lower. The kiss continued, his mouth leaving tender, moist kisses all over her face. It ended with him burying his face between the scented area of her shoulder and neck as he inhaled the cloying perfume clinging to her silken flesh.

Closing her eyes, Caryn curved her arms around Logan's slim waist. "Logan?"

"Ummm." He lay motionless, fighting back the passions threatening to surface and explode.

"What—what we're doing. What we did . . ."

His head came up, and he stared down at her as she regarded him with an impassive expression. "What about *us?*"

After a pregnant pause, in which she managed to control her emotions, she said, "We're going to be together for only a short time, and I believe we're both mature enough not to read more into this—our sleeping together."

A frown settled between his eyes. "What are you saying?"

"I hope you enjoyed sleeping with me as much as I've enjoyed sleeping with you." He nodded. "But that's all it is—our sleeping together, and when it's over it'll be over. No histrionics and no pressure of a future commitment."

His expressive eyebrows shifted. "Are you suggesting we can have a *summer dalliance,* and when the summer ends so will our liaison?"

Caryn hid the pain she wouldn't permit him to see with a gentle smile. She wanted nothing more from Logan except his passion. She did not want him to feel obligated in any manner because she'd offered him her body. Her ex-husband had controlled her life, and when she left him she took it back. And if she was willing to share her body with Logan, it would be on her terms or not at all.

She nodded slowly. "That's the way I want it."

His hands went to her shoulders, tightening and holding

her fast. "What if you become pregnant? I have to assume you're not using any birth control."

She mentally calculated when her period was due. "I'm safe right now, but I won't be in another week."

Releasing her, Logan rolled off her body and lay on his back. "You don't have to worry about becoming pregnant, because I'll assume the responsibility of protecting you."

Caryn reached for his hand and threaded her fingers through his, squeezing gently. "Thank you."

What he wanted to do was scream at her. He wanted to tell her that she was cold, unfeeling, but knew she wasn't. Her words may have indicated indifference to the importance of their sharing the other's body, but the amazing completeness she'd offered him was anything but nonchalance.

He'd burned for her, and when he finally lost himself in her scented limbs the ecstasy she aroused was explosive and satisfying. Unknowingly, she had become the one to assuage his voluptuous, libidinous appetite. A deep peace settled into his being when he confirmed Caryn Edwards was the first woman who had taken him into her body and to complete sexual fulfillment.

The electrical power was restored to Marble Island only after the Army Corps of Engineers, called in at the request of the state's governor, descended on the islands along the North Carolina coast to erect makeshift bridges to link the isolated inhabitants with the mainland.

The Crawford house escaped any flood damage because of its elevated construction, but more than a half dozen of the smaller structures were not as fortunate. Within twenty-four hours insurance company adjusters set up headquarters in a corner of Addie's and conducted business amid the mouthwatering aromas coming from the restaurant's kitchen.

Logan and Caryn went through the task of discarding foodstuffs in the refrigerator and freezer which either wilted or spoiled during the electrical power outage. It was late afternoon when they took a tour of the island, surveying the damage brought on by the unexpected tropical disturbance. Luckily both her car and Logan's four-wheel-drive vehicle were operable and had not sustained any saltwater damage. Others in lower elevations were not as fortunate.

At five o'clock that evening, the sound of the bell in the church's belfry called all inhabitants to the church for an impromptu thanksgiving service for the sparing of human life. Caryn moved closer to Logan and tightened her grip on his hand. He smiled down at her, and she returned it with a dazzling one of her own.

The upcoming Friday night outdoor concert was canceled, but the six businesspeople who made up the island's Chamber of Commerce decided to go forward with the scheduled Saturday night barn dance. There were a few protests, but Elaine Shelton reminded the vacationers that they had come to Marble Island for fun and relaxation, and within minutes everyone agreed.

Addie ended the meeting with the promise of an open house at the restaurant, offering dinner at half the menu price. Randy Bell asked Logan if he and Caryn were coming, but Logan declined. He had only another three weeks on Marble Island, and he intended to spend much of that time alone with Caryn.

"What do you have planned for this evening?" she asked as they made their way back to the house on Watermelon Patch Lane.

Curving an arm around her tiny waist, he pulled her close to his side. "A romantic candlelight dinner under the stars with the most beautiful woman on Marble Island." She tilted her chin at the same time his head came down. He brushed his lips overs hers, inhaling her sweet, moist breath.

"Speaking of candles," she said as they continued their walk along the beach. "I stopped and bought some oil candles yesterday. I thought they would be a pretty addition to the house when your friend and his wife come on Saturday."

Logan nodded. "I have to call Ham and find out if they're still coming. Who knows what kind of storm damage they may have sustained farther down the coast."

"If they don't come Saturday, then they can always come during the week."

"Maybe I'll suggest that. I need this weekend to put the finishing touches on a proposal I'm hoping to fax to my father by Monday."

"How do you like working for your father?"

"He's a hard taskmaster, but he's fair. I learned a long time ago not to challenge him outright once he takes a stand on a project. It has taken many years, but I've learned the subtle art of negotiation."

"I take it you've challenged him?"

"Only once. I was seventeen and I'd just gotten my driver's license, so I volunteered to drive my friends to a party. Jace gave me the keys to his car, but insisted emphatically I come home by midnight.

"Needless to say, I strolled back in after two. We exchanged words, and it was only after he'd clipped me on my jaw and I was sprawled on my ass did I plead temporary insanity. In a heated rage I hadn't remember exactly what I'd said to him, but what I should've remembered was that Jace Prescott had been a middleweight boxing champ at Yale.

"I picked myself off the floor, threw his keys at his feet, and stalked off to my room. My mother came to see me the next day and quoted my inflammatory tirade verbatim. What I said to Jace was unconscionable, and I knew I had to apologize to the man who loved me despite the fact we shared no blood ties. I went to his office to meet with him, but he kept me waiting for two hours even though there was no one in his office.

"His secretary finally let me see him, and I walked over to him, extending my hand. He stood motionless, staring at my hand for what seemed like two minutes, and when he finally looked up to meet my gaze I broke down. It was the first time I'd ever cried wherein I'd permitted either one of my parents to see my tears. And it was also the first time I'd ever seen my father cry.

"We hugged each other, then laughed. Jace patted my cheek, saying he was proud of the man I had become. I kissed his cheek, telling him that I was proud to call him father. The older I become the more I love my parents, and I pray I'll never deliberately hurt them—not for any reason."

Caryn wondered what he'd said to Jace Prescott, but would never ask Logan to disclose something so personal. "How did you meet Marcia?"

"Terrence, her brother, Wayne, and I belong to the National Association of Black Architects. We bonded one year during a national convention in D.C., but after Terrence married Marcia and moved to Asheville, Wayne and I continued the friendship. He was to be my best man."

Logan mentioning his aborted wedding elicited a shiver of awareness. She had just slept with a man who had called off his wedding two weeks ago, and she wondered when he'd made love to her, if he had thought of Nina Smith. Had she become a willing replacement for a woman he'd loved enough to ask her to spend her life with him?

She shook off the feeling of uneasiness. It didn't matter. Whatever they offered the other, would only be for the summer. She would enjoy his protection and his passion, and she when she walked away from Logan she would not look back. At least not with any regret.

The setting for the candlelight dinner under the stars became an ethereal event. Instead of eating on the porch, Logan decided to spread a blanket out on the sand, adding throw pillows from the family room sofa to sit on while they dined on an appetizer of gingery chicken kebabs with a honey mustard sauce, sliced avocado, broiled baby lamp chops served with a Madeira sauce, and a full-flavored fragrant chilled rosé.

After her second glass of wine, Caryn lay down on the blanket and stared up at the quarter moon casting an eerie pale glow on the sand and ocean.

"I think you're a much better cook than I am," she said in a singsong voice.

Logan lay beside her, smiling. "I doubt that. After all, you're the daughter of a very successful master chef."

She closed her eyes. "My culinary skills will never match my father's."

Moving closer, Logan turned on his belly and draped an arm over her flat middle. He couldn't remember when he'd been so relaxed. A cool ocean breeze floated over his body, and he wondered if the air had cooled too much for Caryn to remain outdoors wearing only a pair of shorts and a T-shirt. The storm had broken a record-breaking two week heat wave.

"Let me know when you're ready to go in."

"Are you kidding," Caryn remarked, moving closer to his warm body. "I could sleep out here all night."

Raising his head, Logan chuckled. "I can just imagine you waking up screaming because a crab has decided to feast on your bare feet."

She opened her eyes, their gazes meeting in the ghostly moonlight. "If I wake up screaming, then you'll have to protect me. And knowing you, you'll probably catch the hapless crustacean and cook him."

He held her gaze, and there was only the sound of the incoming tide as lapping waves broke against the sandy beach. "You're right about that, Caryn. You'll always have me to protect you."

Everything that was Logan Prescott swept over her in that instant as she rose and looped her arms around his neck, inhaling his familiar fragrance. She savored the unyielding strength of his hard body and his warmth.

Turning her head, she stared longingly into his eyes, smiling. "Thank you for a wonderful dinner."

Logan's gaze moved slowly over her deeply tanned golden-brown face. "I should be the one thanking you. I was carrying a lot of hatred when I first stepped foot on Marble Island. And knowing I had to share this house with a woman did little to improve my disposition."

"And now?"

Reaching up, he picked at the short curling hairs on the nape of her long neck, rubbing them between his fingertips. "Now I wouldn't want it any other way. You've helped me more than you'll ever know."

Her moist breath swept over his mouth as she inched closer. "Are you saying you like sharing the house with me?"

"I like sharing *everything* with you," he whispered seductively. He displayed the sensual smile that always made her catch her breath as she ran her forefinger down the length of his straight, narrow nose.

"You have a beautiful face, Logan."

He went still, then glanced away. "Men aren't beautiful, sweetheart."

"You are," she countered softly. "Everything about your face is so perfect, so evenly balanced. Your eyes, nose, and mouth resemble those on male statues in European museums. You could've been the model for Michelangelo's David."

A slight smile played at the corners of his mouth. "I look nothing like my biological mother, except for coloring, so I assume I must have inherited my features and height from my father."

"Doesn't it bother you that you don't know who your father is? That perhaps you may have passed him on a street and not known it?"

"The very questions you're asking haunted me at one time, but not now. I've learned to deal with now, not the past."

Caryn nodded. Logan was right. She had let go of her past when she decided never to write Tom's name in her journals. All she and Logan had was now, and she intended to enjoy whatever time given them.

"What do you want to do now?" she questioned so softly he had to strain to catch her words.

"I want to make love to you, Miss Caryn Edwards."

She'd asked and he'd been truthful. And it was time she was truthful—to herself and to Logan. "I *need* you to make love to me."

Together, as if on cue, they rose and picked up the remains of their dinner, carried it back to the house, and put everything away. They worked side by side in silence, cleaning the kitchen while anticipating what was to come.

Caryn retreated to her bedroom and showered while Logan did the same, but when she left the adjoining bathroom to reenter her bedroom she found Logan standing at the window staring down at the beach. He wore a pair of silk boxers, the stark white a brilliant contrast against his sable-brown flesh. Her pulse quickened, her gaze sweeping over his exquisitely proportioned body and lingering on the breadth of his wide shoulders, narrow waist, hips, and powerful calves.

Sensing her presence, he turned slowly and stared at her. She'd wrapped a towel around her head and another around her slender body.

"How long have you been waiting for me?"

"About ten minutes."

She held up a jar of scented cream cologne. "Would you mind putting some cream on my back?"

Moving over to the bed, he patted the mattress. "Lie down."

She complied and lay facedown on the sheet, resting her cheek on her folded arms. Closing her eyes, she shivered slightly when Logan removed the towels. The heat from his large body warmed her limbs as he smoothed the delicate fragrant cream over her back, arms, legs, and feet. Turning her over, he repeated his ministrations, his fingers gliding over her shoulders, breasts, and belly.

Caryn closed her eyes against his burning gaze when his

fingers retraced their path and tightened over the fullness of her breasts. His thumbs lingered around the nipples as they hardened, verifying her rising desire.

Closing his eyes, Logan manually traced the curves and valleys of her form, committing every part of her to memory. And he would need the memories after he left Marble Island because Caryn had set the terms for their brief interlude.

He wanted to tell her of the feelings she aroused in him. But how could he tell her he loved her when all she wanted was a fleeting physical attachment? And wouldn't because it would make him too vulnerable, and he doubted whether he would be able to walk away from Caryn Edwards unscathed.

He wished he could be like some men who took whatever a woman offered, not offering or giving up anything in return. But he knew he was different. Caryn had offered him the gift of her body and he'd accepted it, while he'd returned the gift along with his love—a love she would never hear him openly declare.

Lowering his head, his tongue swept over one nipple, then the other. He teased the turgid flesh between his teeth, she gasping and arching off the mattress.

He reached out and held her hands above her head with one hand when she attempted to push him away. The power failure of the night before had not permitted him to visually feast on her naked body, and tonight he wanted his fill.

Her oversized T-shirts had hidden a lush feminine body which drew his devouring gaze. The shirts hid a pair of full, firm breasts with large dark brown nipples. His eyes closed briefly and opened just as quickly when he envisioned his child suckling at her breasts, but dismissed the vision as soon as it appeared. Caryn would never bear his children because she would never become more to him than a passing summer dalliance.

Lowering his body, he released her hands and traced the outline of her lush mouth with his tongue. Freed, she curved her arms around his neck, pulling his closer, her own mouth staking her claim on his full lower lip.

He returned the kiss, his mouth slanting across hers in hungry abandonment. Her soft moans were his undoing as he gathered her in his arms and carried her out of her bedroom and down the hallway to his.

What followed left Caryn gasping as she lay sprawled across Logan's bed, staring at him in the soft light of a bedside lamp. He divested himself of the silk boxers, paused to protect her, then slipped between her thighs with a strong sure thrust of his powerful hips.

The dormant sexuality of her body had been awakened with his hardness, and she couldn't control her whimpers of delight with the erotic pleasure flooding her whole being. The passion became an ache, becoming stronger and stronger with each thrust as she rose, arching to meet him.

Wanting to get closer, Logan reached down and cupped Caryn's hips, holding her captive and not permitting her movement. He felt the soft crush of her breasts against his chest, inhaled the clean sweetness of her freshly showered body, and he tried measuring the contractions of her fevered flesh pulsing around his rigid sex.

She'd ignited a fire which threatened to incinerate him as the flames of passion grew higher and hotter. His heart pounded uncontrollably in his chest, and he thought if he didn't release his passions it would explode.

A moan of ecstasy slipped through Caryn's lips, followed rapidly by another, then another. She felt the heat of Logan's large body sweep down the length of hers, felt his hardness grow harder while her head thrashed wildly back and forth on the pillow.

The pleasure he gave her escalated and spiraled out of control, sending her hurtling into a fiery blaze of awesome, shuddering ecstasy. She screamed his name at the same time he groaned out hers. Together they climbed the peaks of fulfillment with gusts of desire shaking them long after the turbulence of their passions had quieted and cooled.

Caryn turned away from him, pressing her face to the pillow to stop the words of love from escaping. She hadn't wanted to admit it, but she had made a mistake to sleep with Logan, and she wondered how long it would take before she blurted out her love for him.

Chapter Thirteen

July seventh—

I did it! I slept with Logan. It's not as if I'd planned for to happen, but it did.

I suppose I can blame it on the summer storm that swept up the coast, but that's taking the coward's way out. It's so hard to explain—just like everything which has happened to me since I arrived on Marble Island.

I'd promised myself I wouldn't cut my hair until I turned thirty, and I have. I'd also told myself I wouldn't fall in love again, and I have. And for that I must blame Logan Prescott. I don't know what it is about him, but whatever it is, it won't permit me to follow the dictates of my mind.

Common sense told me not to try to drive back to Marble Island during a tropical storm, but I made the attempt because all I thought about was Logan and how I wanted to be with him. What had begun as a totally wonderful day wherein I treated myself to a day of beauty—haircut, facial, full body massage, manicure and pedicure—ended with my risking my life driving back to the island in a torrential downpour and dangerously high winds.

The moment I heard Logan's voice, felt his arms around me, I realized how much I loved him.

Sleeping with him is an exquisite experience. I'm unable to put into words just how I feel when he's inside me. And the passion he arouses is frightening, unbelievably frightening, because there are times when I want to scream out how much I've come to love him.

Loving him is my secret and will always remain my secret.

Logan scrolled down the screen on his laptop containing the zoning board proposal, listening intently to his father's voice coming through the receiver on the cellular telephone.

"There shouldn't be a question of ingress and egress because the entire development is laid out in a quadrangle," he argued softly. "Look at the plans again, Dad, and you'll see what I'm referring to."

"Hold on a minute, son. There are so damn many papers on my desk that I can't . . . wait a minute, I have it." There was a slight pause. "I see what you mean. It looks good. In fact it looks very good. Nice work."

"Thank you."

"There shouldn't be too much of a debate over this one," Jace remarked, confidence filling his deep, authoritative voice.

Logan smiled, nodding. "I also figured as much." He paused, choosing his words carefully. "Have you had any feedback on new investors?"

"Nothing yet. But I'm confident we'll find someone to finance this construction project."

"I hope you're right, Dad."

"How often have I been wrong, Logan?"

"Not often."

"Precisely. I'm not trying to put any pressure on you to return to Raleigh, but I want you to think about becoming more involved in the firm."

A frown creased Logan's smooth forehead. What was his father talking about? He was practically running the architectural firm. "How much more involved do you want me to be?"

"I want you to take over."

His fingers tightened on the palm-size instrument, squeezing until he left an impression of the telephone on his palm. "When did you decide this?"

"Maeve and I talked about this the day you called."

"She told you why I called off the wedding?"

"Yes. And I don't blame you. But this has nothing to do with Nina Smith or her father. I'll turn sixty-nine at the end of October, and I no longer want the full responsibility of running a company at my age. I've been promising your mother I'd take a few months off and go on an around-the-world cruise with her. I probably could've put her off until next year, but she's given me an ultimatum."

"What's the ultimatum?"

"She'll ask Edwina Mattison to go with her."

"Dad, she can't. Edwina is worse than a blood-crazed shark when it comes to men. You don't want Mama's reputation compromised by vacationing with that woman."

"Precisely."

"When are you thinking of stepping down?"

"As soon as you return. I'd prefer it sooner than later."

Logan's gaze narrowed as he stared out at the beach where Caryn sat on the sand with Domino while the dog sniffed at her bare feet. How could he leave her now? How could he walk away from the woman who had helped him let go of his anger and bitterness? A woman who showed him how to love. A woman he'd fallen in love with.

His expression was impassive. "I'd rather it be later."

"How much later, son?"

"The end of the summer."

"I thought you were only going to be away for a month."

"I've changed my mind." And his change in plans was because of the woman with whom he was sharing a beachfront house. Not only was he sharing the house, but also her bed.

"Then I'll look for your return at the end of the summer." There was no mistaking the disappointment in Jace Prescott's voice.

"I'll call you in a couple of days."

Depressing a button, he ended the call, cursing softly under his breath. His father's decision to retire had come at the wrong time. If Jace stepped down as CEO of J. Prescott and Associates, then he was expected to oversee the day-to-day operations of the architectural and design firm. He would no longer enjoy the luxury of working from home and going into the office two or three times a week. And he also would not have the option of spending weeks at a time on an island like Marble Island. Unlike Caryn, he would not have the summers for his leisure.

He'd contacted Hamilton and Cynthia, putting off their visit until midweek once he realized he wanted more time alone with Caryn. They'd been sleeping together for less than a week, and the anticipation of sharing of her body each night had escalated instead of declining. They usually breakfasted together, but did not see each other again until late afternoon. He often wondered where she went whenever she drove away in her car, yet could not bring himself to ask her. But this morning was different. She had remained on Marble Island.

Staring at the beach, he watched Caryn rise to her feet, her black swimsuit–clad body clearly outlined against the sun-bleached sand and calm gray waters of the Atlantic. She waded into the surf, then turned and glanced over her shoulder at Domino, who appeared reluctant to venture into the ocean.

Logan rose to his feet and whistled sharply between his teeth. The Dalmatian's ears lifted, and he turned quickly and bounded back to the porch. "Stay, boy," he commanded softly. The frisky puppy lay down on the top step, placing his muzzle between his spotted paws.

Man and dog watched while Caryn dove over a wave and swam strongly out into the ocean. Then, as if on cue, both went completely still, staring intently as she disappeared from their field of vision.

Logan moved off the porch and made his way to the beach, his gaze fixed on the area where he'd last seen Caryn. Not realizing he'd been holding his breath, he released it when he saw her swimming back to the shore. Why were his protective instincts so strong with her when they hadn't been with any other woman?

But then he had to ask himself whether she needed protecting. There was no doubt she could handle herself physically, and she certainly wasn't reticent about telling a man what she wanted and did not want. She hadn't hesitated letting him know that she was willing to sleep with him, but wanted nothing more. There would be no declarations of love or talk of a commitment. He smiled as she neared him. Even though she'd denied it, and despite her overall gentle nature, he still thought of her as scrappy.

Her smile matched his. "Why don't you come in? The water's at least seventy-five degrees."

Reaching out, he caught her hand and pulled her to his side, the moisture from her wet body seeping into his shirt and shorts.

"That sounds like a wonderful inviation. Wait here for me to change."

Caryn sat on the beach, her gaze fixed on the ocean when Logan returned wearing a pair of Speedos. She jumped slightly as he sat down beside her and eased her onto his lap.

"A penny for your thoughts," he whispered close to her ear.

Smiling, she rested her head against his shoulder. "They're more like a hundred dollars."

He whistled. "That's rather steep."

"They're rather profound," she said in a solemn tone. And they were. How could she tell him he occupied her waking thoughts and now even her dreams? How could she tell him she loved him so much she ached whenever she thought of not seeing him? That she left Marble Island after breakfast to distance herself from him.

"Can you afford to listen?" she teased.

Tightening his grip on her waist, he pressed his lips to her wet curly hair. "I'll stop you when you deplete my bank balance."

"I feel I'm at a crossroads in my life," Caryn began, closing her eyes. "I love teaching, but I feel as if I could walk away from it without too many regrets. I felt like this at another time when I decided I wanted to change disciplines. Day after day I'd walk into the classroom and watch the blank stares on some students' faces whenever we discussed the works of Charles Dickens, Edith Wharton, James Baldwin, or Toni Morrison. It was as if they didn't care about what these brilliant writers had to say through their written words.

"I taught literature for three years, then took courses to enable me to teach life and career skills. I noticed the different attitudes immediately. I was teaching something most kids could relate to. For them discussing how to manage a limited budget, or how to prepare nutritious inexpensive meals was more to their liking. I love the give-and-take, the challenge of teaching, but there's still something missing. I know it's not my teaching skills, but something within me.

"I feel a restlessness akin to what a nomad feels when she can't settle in any particular place. It's not a yearning to travel because I've done that. I've visited Europe twice, and fulfilled a lifelong passion to see several African countries. I've tried analyzing what it is and can only come up with the justification that I'd moved around too much as a child.

"Every time my parents opened a new B&B, I had to leave my friends at one school to make new ones in a different state. I'd come to think of myself as a gypsy, and there were times when I actually dressed like one. One teacher in particular wrote a note home to my parents complaining about my style of dress—"

"What did they say?" Logan asked, interrupting her monologue for the first time.

"They saw nothing wrong with it. They told her I was very artistic and that I was just expressing myself with long flowing skirts and what I now think of as loads of very tacky jewelry."

"Were you a popular student?"

"Not with the girls, but the boys loved what they said was my 'free spirit.' At that time I wore my hair down to my hips, and I had affected the habit of not putting any oil on it whenever it was humid. Everyone said I looked like a throwback to the hippie and Woodstock era with hair sticking out all over my head."

Logan chuckled, his gaze sweeping over the short, shiny curls clinging to her well-shaped head. "The girls probably hated you because you were so much more beautiful than they were."

Curving an arm around his slender waist, Caryn laughed softly. "You're wonderful for a woman's ego."

"It's not your ego I want to appeal to, sweetheart."

She felt her breath catch in her throat, then start up again, increasing in rhythm until she was almost lightheaded. *No,* she cried silently.

"Don't, Logan," she said, finding her voice. "Don't make what we have more complicated than it should be. You have to know I like you, otherwise I'd never permit myself to sleep with you."

Fighting to control his temper, Logan swallowed back the virulent words poised on the tip of his tongue. She was using him. Using him for her own sexual gratification.

"What is it you want?" His voice was deceptively, calm, soft.

"Friendship," she replied without hesitating.

The hell with friendship, he shouted silently. Friends did not sleep together. And friends were usually honest with each other. He wanted to tell her he loved her, but she did not want his love. If he could, he would pack up everything and leave her and Marble Island, but now that he'd sampled her flesh he knew he was lost, lost in the passion she aroused in him just by existing.

"Friendship is what you want and friendship you shall have." Tightening his grip on her body, he stood up and held her effortlessly in his embrace.

She buried her face in the hollow between his neck and shoulder, eliciting a smile from Logan. He couldn't let her go any more than he could stop breathing, knowing he would love Caryn Edwards until the day he drew his last breath.

They swam, floated weightlessly on the calm waters, then after tiring returned to the house. Logan returned Domino to his cage, while Caryn retreated to her bathroom to shower. She shampooed her hair and had applied an instant conditioner at the same time as the door to the stall opened.

Logan stepped under the flow of the lukewarm water. "I thought I'd share your shower and save water." His midnight gaze caressed her face and body, taking in the rich buckskin-brown hue of her face and a deeper, richer brown on her shoulders and back. It was apparent the sun loved Caryn Edwards. It had kissed her flesh, resulting in beautiful vibrant browns from chestnut to rosewood.

Giving him a saucy smile, Caryn tilted her chin to meet his amused stare. "I didn't know you were also an environmentalist."

"I didn't know it myself until now," he whispered, pulling her wet, naked body to his.

Her hands moved slowly up his hard chest, feeling muscle and sinew as they registered the unleashed power in his upper body. She hadn't realized how wide his shoulders were until now, and she doubted whether her arms would meet around them.

He stood motionless, nothing moving, not even his eyes. She drank in his male beauty with his high, chiseled cheekbones, smooth and nearly poreless black skin, and his perfectly balanced features.

Going on tiptoe, she pressed her mouth to his, his lips parting and permitting her tongue to dance with his. Logan was forced to move when his hands circled her waist, and he lifted her until her head was even with his. Caryn curved her arms around his strong neck, deepening the kiss until she felt their hearts beating in unison.

Their passions rose quickly, and neither remembered when they sank to the floor of the stall and loved the other until time stood still. Simultaneously, their passions exploded, their world tilting on its axis and leaving them gasping in the sweetest ecstasy they had ever known.

Caryn studied her face in the mirror over the vanity, using her fingertips to comb her gel-slicked hair off her forehead and over her ears.

She and Logan had spent most of the morning in bed, sleeping, awakening to lengthening afternoon shadows. They showered again—this time separately after agreeing to dine out.

She smoothed the body-revealing dress down over her flat belly and turned slightly to survey her hips. The black jersey tank dress clung to every curve, ending four inches above her knees. Reaching down, she slipped her bare feet into a pair of three-inch black patent leather sling-strap sandals. Glancing up at the mirror, she saw Logan walk into her bedroom, and there was no mistaking his reaction to her attire. She straightened and turned slowly, meeting his startled gaze.

"I'm ready," she said softly.

Logan opened his mouth several times before he was able to speak. "You look exquisite."

And he hadn't lied. Caryn had brushed most of the curl out of her hair and smoothed it off her face. The style would have looked less than feminine on another woman, but the delicateness of her face shattered that image. The vermilion color on her lips competed with the brilliant color of her gold-green eyes.

Reluctantly, he tore his gaze away from her face and leisurely surveyed her body. The tiny black dress hugged her curves like second skin, offering him a glimpse of tanned womanly breasts rising above the low-cut décolletage. The straps were so narrow, he marveled how they held the garment up. Strong, shapely, smooth legs and well-groomed feet complemented her breathtaking appearance.

How could he escort her into Addie's, where he was certain more than half the men on Marble Island would be lusting after her? Foreign emotions surfaced, he recognized them instantly as jealousy and possessiveness. He didn't want another man to look at her, let alone touch her. How was he going to make it through the summer without going crazy?

Caryn's smile was dazzling. "Thank you."

Her luminous gaze swept over his tall frame. He had elected to wear a flattering shade of pale wheat which blended attractively with his rich, dark coloring. A tailored, finely woven, linen, banded-collar shirt and slacks were complemented by a brown and beige, paisley, silk vest and a pair of brown, woven, leather slip-ons.

Picking up a tiny, black, crocheted purse, she walked over to him. "Let's hope I can remain a lady tonight."

He shifted a questioning eyebrow. "Why shouldn't you?"

"The word is, the single women on Marble Island are after you, and I'd hate for them to disrespect me to my face."

Logan went completely still. Could he hope she was also experiencing bouts of jealousy? That her feelings for him ran deeper than just *friendship* and physical gratification?

"That shouldn't happen because everyone believes we're married."

"Since when does being married stop anyone from going after what they truly want?"

Taking her fingers, he squeezed them gently. "You're right about that, even though I'd never go after another man's wife."

And she would never go after another woman's husband.

The sun was beginning to set, its descent lingering over

the ocean and taking with it a sweltering humidity as Logan led Caryn to his automobile. A knowing smile curved his mouth when he lifted her onto the passenger seat. It would've been impossible for her to make it up into the Jeep with her slim dress and heels without his assistance.

Ten minutes later, he parked behind the rows of stores along Main Street and repeated helping Caryn to her feet. Hand-in-hand they made their way to Addie's, sharing a smile. The two women from New York City stood on line in front of them.

They exchanged pleasantries with Mandisa and Shevonne until they were called for their table. Caryn noticed neither had even deigned her with a cursory glance because they'd stared openly and brazenly at Logan. A surge of pride filled her as she moved closer to him and looped her arm through his. The gesture caused him to move closer while at the same time pressing his lips to her scented hair. Again they shared a secret smile.

They were shown a table for two in a corner, and they spent their dinner talking quietly while staring into each other's eyes. All who noticed them recognized what was that they refused to see—they were in love.

Logan pulled Caryn against him as a live band segued into a slower dance number. After they left Addie's, he'd driven up the coast to a little town populated by vacationers where the median age was under forty. The town's reputation was buoyed by the number of restaurants and dance clubs offering excellent food and a never-ending source of entertainment.

Caryn felt the slow, steady pumping of his heart against her breasts and closed her eyes. The heat of his body stirred the haunting fragrance of his cologne that was so well suited to his personality. It was subtle and hypnotic.

Tightening her grip on his neck, she moved closer, and without saying a word her body communicated her silent confession: *I love you, Logan Prescott.*

She'd stopped asking herself how she could've fallen in love so quickly. And why had she selected him as her object of desire. All she knew was whenever he entered her body, he erased the lingering pain and eradicated the lingering scars.

She'd told herself and continued to tell herself that she was mature enough to walk away from Logan once their summer dalliance ended. She would thank him for the experience, then pick up the pieces of her life to plan for the next phase.

Then she did what she hadn't done in a long time—she prayed. She prayed she would be able to leave him without blurting out she loved him and would love him forever.

Chapter Fourteen

July eleventh—

The Wheatons are due to arrive today, and I hope neither will suspect that I'd been crying. Putting cold tea bags over my eyes helped, but there is still some noticeable swelling.

I don't know what happened to me after Logan and I made love this morning, but without warning I began to cry and couldn't stop. He became quite upset, thinking he had hurt me; however, I lied and told him that I was in the throes of PMS and cry easily during this time. I'm hoping he believed me.

What I couldn't tell him was that making love with him has become akin to a slow dying—a minute at a time.

How can I continue to sleep with him and dissolve into inconsolable tears afterward?

I found myself crying even before we finished making love. The pleasure he offers me is beyond description. He never takes me quickly, but our joining is always a slow, rapturous one. First comes his weight, then his hardness, after that the rhythmic, measured thrusts of his hips. I feel everything—all of him. and at that moment we truly become one person.

Since sleeping together, we usually make love at night and early in the morning when we awake. But yesterday changed that regimen. We made love twice in the afternoon, and it appears as if Logan's voluptuous sexual appetite is as strong, or perhaps stronger than mine. It's as if I want to make up for all of the times I wanted a man after my marriage ended. Now, after sleeping with Logan I'm glad I waited. He has made the wait more than worthwhile.

I'm not certain whether Logan wants more from our relationship, but I can't give him more. I simply cannot chance repeating the same mistake. I refuse to lose control of myself and my life again.

Classes resume August sixteenth and I'm due back for faculty orientation on the eleventh, which allows me less than three weeks with Logan. He'd told me upon his arrival that he was going to stay a few weeks and I assume he'll stay until the end of the month.

Caryn liked Cynthia Wheaton on sight. She was her husband's physical counterpart: tall, slender, tanned, and claimed the same sun-streaked natural blond hair. They looked more like brother and sister than husband and wife with the exception of eye color. Hamilton's were a dark blue, while Cynthia's were a luminous sea green.

Caryn watched a slow, sensual smile cross Logan's face as he stood on the porch, muscular arms crossed over his chest, watching his college friends alight from their car. Cynthia lingered beside the car, hands folded on her hips over an oversized T-shirt. Twin dimples kissed her tanned cheeks as she watched Logan make his way down the porch, her gaze widening appreciably with his approach.

She extended her arms, and Logan did not disappoint her when he folded her to his chest. "How are you, Raven?"

"Wonderful, Tia."

Pulling back, Cynthia surveyed his startling white golf

shirt and matching walking shorts. "So I see," she said slowly. "Tell me, Raven, how did you improve on perfection?"

Logan hugged her again, kissing her cheek. "Ham, your wife is flirting with me."

Hamilton removed two large canvas bags from the trunk of a spacious late-model Mercedes-Benz sedan. "I'd always suspected she was a shameless wench," he said, laughing.

Logan released Cynthia and took one of the bags from Hamilton. "Come on in out of the heat." He led the way up to the porch, smiling at Caryn. His free hand caught her fingers, squeezing gently and pulling her along with him.

Caryn held the screen door open for Cynthia and Hamilton, while Logan took their bags to the master bedroom. They had decided beforehand to give the Wheatons the Crawfords' bedroom because of the adjoining private bathroom and easy accessibility to the first level.

Cynthia smiled her dimpled smile, extending her right hand to Caryn. "Cynthia Wheaton. But everyone calls me Tia."

She shook the proffered hand. "Hello. I'm Caryn Edwards."

Glancing around, Cynthia shook her head. "This place is beautiful. It's more than three times the size of the bungalow we're renting on Gooseneck. Ham and I really would like to thank you and Logan for inviting us to hang out with you."

She wanted to tell Cynthia it was Logan and not she who had invited them. "Logan and I love this place. Come, let me show you around."

Cynthia nodded her approval as she entered and exited rooms the Shelton twins had cleaned earlier that morning. All of the floors and pieces of furniture gleamed, and the fragrance of potpourri and fresh-cut flowers wafted in the living and dining rooms and in the master bedroom. The delicate beauty of vase-filled wisteria, sweet peas, and a profusion of snow-white and pale pink peonies presented a visual feast. And utilizing the special details she had learned from her designer mother, Caryn had added the touches that had made the spaces at their bed and breakfast retreats appear ethereal.

Logan had displayed an inordinate amount of patience when she sent him back to the Winn-Dixie, not once but twice, for several varieties of loose tea. Having the Wheatons as guests would provide the perfect opportunity to serve them afternoon tea.

She and Cynthia retreated to the porch where Logan and Ham sat opposite each other on matching love seat rockers, talking. The overhead fan turned slowly, further cooling the shaded space. Caryn sat down beside Logan, while Cynthia eased her lanky frame down next to her husband.

Dropping an arm over Caryn's shoulders, Logan smiled at her enchanting profile. "I was just telling Ham that we're going to eat on the beach.

"I like the sound of that," Cynthia stated with a dimpled smile.

"We've planned for a presunset beach picnic," Caryn offered as an explanation. The moment she said *we,* she realized she thought of herself and Logan as a couple. Tilting her chin, she stared at him staring back at her.

"What's on the menu?" Hamilton questioned.

Logan continued to stare at Caryn, capturing her gaze and making her his willing prisoner. "Steamed lobster with a tarragon cream sauce," he began.

"Marinated asparagus with an egg salad," she continued. "Prosciutto and melon, a tricolor salad with avocado, tomato, and mozzarella cheese—"

"Enough!" Hamilton interrupted, shaking his head.

"And don't forget the grilled clams and mussels," Logan added.

"I see you haven't changed, have you?" Hamilton questioned. "Everyone used to camp out in Raven's tiny apartment on the weekends because we knew he was always experimenting with a new dish.

"And there were about a half-dozen of you deadbeats who were very willing guinea pigs," Logan countered.

Hamilton laughed and nodded his head. "Even if you botched a dish, it was still better than the swill served on campus."

Caryn exchanged a smile with Hamilton. "And I suppose you guys found time to party your brains out."

Logan shook his head. "I didn't. Not with architecture as a major. Unlike some others I know who decided to major in the dramatic arts."

"Bite your tongue, Raven. We were *serious* drama students," Cynthia said in defense of herself and her husband."

"Are you actors?" Caryn questioned, staring at the attractive blond couple.

Hamilton shook his head. "We haven't acted in years. I'm directing now while Tia's become a script writer. We're part of an independent theater group in Bucks County, Pennsylvania."

The direction of conversation changed from the Wheatons artistic endeavors to Caryn's teaching experiences, then finally to Logan. He gave his friends an update on what he'd been involved in since they last met, while Caryn excused herself. She went into the house to bring out some liquid refreshment, and she was surprised when Cynthia followed, offering to help.

Cynthia rested a hip against a countertop in the kitchen, staring at Caryn. "I hope you won't think me forward, but I couldn't help noticing how Raven looks at you. When we were in college, Ham and I saw him practically all of the time, and not once did I ever see him look at a woman the way he does at you."

Opening the refrigerator, she took out a chilled pitcher of rose tea. "It's been a while since you've seen him. Perhaps he's changed."

"It's been more than twelve years since we've all been together, and in that time anyone can change. But I've seen Raven with enough women to know that you're special."

Caryn felt a rush of heat suffuse her face. "Special how?"

"Firstly, you look nothing like the girls he used to date, and secondly he appears so much more relaxed. Everyone used to tease him, saying he emitted an energy that put anyone who came within five feet of him on edge. He'd walk into a room and you'd know it without even seeing him."

She knew what Cynthia meant. She had felt it the first time she encountered him when he walked into the house calling out her name, and she felt it each time he came to her to make love. Without uttering a word, he'd silently communicated to her what he'd wanted.

"Maybe it's because he's older, more mature," Caryn argued.

"And he's in love with you despite the fact he told Ham the two of you were masquerading as a married couple for the summer," Cynthia retorted.

Caryn felt a rush of uneasiness. It hadn't bothered her that the people on Marble Island thought they were married because it served to thwart the advances of eligible men and women; however, she did not want anyone else to know of their ongoing subterfuge.

"He couldn't love me. He doesn't even know me."

"He loves you, Caryn," Cynthia insisted. "And I suspect you also love him."

"You're wrong," she countered firmly. Logan could not love her, nor would she permit herself to openly admit she loved him.

She filled a large bamboo tray with an assortment of delicately prepared salmon pinwheels, parmesan beignets, and an assortment of cherry tartlets, cherry-nut shortbread cookies, and almond macaroons. She handed Cynthia the tray, who merely raised a pale eyebrow and walked out of the kitchen.

Cynthia's accusation replayed in her head: *And I suspect you also love him.* Was she that transparent? If a woman she'd been introduced to half an hour ago saw what she'd tried to conceal, she wondered if Logan also saw it. She hoped not.

She followed Cynthia to the porch, carrying the pitcher of tea and tall iced tea glasses.

The two couples lay on a blanket, staring up at the navy-blue, star-littered sky. The lingering smells of grilled seafood wafted in the air along with the ever present scent of the ocean. The daytime temperatures had cooled with the setting sun, and Caryn snuggled against Logan, feeding on his body's heat.

"Are you certain I can't get you a sweater, sweetheart?"

"No, thanks," she mumbled against his chest. "Besides, I doubt whether I'll be able to move to put it on. I can't remember ever eating so much."

"Tell me about it," Hamilton concurred, rolling over on his belly and closing his eyes.

"What do you think did us in?" came Cynthia's slurring voice.

"It had to be Logan's lobsters," Caryn declared.

"Yeah, the lobsters," the Wheatons said in unison.

Logan's lobsters, which he called *La Fricassée d'Homard à la Crème d'Estragon*—Fricassee of Lobster with Tarragon Cream Sauce, had been the highlight of the varied menu. Each lobster, weighing an average of four and a half pounds, was served with a rich crème fraîche flavored with sautéed shallots, fresh tarragon, unsalted butter, and freshly ground pepper.

The lobsters had followed their consuming a countless number of steamed clams and mussels, the marinated asparagus spears, a mixed green salad, and several glasses of a cranberry-pineapple vodka punch Hamilton had concocted as his contribution. Painful groans ensued once Cynthia presented her homemade strawberry shortcake, and she promptly returned it to the refrigerator.

The dozen flickering candles in small metal pails lit up the darkened beach, their wavering lights resembling fireflies in the encroaching blackness. The night was still, silent, except for the sounds of gurgling water washing up on the beach with the incoming tide.

Hamilton rolled over again, resting his head on folded arms. "I think I drank too much."

"I told you not to have that last one," Cynthia admonished her husband in a soft voice.

"I was celebrating."

Logan shifted to a more comfortable position. "What are you celebrating, Ham?"

"Fatherhood."

Logan sat up, bringing Caryn with him. "You guys are expecting a baby?"

Cynthia smiled, nodding. "We've decided to sample parenthood. It's about time anyway. We've been married for almost thirteen years, and my biological clock was beginning to gong like Big Ben."

Logan reached over and clapped a hand on Hamilton's shoulder, then kissed Cynthia tenderly on her mouth, offering his congratulations while Caryn mumbled her own good wishes.

She'd wondered why Cynthia hadn't drunk any of the punch, and now she knew. She refused to think of the baby she'd lost, which if it had survived would probably now be a very rambunctious toddler.

She did not want to think of what could've been or what was. She had to remind herself not to dwell on her past. It was only the future that was of any importance.

Caryn realized Hamilton wasn't the only one feeling the effects of the punch as she made an attempt to stand up. Logan caught her as she swayed heavily against his side.

"Do you think you can make it?" he questioned softly.

Squinting up at his shadowed features, she shook her head. "I don't know. Ham should've put a warning label on that punch."

Logan chuckled. "Ham was a bartender in another life, and he made drinks which tasted like Kool-Aid when you drank them, but left you feeling like road kill the following day. I should've warned you about his lethal cocktails."

Holding on to the front of Logan's shirt, she rested her head on his chest. "A fine friend you turned out to be. You're supposed to be looking out for me."

He held her close, supporting her limp body. "I can't be your friend," he whispered near her ear.

"Why not?"

"Because friends don't do what we do with each other. At least not the friends I know."

Her head came up, and she stared at him at the same time as he steered her toward the house. "But we decided it would be friendship and nothing more."

"*You* decided, Caryn. Being friends was your decision, not mine."

She stiffened and pulled out of his loose grip. "You lied to me."

"Wrong, Caryn," he shot back. "How can you believe what we offer each other is nothing more than friendship?"

"That's all it is!"

They stood on the porch under the golden glow of recessed lights, staring at each other, their chests rising and falling in unison.

He arched a sweeping black silky eyebrow. "Now, who's a liar?"

She stiffened as if he'd struck her, but she recovered quickly, flashing a saccharine smile. "I thought you'd be man enough to be able to handle sleeping with a woman without the onus of a commitment."

It was Logan's turn to recoil from her stinging challenge. But instead of retaliating with the sarcastic words poised on the tip of his tongue, he opened the screen door, bowed slightly from the waist, and waited for her to enter the house. Then he closed the door behind her, staring at her staring back at him behind the finely woven mesh screen.

His hypnotic black gaze burned her face, then her chest, and moved lower as it roamed leisurely over her body, communicating he wanted her despite her refusal to acknowledge what they had shared.

"I'm going to make some coffee," Caryn said quietly

before turning and retreating to the kitchen. She did not have to turn around to know Logan hadn't moved because she felt the heat of his gaze on her back. It was the fire and energy Cynthia accused him of possessing. But what Cynthia hadn't realized was she'd always felt his energy. And it was greatest whenever he lay between her thighs.

July fourteenth—

Ham and Tia have been with us for three days, and unfortunately rain and heavy fog for two of those days forced us to remain indoors. But I must admit having them stay with us has been most enjoyable and has help buffer what I feel is a rising tension developing between Logan and I.

Since the Wheatons' arrival we have not shared a bed. Logan came to my bedroom, but I sent him away, telling him I wanted to sleep alone because of menstrual cramps. He retreated, but not before asking whether I wanted him to get something to help ease my discomfort. I know he is still annoyed with me for not acknowledging that our relationship has exceeded the boundaries of friendship, but I can't relent. I can't let Logan know I love him and give up the part of myself which permits me to love him more than I love myself. It has taken a long time, but I've learned to love myself selflessly. And until I'm in complete control of myself and my life, I cannot or will not share it with anyone.

I can see the sun for the first time in two days. There is still a lingering fog which had descended on the island and made driving anywhere nearly impossible. I hope the fog lifts because I'm looking forward to our first Friday night outdoor concert. Printed flyers taped to store windows in the business district advertised prerecorded selections from popular Broadway shows. The flyer also suggested attendees bring a blanket or folding chairs for an informal gathering on the lawn behind the church. The concert is scheduled to begin at eight and end at midnight.

Like Logan, Ham, and Tia, I'm looking forward to getting out of the house.

Chapter Fifteen

Caryn lay on a blanket beside Logan, eyes closed and her head cradled on his solid shoulder. It was the closest they'd been in days, and now that she felt the unyielding strength in his muscular body while inhaling the sensual fragrance of his cologne, she realized how much she'd missed him. They had occupied the same space, slept under the same roof, yet she had missed him.

"Are you comfortable?" he asked softly, pulling her closer to his side.

"Quite comfortable," she replied, not opening her eyes.

Ham and Cynthia lay less than six feet away on their own blanket, talking quietly to each other.

The fog had lifted midday, leaving the skies clear and cloud-free. The humidity had also lessened and the night air was perfect for an outdoor concert.

The lights ringing the church's lawn dimmed at the same time the familiar strains to the opening theme of *West Side Story* came through the powerful speakers set up around the expansive space. Mothers hushed their children, and all talk ceased as everyone settled down to enjoy a summer night filled with music.

Caryn felt herself slipping into a magical world created by the music and the protective warmth of the man holding her to his heart. He shifted her effortlessly until one leg rested between his as she lay half on and half off his body, her thigh pressed to his groin.

"Don't move," he whispered when she attempted to extract herself. Swallowing back a moan, she felt his hardness pressing against her flesh through the cotton fabric covering her thigh. "I want you to know I'll always want you even if you don't want me," he rasped against her ear.

But I do want you, she pleaded silently. She wanted him now, tomorrow, the next day, and she wanted him forever. She loved him just that much.

The taped selections segued to popular hits from *Cats, Jelly's Last Jam, Les Miserables, Phantom of the Opera, The Wiz,* to the classics from *Oklahoma, South Pacific,* and *The King and I.*

As the night wore on, many left surreptitiously, leaving those who decided to remain and enjoy the entire program. Hamilton and Cynthia departed reluctantly, saying she needed more than her usual amount of sleep because of her condition. She was now three months pregnant, but her body had yet to exhibit the obvious evidence of impending motherhood.

"Let me know when you're ready to leave," Logan stated after the Wheatons departed.

Caryn pressed her lips to his warm throat. "I'd like to stay until the end."

He smiled. "So would I."

They stayed until the last note faded away just before the midnight hour, then stood up, folded their blanket, and made their way back slowly to the house on Watermelon Patch Lane.

Logan delayed going upstairs as he went to see to Domino's needs, while Caryn walked up the staircase to her bedroom. She showered, brushed her teeth, then pulled on a lightweight nightgown and fell across the bed. She was asleep less than a minute after she'd extinguished the lamp.

She'd just settled into the throes of a deep, dreamless slumber when she felt the heat and weight. Startled, she sat up, but was pulled back to the mattress just as quickly.

"Go back to sleep, Caryn."

Sighing, she complied, falling asleep in Logan's protective embrace.

"Are you sure you're coming down next weekend?" Cynthia asked Logan as he hugged her.

"Of course," he replied, smiling over her head.

"And if you don't come, then Ham will get it," she said.

Pulling back, Logan frowned at her. "Get what?"

"One of my celebrated, hysterical crying jags."

Hamilton closed the trunk of his car, shaking his head. "Don't do that to me, Raven. I can't stand the woman's tears."

Logan released Cynthia and placed an arm around Hamilton's shoulders. "Come on, man," he said softly. "She's an accomplished actress."

"Oh, no, man. It's different. The tears she throws at me now are not staged. The doctor said it's because of the baby."

An expression of disbelief crossed Logan's face. "You've got to be kiddin' me."

"No lie, Raven. Wait until you're due to become a father. It *ain't* easy," he stated between clenched teeth.

"What are you whispering about, Ham?"

He smiled at his wife. "Nothing, Tia. I was just telling Raven that I hope he won't disappoint us."

Caryn also smiled as she winked at Logan. "Don't worry about us not coming, Tia. We'll arrive early Saturday afternoon."

Her brilliant green eyes shimmered with excitement. "Ham and I want to plan something very special to thank you for your fabulous hospitality."

The two women hugged each other while the men offered the other rough embraces. Hamilton helped Cynthia into the Mercedes, then took his own seat behind the wheel. Logan and Caryn stood together, holding hands and watching as the sedan slowly backed out of the driveway before speeding away and leaving Marble Island behind.

Logan turned to Caryn, smiling down at her. "I think they enjoyed their stay."

"I enjoyed having them."

His eyebrows shifted. "You were a wonderful hostess, and I'd like to thank you for that."

Standing on tiptoe, she touched her lips to his before he could kiss her first. "You're welcome."

Without warning, he swung her up in his arms and headed toward the house. "What have you planned for yourself today?"

Tightening her grip on his strong neck, Caryn rested her head on his shoulder. "Laundry."

"Forget it."

"I can't forget it, Logan. I'm running out of clean clothes."

"Let the Shelton kids do the laundry. Why do you think I pay them."

"By the way, how much are you paying them?"

He climbed the half-dozen steps to the veranda, sat down on a love seat rocker, and settled Caryn comfortably across his lap.

"That's privileged information between employer and employees," he said, giving her a full-mouthed smile.

"Oh, it's like that, Logan Prescott?"

He nodded slowly. "That it is."

"I'd thought you'd gotten over being a tight-ass."

His eyebrows shot up. "You still haven't changed your opinion of me, have you?"

"No." It was her turn to give him a saucy smile.

The gesture entranced him as his gaze widened, taking in the smooth darkness of her tanned skin. He telegraphed the stubborn tilt of her delicate chin and visually traced the outline of her lush mouth. He found it hard to believe that this little slip of a woman had crawled under his skin like an invisible itch he didn't want scratched.

He had come to love the sound of her voice which claimed an unusual accent that made it impossible to identify where she'd grown up; he also loved her passion; a passion that knew no boundaries; an unrestrained passion that always left him reeling with a sense of complete fulfillment once he spilled the soaring lust she always elicited in him.

And in that instant he wanted what his college friends had—a solid marriage and impending parenthood. Before coming to Marble Island, he thought that was what he wanted with Nina, but he realized he'd wanted to marry her for the wrong reason.

His parents had hinted subtly for some time he settle down, and unknowingly he had sublimated their wishes. He'd known Nina for ten years, but had never considered dating her. They were seated together at a wedding for a mutual friend, and before the reception ended they had promised to keep in touch.

He called Nina for a dinner date, then before he realized it they were seeing each other exclusively. He'd told himself that he was in love with her, refusing to acknowledge the infatuation was based solely on a physical dependence.

They dated for a year before he proposed marriage, then decided to wait another year before exchanging vows. What had surprised him was not once had he ever suspected Nina of not being faithful to him, and he had to give her credit for being an expert in deception.

"What do you want to do?" Caryn questioned, breaking into his thoughts.

"How would you like to go boating with me?"

"Sailing?"

He shook his head. "No, rowing."

Her eyes widened. "You want *me* to row?"

Gathering her closer, he pressed his lips to her forehead.

"No. I'll row. We'll order takeout from Addie's, rent a boat, then row over to one of the other islands."

Her right hand searched under the hem of his T-shirt, tracing the defined muscles along his belly and chest. "I'll agree only if we bring Domino."

Closing his eyes, Logan smiled as her delicate fingers caressed his body. "I've watched you with my dog, Caryn. And I remember warning you about spoiling him and turning him into a mush."

"He's not a mush."

"Yes, he is. I've noticed when I let him run free he follows you everywhere."

"That's because he knows I like him."

"And he likes you—a little too much." *Just like his master,* he added silently.

Her hand stopped over his heart. "You sound jealous, Logan. And of a dog, no less."

"You're really pushing it, aren't you, sweetheart?"

"Nope. And stop calling me sweetheart."

"What is it you prefer? Darling? My love? Or perhaps baby?"

She laughed softly. "None of the above."

But he had called her all three in the throes of passion, and there were times when she wondered whether she had said things to him in bed she never would've uttered out of bed.

"You've called me darling a few times."

Her face burned. She had her answer. "That's different," she argued.

"How different?"

"We were making love."

"You call *every* man you make love to darling?"

"There's been only one other man," she said heatedly before she could censor herself.

There was silence, only the soft sounds of their breathing punctuating the space. "Then he was the biggest fool on the face of the earth to lose you," Logan declared in a quiet tone.

Caryn pulled her hand away and struggled to free herself from his embrace as he tightened his grip on her wrist. "Let me go."

"Not yet. Tell me what he did to you."

Her angry gaze clashed with his calm one. "I told you what happened."

Logan shook his head slowly. "No, you didn't. You told me only what you wanted me to know."

"Then consider yourself told and mind your business."

Vertical lines marred the space between his eyes. "I can't. I need to know what it is that keeps us apart. I want to know why you refuse to commit to our having more than a series of quick lays."

She felt a rising panic she wasn't certain she would be able to control. "What's with you, Logan? A lot of men sleep with a woman and never ask for more than a quick lay."

He went completely still, his eyes narrowing as his delicate nostrils flared noticeably, while the skin stretched over his high, sharp cheekbones grew taut. There was something in his stillness that made him appear suddenly dangerous, lethal. She shivered, certain he felt her quaking.

"I'm not a lot of men. So don't even go there, Caryn Edwards."

She felt his repressed rage and wanted to retailiate, but decided she didn't want to argue. Not with him. She had argued enough in the past to last several lifetimes. Besides, she wanted what she and Logan shared to continue until he or she left Marble Island.

Lowering her gaze in a demure gesture, she smiled. "I stand corrected. Now, are you going to let me go so I can get ready to go boating with you?"

Logan's hand fell away as he gave her a look of disbelief. He hadn't expected her to apologize. In fact he wanted to goad her into a confrontation, where in her anger, she would disclose what her ex-husband had done to make her so cautious and guarded with men. He frowned. Why couldn't she just open up and love him as much as he had come to love her?

Caryn slid off his lap and walked into the house, leaving him scowling and staring at the space where she had been.

Dressed in a pair of cotton slacks, a long-sleeve cotton T-shirt, running shoes, and a black baseball cap that belonged to Logan, Caryn sat opposite him in the rowboat cradling Domino on her lap.

Squinting behind the lenses of her sunglasses, she watched the rippling muscles in his arms flex sensuously with the fluid rowing motion. He was dressed entirely in white: shirt, shorts, deck shoes, and baseball cap. The startling whiteness of his attire emphasized the glistening darkness of his sable-brown skin, reminding her of shimmering black and white pearls.

A secret smile softened her mouth. He was beautiful, perfect—in and out of bed.

"What are you smiling about?"

She arched a curving eyebrow. "You."

He returned her smile, his eyes crinkling behind the lenses of his sunglasses. "What about me?"

Caryn hesitated, deciding to be truthful. "I was thinking of how perfect you are. Physically," she added when he gave her a questioning look.

"You're no slouch in the looks department, Miss Edwards."

She shrugged a shoulder. "I'll do."

"You'll more than do. You're an exquisite woman—in and out of bed."

His compliment added more heat to her face with the blazing sun beating down on their heads. "I suppose I'll do in that category, too."

"Wrong, sweetheart. You just don't do. You're the only woman who has been able to satisfy me."

Caryn tightened her hold on Domino, and the puppy

squirmed frantically until she eased her grip around his neck. "I—I never thought you had a problem with—"

"I don't have a problem, " he interrupted. "It was just that I'd never experienced sexual fulfillment. It's like you've climaxed but still want more. You go through all of the motions, yet there's no satisfaction when you're finished."

She nodded. There were times when she had experienced the same emptiness. "It's like scratching an itch, but it continues to itch."

He nodded. "Exactly."

"Why do you think it's different with me?"

Logan stared at her, not missing a measured beat as he continued to row in the direction of a small island less than two hundred feet away tucked in a narrow inlet along the coast.

"Perhaps I'm in love with you."

Her heart lurched in her chest. "Perhaps?"

"Just perhaps," he repeated glibly while winking and flashing a teasing smile.

Perhaps, she repeated over and over to herself until the boat bumped against the sandy shore of the tiny island measuring less than a mile in width.

Logan pulled the oars into the boat and jumped out. He hauled it up on the beach, then extended his hand to assist Caryn as she attempted to disembark with the puppy cradled under one arm and a blanket under the other.

She noticed they weren't the only ones who had decided to picnic on the island. A couple lay facedown on a blanket completely nude, while a quartet less than ten feet away were racing for the water wearing the tiniest swimwear she'd ever seen on a man or woman.

After looping a leash around Domino's neck, Caryn looked up and saw Logan coming toward her, carrying the wicker basket packed with chilled salads from Addie's and a colorful striped beach umbrella.

His gaze wandered over the nude couple and he shook

his head. "I prefer a different view if I'm going to eat," he whispered, smiling.

"So would I," she concurred.

They walked several hundred yards and found a spot to their liking. Caryn spread out the blanket while Logan set up the umbrella. He opened the large basket and withdrew a dish wrapped in plastic for Domino and filled it with chilled bottled water. The dog lapped up the water, then sank down on a corner of the blanket, yawned, then closed its eyes. Within minutes they heard a soft snoring.

Caryn removed her cap, fluffed up her shortened hair with her fingers, and sank down to the blanket. A cooling breeze swept under the umbrella as she rolled over on her belly and rested her head on folded arms. Logan eased his tall frame to the blanket, his face close to hers. He'd removed his cap and she stared at the shimmer of moisture clinging to the strands of his short, coarse, black hair.

Reaching out, she pulled several strands with her fingertips, realizing for the first time there was no indication of a curl. "Why do you wear your hair so short?"

His eyes widened slightly before he closed them, shutting out her questioning stare. "The longer it grows, the more stubbly it gets."

"It won't lie down or curl?"

He shook his head, opening his eyes. "Any more questions?"

Her mouth gaped, then snapped shut. "Are you telling me to mind my business?"

Rising on an elbow, his free hand touched her cheek. "Not at all. I'd never say that to you."

"Touché, Logan." She remembered telling him to mind his business when he'd asked her about her ex-husband.

Logan's forefinger toyed with the diamond stud earring in her pierced lobe. "After I thought about it, I realized I had no right to pry into your private life. Just because we're sleeping together that doesn't permit either one of us carte blanche to know the other's personal secrets."

Leaning forward, she pressed her forehead to his and brushed her lips across his mouth. "Thank you for understanding. It's not that I don't want to tell you about Tom, it's just that I can't. Not now."

The fingers of his right hand curved around the back of her head as he increased the pressure of her mouth on his. "It's okay," he crooned between soft, nibbling kisses. "Everything is going to work out between us."

I pray you're right, she mused, giving into the drugging power of his potent mouth.

They spent more than five hours on the tiny island, napping, dining on the chilled-packed dishes purchased from Addie's, and reading aloud to each other from the collected works of Edgar Allan Poe. Caryn lay, eyes closed, listening intently as Logan read "The Raven" and "Annabel Lee," his sonorous voice rising and falling with the striking musical imagery of the popular poems.

The lazy, hazy summer day also affected Domino, he preferring to yawn, stretch, and doze to running around and exploring his new surroundings. The most energy he expended all afternoon was to climb up on Caryn's back and promptly fall asleep.

She stared at a stunned Logan, spreading her hands outward. "I did nothing to elicit this," she protested, pointing over her shoulder.

He mumbled a four-letter expletive under his breath, then apologized. "I'm sorry, Caryn. I didn't mean to say that."

"Yes, you did, Logan Prescott. And don't blame me for your pet's behavior."

"I'm not blaming you. The animal's hopeless."

"And don't call him an animal. He's not a wild creature who roams the woods eating carrion."

Logan forced back a smile. "Now that he's a certified mush, I suppose you're going to train him to bite me."

"Never," she said, sticking out her tongue.

His laughter bubbled up and out, the sound full and rich. "What am I going to do with the two of you?"

Caryn wanted to say, *just love us,* but didn't. She flashed him a sensual smile that made his heart turn over in anticipation. It had been days since he'd made love to her, and not only did he want her but he also needed her.

Chapter Sixteen

Logan walked into Caryn's bedroom at the same time as she made her way out of the adjoining bathroom, one towel wrapped around her head and another over her breasts.

She knew he'd showered and shaved because she could smell the natural odor of his skin mingling with the fragrance of a scented soap and matching aftershave.

Taking long, determined strides, he closed the distance between them and swept her up in his arms. She opened her mouth to tell him she still had to moisturize her body, but the words were swallowed back once he covered her mouth with his, robbing her of her breath.

Clinging to his neck, she trembled as she felt the rapid pumping of his heart against her bare breasts. She did not have to glance down to see whether he was aroused because she knew he was.

Their mouths still joined, he took her to his bedroom and placed her on the bed, his body covering hers, and she welcoming his weight. It was later, much later, that Caryn remembered what had occurred between them.

He'd removed the towels, then his mouth and tongue

were everywhere: tracing the outline of her lips, in her ears, along the column of her throat, over her breasts, under her arms, and up her inner thigh. She wasn't given an opportunity to recover from one shock before she was assailed with another.

His tongue searched and teased the nodule of flesh at the apex of her thighs, eliciting heat and chills at the same time. Reaching down, she tried pushing at his head, but he caught her wrists between his long, strong fingers and held her fast while he feasted on her throbbing flesh.

Arching, she was unable to stop the soft moans escaping her parted lips. The moans slipped into groans, then into a keening that rose and held like a sustained note.

Her entire body was on fire, throbbing with a desire akin to pain if she didn't release it. "Logan. Oh, Logan. Please, Logan." His name became her mantra as she pleaded for release.

Logan heard her entreaty. He moved up her body and reached for the plastic pouch on the bedside table. Seconds later he moved over her trembling form, staring down at the passion dilating her pupils and erasing all traces of gold from her eyes. Easing his hardness into her body, he gasped audibly from the exquisite pleasure of becoming one with Caryn as she closed her eyes.

Pressing his greater weight down on her slender body, he whispered roughly in her ear. "Are we still friends, sweetheart?" he taunted, punctuating each word with a strong thrust. Opening her eyes, Caryn stared up at him as if she'd never seen him. "Do friends do this to each other?" he whispered, quickening his thrusting and rolling his hips heavily against hers. "Do they?" he continued.

Curving her arms around his neck, she buried her face against his shoulder and mumbled a quivering, "No."

The single word broke the dam, and a torrent of passions rained down like the fury of an erupting volcano. A rising desire swept them up, buffeted them sideways, then took them on a ride of free fall before they were shattered into minute particles where they collapsed in a flood tide of complete and utter sexual fulfillment.

Logan went still, savoring the lingering pulsing aftermath of completion as he counted the thundering beats of his heart slamming against his ribs. For a brief moment he had experienced *le petit mort*—the little death—in the arms of the woman he had come to love above all others.

His body quieted and it was then he felt her trembling. Withdrawing from the warmth of her soft body, he reversed their positions and held her gently.

Caryn bit down hard on her lower lip, fighting back tears. Curling into a fetal position atop Logan's sweat-drenched body, she closed her eyes and went to sleep.

July twenty-second—

Logan and I are leaving within the hour for Gooseneck Island. He called Ham earlier this morning confirming our arrival for one this afternoon.

Even though I look forward to seeing Ham and Tia again, I'm ambivalent about leaving Marble Island. This past week has been wonderful. I can't describe what I've shared with Logan with any other word except—honeymoon.

We've pretended to be married, but somehow I truly feel married. Without the exchange of rings or vows I feel loved, protected, and as if I'm the only woman on the face of the earth. My happiness runneth over.

Instead of our desire for each other decreasing, it has increased. I never tire of making love with Logan, and he always appears as eager as I am.

I was beginning to think we were becoming sex addicts, but quickly dispelled that notion because the times we don't make love we're content just to lie in bed together listening to music or reading to each other. Our relationship out of bed has become very comfortable. We respect each other's privacy and alternate days preparing meals and dining out.

Domino is growing so quickly, I find it difficult to pick

him up. Logan stopped complaining about me spoiling him, and lets me have my way with the mush.

My love for Logan has grown deeper and when I leave Marble Island I will take my love for him with me. He has become friend, lover, and the man I will love forever.

Hamilton and Cynthia were waiting for them as they maneuvered alongside their shiny black Mercedes sedan with Pennsylvania plates on the sand-littered driveway. Caryn waved, flashing a grin as she waited for Logan to circle the Jeep and help her down, while Domino barked excitedly when he recognized the two people who had shared his domicile a week ago.

Logan swung Caryn to her feet, then unloosened the leash around the roll bar, releasing Domino.

Cynthia moved forward to greet her guests, her hair swept up in a ponytail and making her appear much younger than thirty-five.

She kissed Caryn's cheek, then offered her lips to Logan. "I'm glad to see you're both wearing deck shoes."

Logan held her at arm's length. "Where are we going?"

"Sailing," Hamilton, announced, extending his hand to Logan.

He took the proffered hand as a wide grin softened his features. "For how long?"

"How long do you guys want to stay?"

Logan glanced down at Caryn, shrugging his shoulders. She raised her eyebrows and lifted her own shoulders. "Caryn and I packed enough clothes for three or four days."

Hamilton dropped an arm around Caryn's shoulders and kissed her cheek. "You won't need clothes if you brought bathing suits."

Logan's gaze narrowed as he stared at Hamilton, then Cynthia. "How long a sailing trip have you planned for, and where are we going?"

"Sunny Puerto Rico," Cynthia announced, rolling her

r's. "We'll sail down, take in some nightlife, then come home."

Caryn turned to Logan, her eyes wide. "I didn't pack clothes for—"

"Don't worry about it," he said softly, interrupting her. "I'll buy us what we'll need once we dock."

Letting out her breath, she nodded. She thought they were going to spend a few days on Gooseneck Island, but instead she was sailing to Puerto Rico with the Wheatons, Logan, and Domino.

Cynthia moved closer to Caryn and looped her arm around her waist. "I wanted to tell you what Ham and I had planned, but we wanted it to be a surprise."

Caryn smiled at the taller woman. "And it's a very nice surprise."

"A driver will be here any minute to take us to the marina. When I found out that I was pregnant, Ham and I decided to take a month off and celebrate. It's been a long time since we've taken a *real* vacation, and having you and Raven along will make it special."

The sound of an engine garnered everyone's attention, and within minutes a man maneuvered a classic, wood-paneled station wagon behind the other two vehicles.

Caryn and Cynthia sat on a row of seats in the back of the station wagon, while Hamilton and Logan helped the driver store their luggage in the cargo area. The entire process took less than five minutes. Domino jumped into the car, turned around several times, then settled himself between Caryn's feet. Scratching the puppy behind his ears, she smiled at Logan as he sat down beside her, noticing the beginnings of a grin as he shook his head and drew his finger across his throat in a slicing motion.

Tilting her chin, she gave him a haughty look, then glanced out the window as the car backed out of the driveway. Her pulse quickened in anticipation of sailing down to the Caribbean with Logan. She never would've imagined when she first stepped foot onto Marble Island she would share the house with a man—a man she had fallen in love with; a man she wanted to spend the rest of her life with.

Caryn lay on a canopy-covered deck chair of the *Maggie E,* closing her eyes. After boarding the yacht, she was shown to a cabin where she quickly changed into a swimsuit before returning to the deck. The overhead sky was cloudless, the sun brilliant, and a rising sea breeze cooled her exposed flesh at measured intervals.

The *Maggie E* was a magnificent gleaming white seventy-five-foot sailing vessel which boasted a polished teakwood deck that was as soft to her bare feet as absorbent cotton. The highly trained crew of three were friendly, silent, and amazingly imperceptible.

Logan and Hamilton hadn't changed, but leaned against the railing talking animatedly with each other while Domino found a shady area and had settled down to sleep. Cynthia crossed the deck and lay on a matching deck chair next to Caryn's. She had also changed into a swimsuit, but had added a lightweight, long-sleeve blouse to prevent her fair skin from burning. The form-fitting swimsuit accented her thickening waist, and it was the first time Caryn saw her as a pregnant woman.

"Is this not the life?" Cynthia questioned with a wide smile.

Caryn nodded while inhaling a lungful of sea air. "It's incredible."

"I love this ship," Cynthia continued. "Ham's dad bought it for his wife for their forty-fifth wedding anniversary. Her name is Margaret Elizabeth, but she insists everyone call her Maggie E."

Turning her head, Caryn stared at Cynthia from behind the lenses of her sunglasses. "It's nice to have that kind of money."

"And you'd better believe the Wheatons have loads of money. They're descendants of one of Connecticut's founding families who had made their money by shipping goods between here and Europe before expanding into marine insurance and investment banking. It took them a long time to accept me, but now that I'm carrying a Wheaton things have changed."

Caryn sat up, noticing the frown between Cynthia's eyes. "Are you saying they didn't want you to marry Ham?"

"They loathed me on sight."

"But why?"

"Because they were rich, very smart, and were able to see what so many others hadn't been able to discern up to that point. Before I married Ham, I was Cynthia Jones from Evansville, West Virginia—population three hundred thirty-four. Even before they closed the coal mines, I doubted whether the population was ever more than five hundred. I was the sixth of eight children of Jimmy and Patty Ann Jones."

"But you don't sound as if you're from West Virginia."

"You forget I'm a trained actress. *A very good actress,*" she said, stressing each word. "I hated Evansville, the coal dust, and I hated having to share a bed with three of my brothers and sisters. All I ever dreamed of was getting out. And I figured out at a very early age that I had three things going for me. I had a quick mind, long legs, and I had inherited good teeth. Perfect assets for an actress.

"Once I realized I had a photographic memory, I used it to my best advantage. I studied very hard, graduated valedictorian, and received a full scholarship to Yale for the dramatic arts. The moment I arrived on campus, I knew I was different. Everyone was polite, but so Ivy League. Whenever I opened my mouth to speak, anyone who heard me stopped and stared. It was then I began my metamorphosis.

"I waited tables to earn extra money and instead of using the money for clothes or to take in a movie I gave it to a voice coach. My roommate was a gorgeous black girl from New York, whose mother had been a model. I watched her style her hair and put on her makeup and asked her if she would teach me. Within three months I'd lost the West Virginia twang, changed my hairstyle, and learned to apply makeup like a professional."

"What about clothes?" Caryn asked, totally engrossed in Cynthia's Cinderella story.

"My mother taught all of her daughters to sew, which came in handy once I bought a secondhand portable sewing machine. I made a lot of my clothes, and every once in a while I'd make something for my roommate, Vivienne. She had tons of beautiful clothes, but she was gracious and always wore what I'd made for her.

"We became very close, and when she began dating Logan Prescott she asked me to double date with his friend, H. Hamilton Wheaton II. I later found out the *H* stood for Hiram. Ham's father is also named Hiram, and they called Ham by his middle name to distinguish between the two. Our first date was a disaster."

"What happened?"

"I wouldn't listen to Vivienne when she told me that I was overdressed. The guys were supposed to take us to an upscale restaurant in New Haven, and I wanted to make a good impression but ended up looking like a five-dollar painted hooker on New Year's Eve. I had on a pair of high heels and a dress that was better suited for a dance club, while Vivienne wore a simple wool wrap skirt with a matching bolero jacket and a white silk blouse with a jewel neckline. I took one look at Ham and Logan with their tailored slacks, sports jackets, and ties, and started bawling like a trapped pig." Cynthia laughed, recalling the events that followed, and to her surprise Caryn also laughed.

"What happened after that?" she questioned.

"The guys were so shocked, they just stood there staring at each other. I knew who Ham was because we were both drama majors, but I never thought I'd ever go out with him. One of the more popular freshman guys had agreed to go out with me, while all I could do was cry and ruin my carefully made-up face. Mascara had run down my cheeks and dripped onto my dress. As we would've said back in Evansville, I was souping snot.

"Logan, being the most perceptive, suggested we all change and go to a popular off-campus burger joint. He literally changed my life that night. The guys went back to their dorm rooms and exchanged their ties and jackets for turtlenecks, while Vivienne and I opted for slacks and sweaters. I dismantled my elaborate French twist hairdo, and I tried covering the red blotches on my face with makeup, but in the end decided just to wear lipstick. Ham won me over when he said he preferred my hair down and my face without the blush, eyeliner, and mascara.

"That one night taught me more than I'd learned in my first eighteen years of life. It taught me about class, which has nothing to do with the amount of money a person has in the bank. It was about family lineage, upbringing, manners, and an unwritten code of behavior. The other three had it and I didn't.

"Ham said he liked me for myself and after a while I decided I, too, liked Cynthia Jones from Evansville, West Virginia. That was who I was and who I would remain. Over the years I've learned what is socially acceptable and what isn't. But what you see is what you get."

"What happened when you met his family?"

Cynthia studied the unadorned gold band on the third finger of her left hand. "I met them for the first time over a Thanksgiving recess. They were speechless—all but Ham's cookie-cutter Barbie doll triplet sisters. The girls were only twelve, and as privileged, overindulged little cherubs they quickly reminded me that I'd eaten my salad with the wrong fork. Ham's mother took to her bed after dinner and remained there until we returned to school. His father didn't know I'd overheard him telling Ham that I was an ignorant trailer park tramp who would deliberately get pregnant to entrap him into marrying me. I wanted to tell Hiram that I'd never lived in a trailer park, and even though I'd been dating his son for almost a year I had yet to sleep with him.

"I had just begun my senior year when I tested for a small part in a movie and got it. The day I told Ham he proposed marriage, and I was faced with the biggest dilemma of my life. Do I leave school and go to California or stay and marry Ham. By that time I was so hopelessly in love with him that I turned down the part. We were married by the campus chaplin, moved into a tiny apartment in a less than desirable part of New Haven, and mapped out our future."

Caryn shifted an eyebrow. "I thought you said Ham came from a wealthy family."

"He did, but at the time he was receiving a modest monthly allowance from his trust fund which wasn't enough to move into one of the better neighborhoods. Logan was also living off-campus, but his studio apartment was in a wonderful area of the city. Unlike Hiram and Maggie E, Logan's parents did not monitor the women he dated.

"The day Ham celebrated his twenty-fifth birthday he assumed complete control of his trust fund. We moved from Connecticut to Pennsylvania, purchased a dilapidated old farmhouse set on four acres, renovated it, then invested in a theater company."

"You are a true living and breathing Cinderella."

"You're right about that," Cynthia acknowledged with a bright, dimpled smile. Her smile vanished, her forehead furrowing. "I'll never be as close to my in-laws the way Ham is with my family, but I have to remember the child I'm carrying is as much Wheaton as it is Jones. And Maggie E was the first to remind me that if it is a boy, then the Wheaton name would continue for another generation."

Reaching up, Cynthia pushed her sunglasses atop her head. "For heaven's sakes," she drawled, lapsing into the cadence of her childhood, "I been jawing to beat the band. What's going on between you and Raven?"

Caryn shrugged a bare shoulder. "Nothing."

Cynthia snorted delicately. "I know he told Ham he'd called off his wedding a little more than a month ago, but what I can't understand is that he doesn't seem to be too broken up over it. And I have a feeling you're responsible for that."

"You and Ham have known Raven a lot longer and much better than I, and if there's one thing I've learned about him is that he's a survivor. I don't think he will permit anyone or anything to upset his emotional equilibrium for any extended length of time."

"You're right about that, Caryn. But when are you going to admit that you're as much in love with Raven as he is with you?"

Never, she said silently. Staring out across the deck where Logan stood, she allowed her gaze to caress the length of his tall, powerfully built body. It lingered on his distinctive profile as he smiled at something Hamilton had said. Closing her eyes, she realized she had come to know every inch of his flesh—with or without his clothes. She had come to gauge his mercurial moods just by watching his body language, knowing when he was tense or relaxed, when he wanted her or when he wanted to be alone.

She opened her eyes, and without warning he shifted his head and stared at her behind the lenses of his sunglasses. She felt the pull across the expanse of the deck, knowing at that exact moment in time he wanted her—as much as she wanted him. Their shrouded gazes fused as they shut out all and everything around them.

"I can't admit it, Tia, because you're wrong," Caryn whispered, knowing the moment the words were uttered that she'd openly lied about not loving Logan.

Chapter Seventeen

The captain of the *Maggie E* dropped anchor off the coast of Savannah in time to join his crew members for an on-deck dinner under the stars in a clear summer night sky.

Caryn, Logan, Hamilton, and Cynthia reclined on deck chairs while listening to CDs on a small but powerful sound system playing Sade, the Rippingtons, and a greatest hits compilation from Motown: the Supremes, Marvin Gaye, the Four Tops, and the Temptations.

Everyone was content to sit and listen until *The Big Chill* soundtrack slid into place on the carousel. Caryn sat up, completely startled as Logan, Cynthia, and Hamilton jumped up, singing and dancing with Marvin Gaye's "I Heard It Through The Grapevine," followed by the Temptations' "My Girl."

Caryn was as transfixed by the trio's theatrics as the crew, who had left their dinner to watch the impromptu performance. Cynthia's understated sensuality surfaced as she performed the Aretha Franklin anthem, "(You Make Me Feel Like a) Natural Woman," and "The Tracks of My Tears." Logan was as uninhibited as his college friends when he mimicked the dance steps of the Temptations as he led them through "Ain't Too Proud to Beg." It ended to rousing applause, whistles, and tears streaming down Caryn's face as she doubled over in laughter. The captain, chef, and steward returned to their dinner, their muted laughter floating in the warm air.

She held out her arms to Logan, hugging him tightly. "You were wonderful," she whispered, registering the runaway pumping of his heart.

His mouth swept over an ear before finding her lips. "So are you," he whispered back. Holding Caryn close to his chest, he smiled over her head at the Wheatons. "The last time we put on this performance, you guys almost got me evicted from my apartment."

Cynthia leaned against her husband's side, a hand cradling her belly. "It wasn't only us, Raven. Remember, we were only two. There had to be more than thirty people in your apartment that night."

Caryn listened to the lively banter between the three friends and suddenly she felt left out, estranged. Cynthia and Hamilton were Logan's friends, not hers. And the memories they had shared would bind them together for a lifetime, even if their paths never crossed again.

But she would have different memories—memories of the summer storm that had propelled her into Logan's arms and his bed, along with the summer passion he had offered her.

Unknowingly he had helped her to heal and to trust. He had helped her to open her heart to love again, even though he would never know how much she had come to love him.

Hamilton ruffled his wife's tousled sun-streaked hair. "I think it's time I put you to bed, wannabe diva."

Cynthia dropped her head to his shoulder. "You won't get an argument out of me tonight." She waved to Caryn and Logan. "Good night, guys."

"Good night," they returned in unison.

Logan waited for them to go below deck, then picked

up Caryn and swung her around until she pleaded with him to stop. He made his way over to a deck chair and sat down with her straddling his thighs.

"Logan," she chided softly. "How do you think this looks?"

Tilting his chin, he smiled up at her. Both their faces were shadowed in the tiny lights ringing the ship. "Exactly what it is. I'm holding my girlfriend while we study the stars."

Her gaze slipped lower. "I wasn't aware I was your girlfriend."

"Oh? And just what did you think you were?"

She shrugged a bare shoulder under her strapless dress. "A friend, or perhaps your roommate."

Much to her surprise he laughed, the sound rising and floating out over the calm ocean. He shook his head. "Oh, no, baby doll. You're much more than that." Shifting, he pushed to his feet and stood up, still holding her to his chest. "And in case you've forgotten, I have just the thing to remind you."

Five minutes later Caryn lay in Logan's arms, feeling the gentle motion of the ship swaying under them as he wordlessly demonstrated how unlike friends they were. She successfully swallowed back the moans of passions scorching her mind and body. The fire blazed uncontrollably, sweeping them up in an inferno that refused to be quenched until hours later when they finally fell asleep as dawn touched the horizon and the *Maggie E*'s crew stirred to begin another day at sea.

July twenty-fifth—

We're due to dock in San Juan Bay within the hour. After spending three days at sea—with layovers in Savannah and Miami, I'm more than ready for terra firma. The time we spent in Miami was magical, and the Spanish flavor of the city has gotten all of us in the mood to enjoy all that Puerto Rico has to offer.

Logan and I did not get too much time to tour the city

because we spent hours shopping for clothes. We left the trendy boutiques in Miami Beach with shoes, slacks, jackets. dresses, and exquisite accessories. Before returning to the Maggie E, *Logan stopped at a bank to purchase travelers checks. He ordered several books in various denominations with both our signatures. He teased me, saying he thought I'd need a little spending change.*

Ham and Tia plan to spend five days in Puerto Rico before returning to the mainland. I project we'll return to North Carolina the beginning of August, which will give me only another week before I return to Asheville. I don't want to think about leaving Logan because I know I will start crying and won't be able to stop. He's never to know that I love him, now and forever.

The beautiful island of Puerto Rico came into view, giving credence to its claim as the Shining Star of the Caribbean. Hundreds of boats—from cruise ships to sailboats—were docked in the harbor. Caryn felt Logan move behind her as she stood at the rail, watching the fronds of palm trees in the distance sway in a warm, gentle breeze.

Smiling, she closed her eyes as he pressed closer. "Puerto Rico is beautiful, Logan. It's only a thousand miles southeast of Miami, yet I've never thought of visiting the island."

Curving his arms around her waist, Logan lowered his head and inhaled the sweet fragrance of her freshly shampooed hair. "I've been here once," he admitted. What he didn't tell her was that he and Nina had come to the island after she'd accepted his marriage proposal.

Caryn opened her eyes and turned in his loose embrace. "Was it for a special occasion?" she questioned perceptively.

His lids lowered over his eyes, not permitting her to gauge his reaction to her query. "At the time it was," he answered truthfully.

She hesitated, her breasts rising and falling heavily under her blouse. "And now?"

Releasing her waist, Logan cradled her face between his

palms. "What I have with you is beyond special. You've changed me so much that I can't even describe what I've become."

Lowering her gaze, she smiled up at him through her lashes. "Is that a good thing?"

He nodded slowly. "A very good thing."

"If that's the case, then I'm glad I met you, Logan Prescott."

"And I you, Caryn Edwards."

Hamilton walked across the deck, holding Cynthia's hand as she exchanged parting words with the captain. "I don't know about you two lovebirds, but we're ready to go ashore." His dark blue eyes grew serious. "Raven and you, Caryn, can have the option of either staying aboard the *Maggie E* or at my folks' condo while ashore. It's your call because there's plenty of room at the condo."

Logan was as surprised at Hamilton's suggestion as Caryn. "Where are you and Tia staying?"

"We've opted for dry land."

Caryn shook her head, giving Logan her answer. "Then we'll stay on the *Maggie E.* I think Domino would much prefer the run of the ship to being enclosed by four walls."

"Damn," Hamilton swore softly under his breath. "I forgot about the dog. It's just as well because pets aren't allowed."

"You don't have to baby-sit us," Logan stated, trying to reassure their hosts he and Caryn would feel more than comfortable on the island by themselves. "I know you and Tia are here to unwind before you return to the States. How about we do our own thing during the day, then get together for dinner each night?"

Hamilton quickly agreed and gave Logan the address and telephone number of his parents' San Juan residence, before the two couples went ashore. Logan and Caryn waited for the Wheatons to hail a cab, then headed on foot toward the historic Old San Juan.

"Old San Juan is a National Historic Zone," Logan explained as he held Caryn's hand firmly while leading her down a narrow, cobblestone street with thick-walled colonial buildings.

They spent hours touring the seven square blocks of homes, municipal offices, shops, and art galleries. The soaring ninety-degree heat and her sandaled feet forced Caryn to give in to Logan's entreaty that they return to the ship.

Logan found Domino with the steward, whose turn it was to remain on board. The crew members had each elected to spend at least eight hours on board when in port. Hiram Hamilton Wheaton I paid them well, and had given explicit orders that his *Maggie E* was never to be left without someone aboard when docked other than home port.

Curving an arm around her waist, Logan kissed Caryn's forehead. "Why don't you get something to drink, then take a *siesta* while I groom Domino before I feed him."

She needed no further prompting. San Juan was hot. Much hotter than she had expected, and her feet hurt from walking the cobblestone streets in sandals. The Italian-made shoes were pretty but not practical for the sixteenth-century city streets.

Making her way into the galley, she poured herself a glass of fruit juice from the refrigerator, drank it, then made her way to the cabin she shared with Logan.

The space was large and well appointed with all of the conveniences of one's own bedroom. It contained a queen-size bed, double dresser, bedside tables, triple closet, and an adjoining shower.

Stripping off her blouse and slacks, she draped them over the back of a chair. Then she removed her underwear before stepping into the shower. She lingered under the steady flow of lukewarm water, washing her hair and body. Reaching for a thick, thirsty bath sheet, she towel-dried her hair, then patted her body, making certain to leave a layer of moisture to cool her fevered flesh.

When she opened the door to the shower stall and stepped into the bedroom, Logan was already there. He sat on a chair, sans shoes and shirt, waiting for her. There was a flicker of banked passion as his gaze moved leisurely over her naked body.

He moved fluidly off the chair, reminding her of a large, graceful bird rising above the water before taking flight. She went still, unable to move when he placed one bare foot in front of her other with a deliberate slowness that made her heart stop at the same time her pulse raced.

She felt like a helpless creature, paralyzed while trembling inwardly with the approach of a larger, more dangerous predator. She realized she did not fear Logan as much as she feared herself. How could she continue to see him, sleep with him, pour out her passion, and not tell him what lay deep in her heart?

How could she not tell him that she loved him, wanted to become his wife and the mother of his children?

Logan's gaze registered the fluttering pulse in her silken throat as he moved closer. His right hand came up slowly and curved around her neck, fingers splayed over her cheek. Lowering his head, he breathed in the scent of her clean flesh. His mouth hovered above her, feeling the moist caress of her breath over his lips.

Then he took her mouth, slowly increasing the pressure until her lips parted and permitted him access. He was not disappointed when Caryn rose on tiptoe and curved her arms around his neck. The full softness of her firm breasts pressing against his bare chest was a shock to his system when the nipples hardened with her rising desire.

Logan had stopped asking himself if he would ever tire of her because he knew the answer even before the thought was formed in his head. But what he refused to ask himself was whether he could leave Caryn or permit her to walk away from him when the time came for her to leave Marble Island.

And he had to admit to himself, he feared the worst. Caryn Edwards would and could walk away from him as easily as he had walked away from Nina.

There were times after he and Caryn had made love that

he lay in bed beside her wondering how she could offer him so much passion without declaring what they shared went beyond friendship.

He'd slept with women he didn't love, but he never gave them all of himself as he'd done with Caryn. With her he never held anything back, and doing so he had become vulnerable. The woman in his arms was the only human being capable of destroying him totally—body and soul.

He'd told himself over and over that he compromised himself each and every time he joined his flesh with Caryn's. That she had become his opiate, an addictive drug he was helpless to resist.

His arms curved around her waist, and he lifted her off her feet until her head was level with his. Pulling back, he stared at her staring back at him. Her eyes were wide, her face flushed under her deeply tanned skin, her parted lips swollen from his sensual assault, and the color of her eyes a deep jade green.

Logan opened his mouth, the words *I love you,* poised on his tongue, but he swallowed them back. And in that instant the pain knifed his heart, causing him to inhale sharply.

He'd thought that loving her would be wonderful, magnificent, yet it brought only pain. A pain he would not permit her to see. A wry smile curved his strong mouth as he lowered her to the floor.

"Wait for me to shower, then I'll join you in bed," he said in a quiet voice he did not quite recognize as his own.

Caryn was noticeably subdued as she sat beside Logan in a restaurant at a luxury hotel situated along the Condado Beach area. She had sensed the change in him after he'd showered that afternoon before coming to her. His love-making was strong, but was tempered with a desperation which hadn't been there during their previous encounters. And instead of holding her until they both fell asleep, he'd turned away and lay motionless until she slept. When she awoke he was gone.

She'd washed, dressed, and found him on deck, playing an intense game of chess with the chef. He hadn't glanced at her, but patted a chair beside him for her to sit. She complied, sitting and watching the two men play until she grew bored then spent the next hour and a half relaxing on a deck chair with Domino at her side. The game ended without a winner, and only then did Logan inform her that they were to share dinner with the Wheatons at seven.

She had taken special care when she dressed for the evening, hoping it would lift her sagging spirits. She had selected a black silk tank dress ending midcalf with a generous slit that allowed for a view of her smooth, tanned legs. Three inches of black patent leather sling-strap sandals, with one strap crossing her instep and ending around her heel, added height and definition to her strong, well-shaped legs. She had applied a styling gel to her short hair and brushed it off her face until it lay against her scalp without any hint of a curl. A pair of large faux pearls earrings with a matching single-strand necklace rested on the fullness of her exposed breasts, a layer of mascara and deep copper lipstick complemented her simple, but elegant appearance.

Caryn had garnered the reaction she sought from Logan when he saw her. He'd stared, his mouth gaping for several seconds before he whispered how beautiful she looked. She had gone up on deck to wait for him to dress, and she had been equally stunned when he joined her. He had also elected to wear black—an exquisitely tailored linen suit; white silk shirt; and a patterned silk tie with muted shades of black, white, gray, and jade green. The stark whiteness of his shirt highlighted the deep, dark hue of his sable-brown face, and on more than one occasion a female head turned in his direction as he made his way through the restaurant.

Curving an arm around Caryn's waist, he leaned closer

and pressed his mouth to her hair. "Are you hungry, sweetheart?"

Tilting her chin, she smiled up at him. Her pulse quickened when she registered the potent magnetism Logan Prescott emitted by breathing. "A little," she lied smoothly. She had barely eaten all day; however, her uneasiness would not permit her to put a lot of food into her stomach.

She had speculated all afternoon what had happened between her and Logan which would not permit her to feel at ease with him. Then she wondered if they had made a mistake to leave Marble Island. It was there they had found each other, offered the other healing, and it was on Marble Island where she had fallen in love with Logan Prescott.

Cynthia's sea-green gaze studied the menu. "I'm hungry enough to eat a whole pig."

Hamilton ran the back of his hand over her cheek. "Do you think it's good to give the baby pork?"

The golden curls piled atop Cynthia's head shook when she turned and glared at him. "You've got something against pork, Hiram Hamilton Wheaton?" she asked, folding a hand on her slim hip. "Because I'll have you know that women have fed their babies pork since the beginning of time if it was the only meat they could get their hands on, and we're still here to talk about it."

Hamilton flushed furiously under his tan. "I didn't mean it that way, Tia. I was just concerned about your intake of cholesterol."

Cynthia kissed his cheek, then swiped away a smudge of deep rose color with her thumb. "Thank you, Ham, but you forget that I am as strong and healthy as a plow horse."

Hamilton smiled into her eyes. "I'd never think of you as a plow horse, gorgeous. You're more like a palomino thoroughbred."

Caryn and Logan smiled at the interchange between the blond couple. It was apparent they still were very much in love.

"What are you having?" Logan asked Caryn.

She stared at the menu, reading the selections listed in both English and Spanish. "I don't know. I'm leaning toward fish, but since coming to Marble Island I've had more fish in three weeks than I've eaten all year. Perhaps I'll go for a meat dish."

In the end the two couples decided to order a variety of dishes with beef, pork, fish, and chicken. They all agreed on accompanying platters of white rice, pink beans, and *tostones de plátano,* fried green bananas, and a melt on the tongue *flán de leche condensada*—a caramelized condensed milk custard.

Two hours later Caryn dabbed the corners of her mouth with a cloth napkin, shaking her head in amazement. She could not believe she had eaten so much.

"Not hungry, huh?" Logan whispered close to her ear.

She poked him in the ribs with a finger at the same time as she gave him a tight smile. "I've got to get up and walk this off," she stated between clenched teeth.

Logan nodded and signaled the waiter. "I'll take care of the check," he informed Hamilton, reaching in the breast pocket of his jacket and withdrawing a credit card case. Hamilton inclined his head.

Cynthia let out a satisfied sigh. "Now, where are we going?"

Caryn rose to her feet when Logan pulled back her chair. "I'm ready to do a little partying." She had successfully shed her dark mood and was ready for a night of fun.

Holding on to her husband's arm, Cynthia, said, "Let's go to a club and dance."

"Logan?" Hamilton questioned, as Logan signed the credit card receipt.

He glanced up, nodding. "Count me in."

Caryn studied Logan's clearly defined profile as he signed his name with a flourish. Once again she was taken with his physical perfection. *Even his hands are exquisite,* she thought, staring at his long, tapered fingers. Then she thought about the man and woman who had lain together to beget him, smiling. If they saw him as a man, she knew they surely would have been pleased with their creation.

Logan put away his credit card, then curved a protective arm around Caryn's waist. "We'll have the concierge call a driver to take us into Old San Juan. There are quite a few clubs for us to choose from."

An hour later the two couples pushed their way through a throng of tourists standing shoulder-to-shoulder at a bar until they found two small tables in the back of the nightclub. The sounds of raised voices speaking English and Spanish punctuated the air.

An attractive young waitress sauntered over to them, her loose hips keeping tempo with the pulsing Latin rhythm coming from the powerful sound system.

"Buenas noches, señors y señoras. May I get you something to drink?" She switched with easy facility between Spanish and English.

Hamilton and Logan ordered rum concoctions, while Caryn and Cynthia opted for virgin piña coladas.

"I've got the drinks," Hamilton stated firmly when he spied the waitress returning to the table with a tray filled with their order.

Cynthia frowned. "Must you guys always fight over the check?"

Logan arched a sweeping eyebrow. "You wouldn't understand, Tia." He took a sip of his drink, nodding his approval. It's a *man* thing." Cynthia's mouth dropped as her face flooded with a rush of color.

Caryn caught Logan's hand and urged him to his feet. "Let's dance, darling," she hissed between her teeth. He gave her a startled look, but complied, permitting her to lead him out to the crowded dance floor. "You've just came down with a classic case of foot-and-mouth."

Pulling her against his body, Logan swung her into a smooth dance step. "Foot-and-mouth?"

"You just put your foot in your mouth, Logan Prescott. Don't ever tell a woman about what's a *man thang.*"

"Men are supposed to argue about who will pick up the check."

"That's just being silly."

"What do women do?"

"We usually divide it evenly among us. That way there's no 'I paid last time and now it's your turn.' It saves us from getting catty."

He chuckled. "That's very diplomatic."

"That's because we are diplomatic, practical, and—"

Her words were cut off when he lowered his head and moved his mouth over hers, devouring its softness.

"Are you telling me to shut up?" she whispered against his firm lips.

Tightening his hold on her slender body, he chuckled. "I'm not even going there, sweetheart."

Closing her eyes, she rested her forehead on his shoulder, inhaling the scent of his cologne clinging to the linen fabric. Pressed against his chest and thighs, she felt every hard line of his body, glorying in his cloaking protective warmth and strength.

The tempo changed to an upbeat salsa, and within seconds Caryn found herself dipping and swaying to the Latin rhythm as she followed Logan's expert lead. She had danced with him more than she had with any other man in her life. He spun her around and around with one hand, then caught her and dipped her lower until her head was only inches above the highly waxed floor.

"Logan!" she gasped breathlessly when he clasped her close to his chest once again.

"I wouldn't have let you go," he whispered in her ear. His right hand moved down her spine, his fingers splaying over her hips and pulling her closer. He groaned deep in his throat when he felt her breasts swell against his chest. It was then Caryn's turn to moan when his hardness searched against the silk of her dress, burning her groin with his rising, scorching heat.

"No," she whispered frantically. "Not here, Logan."

"Tell that to my body," he gasped.

She felt her body grow heavy and heat up with his hardening flesh. If he didn't stop she would beg him to make love to her right on the dance floor.

"Take me back to the table. Now!"

He released her, but held on to her shoulders as she walked in front of him until they reached the table. He seated her, then sat down.

Caryn picked up her drink, unable to look at Hamilton and Cynthia staring first at her, then Logan. *How could he?* she raged inwardly. How could he make love to her in public, and in front of his friends, whom she was certain saw everything?

"Dance with me, Ham," Cynthia ordered her husband as she pushed to her feet.

Waiting until the Wheatons were out of earshot, she rounded on Logan. "What was that all about back there?"

Shifting his eyebrows, Logan slowly stirred his drink. He was back in control. "We were dancing, Caryn."

"Wrong. We were making love on the dance floor."

His head came around slowly and he stared down at her, his gaze narrowing. "I don't need a dance floor to make love to you, Caryn Edwards. Each time I touch you, I make love to you. Whether it's holding your hand or helping you into or out of a car, I'm making love to you." He leaned closer. "Whenever I look at you, I'm making love to you. And if there's a problem, then it's yours, Miss Edwards, not mine."

Fury choked her as she struggled to come back at him. Shifting slightly, she turned away and picked up her drink. The icy liquid bathed her throat, temporarily extinguishing the heat in her face. Swallowing, she realized the drink was too sweet, too much like a milk shake. She reached over and picked up Logan's drink and put it to her lips. It was liberally laced with rum, but she welcomed the burning sensation, refueling her temper again.

"I don't like public displays of affection." The moment

the words were out of her mouth, she knew she couldn't retract them. It was what Tom said to her whenever she held his arm or touched his hand in public.

Logan's gaze narrowed when he saw a shimmer of unshed tears fill her eyes. "What's wrong?" he questioned softly.

Tilting her chin, she closed her eyes. "Nothing."

His fingers curled around her upper arm. "Stop lying to me, Caryn."

"You don't understand, Logan. You can't understand." The words were torn from her throat.

"Try me," he crooned. "You know I'm a good listener."

Opening her eyes, she let out her breath in a lingering sigh. "Not now."

"When?"

Shaking her head, she bit down hard on her lower lip. "I don't know."

His hand moved up to her neck, his fingers massaging the tight muscles across her shoulders. "Remember, Caryn, I'm here if you need an ear or a broad shoulder."

She nodded numbly. "Thanks."

He's so patient, she mused. And she felt like a shrew for snapping at him. Why couldn't she just open up and tell him of the verbal, emotional, and physical abuse she had permitted to go on unchecked? Why couldn't she tell him she had become a willing victim because she feared losing a man who had become her first lover?

An incredibly young-looking American sailor wearing a leering expression approached their table. His dark eyes swept appreciably over Caryn. Standing at attention, he extended his right hand.

"May I dance with the lady?"

Logan went completely still, then rose slowly to his feet, eclipsing the man by at least four inches. "Beat it!" he ordered softly. The sailor affected a neat salute, then turned and walked away.

Caryn doubled over in laughter as Logan sat down, trying valiantly not to laugh. "Did you see that clown?" he sputtered. "Did he really think he was going to dance with you?"

She dabbed at her moist eyes with the edge of a cocktail napkin. "He was kind of cute."

Sobering, Logan stared at her. "You really think so?"

She also sobered. "First you were jealous of Domino and now it's of a boy who's probably on his first shore leave."

"This is the second time you've accused me of being jealous."

"Well, are you?"

His gaze inched over her face, feature by feature. The seconds stretched into a minute before he finally responded. "I suppose I am."

Caryn felt her heart beating outside her chest. She had her answer. If he was jealous, then that meant she was more to him than someone he just slept with. What she didn't want was for him to love her because it only complicated their having to leave each other.

He stood up, extending his hand. "Let's dance again. I promise to behave."

She put her hand in his, smiling. "Do you know how to behave, Mr. Prescott?"

"Not really," he teased, leading her back to the dance floor.

Chapter Eighteen

It was past midnight when Logan and Caryn returned to the *Maggie E.* She let out a small cry of surprise as Logan swept her up in his arms and carried her to their cabin.

"I can walk," she whispered, hoping not to wake up the sleeping crew.

"Why are you being a tight-ass, Caryn?"

"I'm not."

"Yes, you are. Why can't you permit me to court you properly?"

"Noooo, Logan. No courting."

"And why not?"

"Because . . ."

He pushed open the door to their cabin, then kicked it closed with his foot. "Because what?"

She dropped her head on his shoulder. "Because I don't feel so good right now."

He smiled, attractive lines fanning out at the corners of his eyes. "It serves you right. You shouldn't have touched my drink."

"What was in it beside the rum?"

He place her on the bed and sat down beside her. "*Rums.*

There were three different kinds of rum with a mixture of tropical fruit juice."

Placing the back of her hand over her forehead, she closed her eyes. "I think I'm drunk."

Logan removed her shoes, then turned her over and unzipped her dress. "You're hardly drunk, sweetheart." He eased the dress off her shoulders and pulled it down over her hips. Seeing her clad in a pair of black lace bikini panties with a matching strapless bra caused his mouth to go dry. The light from the bedside lamp spilled a ribbon of gold over her slender, tight body.

He unhooked her bra and removed it, but left her panties on. The tiny scrap of fabric was enough to provide a barrier against her nakedness and would serve as a reminder that she would not share her body with him this night.

He undressed, leaving his clothes on a chair, then slipped into bed beside Caryn, Reaching out, he turned off the lamp, plunging the cabin in darkness.

July twenty-eighth—

We've been in beautiful, romantic Puerto Rico for four days, and it has been four wonderful days.

Ham and Tia are celebrating a second honeymoon, while Logan and I are not only discovering the island. but things about ourselves. At least I am.

I've come to terms with the fact that I love him. I no longer fight my feelings. And now that I can admit it to myself I don't feel so tortured. The only thing I'm not ready to do is talk about my failed marriage or ex-husband. What I don't want is for Logan to see me as a weak idiot.

My outburst after we'd left the dance floor the other night—I'm still trying to make some sense of my reaction. It was not the first time Logan and I had danced together nor was it the first time he had become aroused when were dancing together. I think my reaction had something to do with Ham and Tia seeing us together. I've denied my feelings to Tia so many times that she knows I'm lying. And I'm certain she saw right through me when I was dancing with Logan. Only a blind person would not be able to see what had passed between us. I was embarrassed. There is no other word to explain my behavior. Now I know I'm not as mature as I'd like to believe I am. Still more insecurities left over from my failed marriage.

Logan rented a car yesterday, and we toured El Yunque rain forest. We hiked along the trails, overwhelmed with the beauty of viewing a minute portion of two hundred forty different tree species and over two hundred types of ferns. The guide reported four forest zones grow at different elevations along the slopes. Seeing the exotic heliconia was breathtaking. The leaves looked like those of a banana plant, but instead of producing bananas it yields yellow or red lobster-claw brats that grow up to a foot. After recognizing hibiscus poinsettias, and bougainvillea growing in abandonment, I purchased an assorted bouquet from a flower vendor in San Juan and gave it to Ham and Tia for their apartment.

I've learned to order food in Spanish, which surprised Logan when we stopped at a small roadside stand. He gave me a skeptical look until he tasted the bacalaitos, asopao, *and* pasteles. *The* pasteles *have become my favorite—pork filling surrounded by a soft mixture of green bananas and* yautía *wrapped in plantain leaves and boiled. I'm told they are very popular at Christmastime.*

This morning Logan and I will take a short hop over to St. Thomas to shop. We invited Ham and Tia, but they declined. They plan to sail on the Maggie E *for a fishing expedition. They've offered to look after Domino, who has become my constant companion. He rarely looks at Logan except when he wants to eat. Logan says he's going to change his name to Traitor because he's become a certified mush.*

I have to close because I hear Logan calling to say we're ready to leave for the airport for the flight to St. Thomas.

Caryn held on to Logan's hand throughout the thirty-minute flight from Puerto Rico to St. Thomas. She chided herself for not having an empty stomach each time the commuter plane dipped and swayed before the pilot landed the small aircraft smoothly.

Logan cradled Caryn to his chest, pressing his lips to her moist forehead. "It's over, baby,"

"It's not over, Logan. We still have to fly back," she moaned.

"Do you want me to charter a boat for our return trip."

Pulling back, she stared up at his solemn expression. "When?"

"Now."

"You want to leave now?"

He nodded. "I will if you're not feeling well."

She gave him a stunned look. "But I came here to shop."

"You feel up to shopping?"

"Logan Prescott. I did not endure that harrowing flight so I could go back to Puerto Rico without shopping."

"Okay," he drawled, smiling. "Let's find a taxi so we can shop until we drop."

Caryn thought of Puerto Rico as romantic and St. Thomas as sensual. Clear blue-green water surrounded an island of steep green hills. A taxi driver took them to Charlotte Amalie, a bustling picturesque town with narrow streets and quaint Danish colonial architecture. They stopped counting at ten the number of cruise ships and yachts docked in the harbor. The duty-free shops offered many discounts on liquor, fine jewelry, cameras, watches, perfumes, silks, and lace.

She and Logan strolled the narrow streets, entering and exiting many shops while deciding on what they wanted to purchase.

Four hours later, laden with shopping bags containing perfume, fine jewelry, and watches for her niece and nephew, Caryn climbed aboard the commuter plane and closed her eyes. Logan secured his own shopping bags, fastened his seat belt, then held Caryn's hand as the plane taxied for takeoff.

He had purchased gifts for his parents, his personal secretary, and for the Wheaton's unborn child. He had also purchased a gift for Caryn. He knew she would be pleased with his choice because he'd watched her admiring the necklace although she'd refused to try it on.

Squeezing her fingers, Logan smiled at her. "We have just one more day before we go back to the States."

She nodded. "There's so much more of Puerto Rico I'd like to see, but there's isn't enough time."

"We can always come back."

"When?"

"Whenever you have a school recess. I can call you—"

"Don't, Logan," Caryn interrupted. "Let's not plan beyond today."

"Are you saying you won't come back here with me?"

"I'm not saying anything. What I am saying is that I don't know where I'll be next summer."

"None of us know where we'll be tomorrow, but that doesn't mean you can't plan."

"You're right about that because I surely didn't plan to come to Puerto Rico when I left Asheville for Marble Island."

He flashed a wide smile. "It has been a summer of surprises."

"Tell me about it," she said mysteriously.

And it was. She hadn't planned on meeting a man, and she hadn't planned on falling in love. It was a summer to remember.

All plans the two couples made for their last day in Puerto Rico were quickly dashed by a heavy tropical downpour, and the Wheatons returned to the *Maggie E* to wait out the rainy weather.

Caryn lay on her bed, reading. She'd found a recent *People* magazine among a stack in the dining room and had begun to read every word on a page. Logan had retreated to the galley where he and Hamilton joined the crew members in a very vocal poker game.

The sound of rain tapping against the porthole and the rocking motion of the anchored ship lulled her into a state of total relaxation until she had to struggle to remain awake. A noise caught her attention and she listened intently. It came again. Someone was knocking on the door.

Pushing up on an elbow, she closed the magazine. "Come in.

The door opened slightly and a curly, sun-streaked head appeared. "Do you mind company?"

Caryn sat up, smiling. "Not at all. I've found myself reading the same words on the same page for the past fifteen minutes.

Cynthia walked in and sat down on the bed. Caryn shifted, giving her more room. Pressing her head against the pillows propped up against the headboard, she closed her eyes. "Today is the first day I really feel pregnant."

Caryn glanced over at the very noticeable mound under Cynthia's oversized T-shirt. "Maybe that's because today you really look pregnant."

Nodding, she placed a hand over her rounded belly. "First my belly was flat, then wham! I look like I swallowed a honeydew melon."

"How are you feeling otherwise?"

"Wonderful."

"When are you due?"

"The middle of January. And with my luck I'll probably go into labor during a snowstorm."

Caryn laughed. "Bite your tongue."

"That's what Ham says whenever I tease him about getting me pregnant in the spring. The next time we'll try for the fall like most teachers do. That way I'll deliver either late spring or early summer."

Adjusting a pile of pillows behind her shoulders, Caryn stared at Cynthia. "Do you and Ham plan on having more children?"

She shrugged a shoulder. "Probably one more before we get too old. How about yourself? Do you plan to have any children?"

"I'd like a couple. But I want to be married first."

"What are you waiting for?"

"I'd like to find Mr. Right."

Turning and shifting her body to her right side, Cynthia stared at Caryn. "You have Mr. Right."

"Logan?"

"Yes! Logan Prescott."

Closing her eyes, Caryn shook her head. "It's not that easy."

"Why not?"

She opened her eyes, staring across the room. "I was married once."

"And?"

"It was a disaster."

"That doesn't mean it wouldn't work with Raven. He can't be anything like your ex-husband, otherwise you wouldn't have come to Puerto Rico with him."

"That's for certain.

"Then what's the problem?"

"There's no problem. Logan and I are friends, and nothing more."

Cynthia snorted delicately. "I *believe* you guys are a little bit more than friends."

"Okay. We're friends who happen to sleep together."

"I knew that the moment we were introduced."

"How did you know?"

"The way Raven looked at you. And whenever he touched you there was a possessiveness that was so apparent even Ham mentioned it."

Caryn winced. "It's like that?"

"Yeah, it's like that." A secret smile curved Cynthia's mouth. "I don't know if you realized it, but when the two of you were dancing in that club in Old San Juan you were downright shameless. I almost slapped Ham to get him to stop gawking."

Heat flooded her entire body and her face burned in remembrance. "Don't remind me. I've never been so embarrassed."

"Don't be embarrassed. You had every woman in the club throwing daggers at you. Even I was jealous."

Caryn sat up straighter. "Jealous because Logan decided to use the dance floor to make love to me?"

"Hell, yeah. I love Ham to death, but he'll never become one of *People* magazine's sexiest men alive. Now, Raven would definitely be in the running. Women were always throwing themselves at him, but he was very discriminating. He usually dated tall, dark-complexioned women. That's why I was surprised when I saw the two of you together."

"I hadn't planned to spend the summer on Marble Island with Logan." Caryn explained how she had come to share the house with him.

"So, the two of you were sort of thrown together?"

"Exactly," Caryn said smugly.

"Oh, how romantic."

"If you say so."

Cynthia's expression sobered as she stared at Caryn. The cabin was silent as the two women sat regarding each other. "I know I'm a wretched busybody," Cynthia said after an interminable pause, "and I won't get mad if you tell me to mind my own business. But there's one thing I have to know."

"What?"

"Are you using Raven?"

Caryn's body stiffened in shock. What was Cynthia accusing her of? "Using him how?"

"Are you sleeping with him to punish your ex-husband?"

Annoyance replaced the shock. "How dare you accuse me of using Logan. What I feel for him has nothing to do with my ex-husband."

Cynthia arched a pale eyebrow. "So you do love him?"

"Of course I love him," she said recklessly. "I'd never sleep with a man I didn't love."

Cynthia reached over and hugged Caryn, then kissed her on both cheeks. "Thank goodness."

"Now I suppose you'll go and tell him."

"No, Caryn, I won't. If Raven doesn't realize you love him, then he's a fool."

"I don't think he's a fool. It's just that I'm very good when it comes to pushing him away. There are times when I ask myself whether he's using me to forget his ex-fiancée, then I say it doesn't matter because once I leave Marble Island everything I've shared with Logan Prescott will end. He won't owe me anything and vice versa."

"It all sounds very adult to me."

"Because we are adults, Tia. Logan and I are carrying emotional baggage that shouldn't be unloaded on each other. I need to be able to come to Logan not worrying about whether he'll be faithful or supportive. Not only do I want to love him, but I always have to trust him. I don't want to marry a Dr. Jekyll, then wake up to find Mr. Hyde."

"Is that what happened to you, Caryn?"

"Yes."

Cynthia clapped a hand over her mouth. "Oh, sweet heaven. You poor thing."

Caryn managed a tight smile. "It's okay, because I got out in time to save myself."

Cynthia hugged her again before sinking back down to the mound of pillows cradling her shoulders. The women lay on the bed talking for the next hour, offering vignettes of their childhood. Caryn told her everything with the exception of who she'd married and the abuse she'd had endured from the man she'd pledged to love until death parted them.

They returned to Gooseneck Island the second of August at sunset. Domino wound himself around Caryn's legs, seemingly relieved to be back on dry land.

She hugged Hamilton, then Cynthia. "I'll never be able

to thank you for a wonderful week," she said to the now very obviously pregnant blond woman.

"We thank you and Raven for helping us celebrate our last fling with freedom before we're faced with baby formulas, disposable diapers, colic, and teething," Cynthia teased.

"And I'm willing to bet you'll love every minute of it."

Hamilton wound an arm around his wife's thickening waist. "I'm certain we will. I've waited a long time for this event."

Logan, having stored the last of his and Caryn's luggage in the Wrangler, walked over to join her and the others. "Ham and Tia, what can I say except thank you very much for a wonderful surprise."

Hamilton inclined his head. "When do you want to get together again?"

"You have my numbers. Give me a call."

"Will do, Raven."

Logan handed Cynthia two gaily wrapped packages. "Here's a little something for the baby from Caryn and I."

She took the gifts, her eyes filling with tears. "Raven—you guys didn't have to." She sniffled loudly. "You'd better go before I start bawling my eyes out."

Caryn hugged and kissed her new friends again, feeling as if she'd known them for years. Cynthia clung to her neck, weeping. "He loves you," she sobbed in her ear.

I don't want him to love me because it'll make my leaving him so much more painful, she whispered back silently. Easing out of Cynthia's embrace, she walked over to the Jeep and pulled herself up without waiting for Logan to help her. She was already seated and belted in when he picked up Domino and placed him behind the front seats.

Logan swung up onto his seat in one fluid motion. He glanced at her before turning the key in the ignition. He switched on the headlights, put the four-wheel-drive vehicle in reverse, then backed out of the driveway. A wave of sadness shrouded him when he realized seeing his college friends again reminded him of what had eluded him for years—his loving a woman enough to marry her.

But he'd miraculously found love since coming to Marble Island. He had fallen in love with a woman who kept him at a distance; a woman who offered him her body and her passion, but withheld what he needed most.

The drive, which would have normally taken an hour to return to Marble Island, was accomplished in half that time as Logan exceeded the speed limit by more than twenty miles per hour. The drive commanded all of his concentration because of the dark, single-lane road.

He maneuvered into the driveway of the Crawfords' house beside Caryn's car, shutting off the engine. Shifting to his right, he glanced at Caryn. The silvery light from a full moon showed her head hanging at a grotesque angle. A tender smile softened his features. She had fallen asleep.

"Stay, boy," he whispered to Domino when the dog rose to his feet, whining softly.

He retrieved the keys to the house, then gathered Caryn in his arms. She stirred, mumbling softly to herself, then settled back to sleep by the time he'd opened the front door. He flicked a switch on a wall in the entry, flooding the upper level with light. Making his way slowly up the staircase, he stared down at her face relaxed in sleep, his heart welling with emotion.

Caryn hadn't slept much the three days they were at sea for their return trip. Most nights she had sat on deck, staring out at the ocean. Their last night at sea she had refused to come to bed and wound up napping on the deck chair.

Logan walked into his bedroom and placed her gently on the bed. She would sleep with him this night. He would make certain of that.

Chapter Nineteen

Caryn turned over, encountering a solid object. Opening her eyes, she saw a wall of dark brown flesh, realization dawning. She was in bed with Logan. She hadn't slept with him the past three nights because she needed time to withdraw, time to decrease her emotional and physical dependence on him. Moving a leg, she eased her body toward the edge of the bed, but was thwarted when a large hand snaked out and held her fast.

"Where do you think you're going?"

Glancing over her shoulder, she saw Logan frowning at her. "I'm getting up."

Exerting a minimum of pressure, he pulled her back until she lay over his chest. "No, you're not."

Something in his voice, the command, sounded so much like Tom's that she snapped. Raising her free hand, she swung at him, but found herself lying flat on her back with Logan looming over her, his superior weight pressing her down to the mattress.

"What is the matter with you, Caryn?"

"Nothing," she screamed in his face, trying unsuccessfully to free herself. "Let me go!"

He eased his hold on her body but would not let her up. "What's going on with you?" Holding her shoulders, he shook her gently. "Come on, baby. Tell me what he did to you."

His calling her baby was her undoing. All of the shame and pain she'd carried for years swept over her, and she bit down so hard on her lower lip that she drew blood.

"No, Logan, I can't," she sobbed. "Please, please don't ask me again."

Gathering her close, he reversed their positions while placing tender kisses on her wet cheeks. "It's okay, sweetheart. Everything will work out. I'll take care of you."

The moment he said the words, he realized he'd repeated what he had promised the night of the storm. The night she had come to him—soft, passionate, and vulnerable.

He held her until the stiffness left her limbs enough for her to relax. He now knew without a doubt it was the shadow of her ex-husband that kept her from loving him. *He must have been a monster,* he seethed silently. A monster who had terrorized her until she somehow found the courage to escape him.

"What do you want from me, Caryn?"

She jumped slightly at the sound of his voice against her ear. Settling her legs more comfortably between his, she shook her head.

"Nothing, Logan."

He stiffened momentarily, held his breath, then let it out slowly. All she had to do was ask, and he would give her anything she desired. Anything within his grasp.

"You've given me all I'll ever need," she continued softly, her warm breath feathering over his throat. "And when I leave Marble Island, I want you to know that I'll never forget you."

He refused to think of her leaving Marble Island—leaving him. But he knew eventually the time would come when he, too, would have to leave.

"When are you leaving?" He was certain she could hear the anguish in his voice.

"I have to leave by August ninth."

"Why so soon? Don't classes begin the middle of the month?"

"I have orientation on the eleventh."

"That gives us only another week together."

Her eyes filled with a fresh wave of tears. "Then we'll have to make it a week to remember."

Logan swallowed the lump rising in his throat. "Yes, we will."

August fourth—

Logan and I have been back on Marble Island for two days, and it's not the same. We have not slept together since our first night back. I lay in my bed waiting for him to come for me, and he doesn't. It's as if he knows we have to pull back to prepare for our final departure.

Even Domino senses something is wrong. He's stopped following me and now stays close to Logan.

I feel so alone, so empty. How can that be when he still lives in the house with me?

We continue to take our meals together, but there's not much conversation. We've become two polite strangers who happen to share a house. He did ask me if I would go to the outdoor concert with him tonight and I said I would. It will be the last concert we'll share. It has been billed as International Night. featuring vocalists and musicians from around the world. It should top off a wonderful summer for me.

It was apparent the days were getting shorter and the nights cooler, yet that had not lessened the enthusiasm of the vacationers who had planned to remain on Marble Island until the Labor Day weekend.

Caryn had spent the day packing. She still had another four days on the island, but she did not want to wait until the last minute to begin the onerous task. She was returning to Asheville with more than she'd left with. The clothes Logan had purchased for her for their Puerto Rico excursion added much more weight to her pullman and garment bag.

Glancing at her watch, she realized she had to rush to get dressed if she didn't want to be late for the concert. Stripping off a T-shirt and a pair of shorts, she took a quick shower.

She was dressed and had brushed her hair when Logan knocked on her bedroom door. Smiling at him, she said, "I'm ready."

Logan returned her smile. "You look cute tonight."

Caryn glanced down at the forest-green, cotton, jersey, drawstring pants with a matching long-sleeve shirt, she had pulled on over a white tank top. Her deck shoes were the same forest green.

"Thank you."

Extending his hand, he grasped her fingers. "Let's go or we'll be late."

She glanced at her watch. It was seven-fifty. The concert always began promptly at eight.

Logan led her down the staircase and out to the porch. Domino, who lay in a corner on the porch, stood up. The puppy was now completely housebroken and could be trusted to have the run of the house and porch.

Logan whistled softly through his teeth. "Let's go, boy. Inside." He held the door open and the dog bounded into the house, standing at the screen door and whining softly. "We'll be back soon." He lay down even before Logan closed the door and locked it.

"I'm going to miss Domino," she said quietly as Logan picked up a blanket from a rocker.

He chuckled. "I'm thinking of giving him to you. I have no need for a mush dog."

Caryn looked up at him and smiled. "Are you serious?"

He gave her a long, penetrating look, then nodded. "Do you want him?"

"I'd love him."

"Are you allowed to have pets where you live?"

"Yes. I'm renting a small house. It even has a yard in the back where he can run free."

"If that's the case, then he's yours."

She stopped, forcing Logan to stop with her. "You'd really give me your dog?"

A slight frown settled between his dark eyes. "I'd give you anything you'd want, if it would make you happy."

"What makes you think I'm not happy?"

"There are times when I see a sadness you can't hide, Caryn. A sadness that weighs you down—"

"Don't analyze me, Logan," she interrupted.

"I'm not analyzing you," he countered angrily.

Closing her eyes, Caryn counted to three. Opening her eyes, she flashed a tight smile. "Let's not fight. We don't want everyone to think we're having a lover's quarrel."

Leaning over, he kissed her cheek. "And, we wouldn't want everyone to know that we don't love each other, especially if they believe we're married."

She nodded numbly. It had become a summer of deception. They'd lied about being married, and she had lied about not loving him. Only Cynthia knew the truth, and had promised not to tell Logan. But, she hadn't promised not to tell Hamilton. Closing her eyes, she prayed silently that Cynthia would keep her secret.

Caryn lay beside Logan, not touching, and staring up at the darkening sky. She inhaled the familiar scent of his sensual cologne, felt his warmth and wanted so much to touch him.

Touch me, Logan, she urged him silently. *Make the first move.* But he didn't, and as soon as the lights dimmed, she closed her eyes, shutting him out.

Logan regretted coming to the concert the moment he heard the opening notes of the Sarah Brightman and Andrea Bocelli duet, "Time To Say Goodbye."

Pain, sorrow, and loss merged, threatening to swallow

him whole. The pain he'd experienced when he saw Nina with Wayne was nothing compared to what he was now undergoing. The pain eased, becoming a slow, seething rage. The love he felt for Caryn bordered on a loathing, a loathing for making him vulnerable.

Caryn Edwards had done to him what no other person had been able to do to him in thirty-five years. She had stripped him bare where anyone or anything could destroy him with a touch or a look.

Turning his head, he glanced down at her, his hands tightening into fists. He felt brittle, brittle enough to shatter into millions of pieces. He saw her shaking and thought maybe she was laughing, but as he leaned closer he realized she was crying. She was crying without making a sound.

His fingers unclenched as he pulled her against his body. Pressing his lips to her forehead, he cradled the back of her head.

"Oh, Caryn, don't do this to me, to us," he gasped, struggling for control.

"I want to go home."

Logan also had had enough. Standing, he helped her to her feet, then picked up the blanket. There was only the sound of their breathing on the return drive to the house. Each did not want to intrude on the other's chaotic emotions.

Caryn walked into the house before Logan and raced up the staircase. She made her way into her bedroom and closed the door. She stood in the dark, unable to turn on the light. The light would reveal her luggage sitting in a corner; it would remind her of how short her time was on Marble Island. And when she put those bags in her car and turned the key in the ignition, it would be over. Everything she had shared with Logan Prescott would come to a crashing end.

She finally pushed off the door and undressed in the dark. Her movements were measured, precise as she folded each piece—even her panties. She placed the pile of clothing on the foot of her bed, then lay facedown on the bed.

"I love you, Logan," she whispered to silent space. The four words lingered in her mind as she fell into a deep sleep.

Logan paced the porch for over an hour, wanting to go to Caryn, then berated himself for weakening. He loved her. And he'd tried every way he could to tell her, but she'd rejected him over and over.

He heard whining and knew it was time for the dog's last outing. Opening the door, he let Domino out. He didn't have to wait long for the Dalmatian's return.

Logan shook his head. Now, who's the fool, he thought, staring at his pet. He had offered Caryn his dog because she wanted him. He would miss Domino, but knew he would get an excellent home.

"She loves you more than she loves me," he said to the dog.

He locked the front door, turned off the light, then made his way to the upper level, his footsteps heavy on the stairs.

Standing at the top of the stairs, he stared at the closed door to Caryn's room. He couldn't remember when he'd seen the door closed. His footsteps were determined as he walked the length of hall and turned the knob. It opened. At least she hadn't locked it.

He stood, stunned. It could've been a repeat of his first night on Marble Island. Caryn lay on the bed, naked, in the full moonlight. The same surge of desire gripped him, and his knees buckled slightly.

The last time he'd taken a cold shower. But that was before he'd tasted the burning sweetness of her lush body. And he wanted her—once more before it was time for their final goodbye.

Logan did not remember removing his clothes, nor did he remember slipping into bed with Caryn. But what he did remember the moment he pushed into her moist, hot body was that he hadn't protected her. The first and last time he would make love to her it would become a risky game of chance.

Caryn awoke to Logan's hard flesh filling every inch of her. Any and all vestiges of sleep vanished as she curved her arms around his neck, lifted her hips, and followed his lead in a dance of abandoned desire.

He alternated the rhythm, slowing with a heavy, surging rolling of his hips before quickening to a frenzied, uninhibited thrusting that left her taking in deep gulps of air.

She felt his pulse outside of his body, heard it pounding in her head. His body pressed hers down to the mattress, his fingers entwined in the sheets in a punishing grip which would have left angry bruises on her flesh had he held her.

"Baby! Oh, baby," he groaned over and over, the endearment becoming his mantra.

Caryn felt her heart melt and turn over as she raised her legs and circled his waist. The motion brought him closer, deeper, and with it a rush of passion as the floodgates opened, drowning both with a scorching inferno that pulled them under where they had stopped existing as separate entities, becoming one in the same.

"Darling," Caryn sighed, her body shaking uncontrollably from her awesome release. A final, lingering shudder shook her simultaneously with the aftermath of Logan's violent climax.

He collapsed heavily on her slight frame, gasping for much-needed oxygen to fill his burning lungs. He had taken her without his usual foreplay, and she had welcomed him into her body; the pleasure she'd offered was pure, explosive. A pleasure akin to a sweet agony where she had communicated her final goodbye.

Caryn pushed against Logan's shoulders and he rolled off her. She slipped off the bed and headed for the bathroom. The light from the full moon silvered the space where she did not have to turn on a light. She moved as if in a trace when she opened the door to the shower stall, stepped in, and turned on the water. She stood under the stream of the lukewarm water, crying uncontollably.

She cried for her lost innocence; an innocence to one so undeserving, and she cried for all of the times she hadn't cried when Tom humiliated her; and finally she cried for the tiny life which was never offered the possibility of surviving to term.

But what she would not cry for was the time she'd spent with Logan. Falling in love with him had become a great source of joy. Unknowingly he had taught her she could love, and that she could also walk away from someone she loved. He had taught her more in four weeks than she'd learned in four years of marriage.

Picking up a bottle of shower gel, she lathered her body, washing away the odor of Logan's body and the passion they'd shared. She completed her shower of renewal, shoulders squared, and in complete control of herself for the first time in her life. She knew what she had to do.

After toweling her body dry, she went through her ritual of moisturizing her moist flesh, before walking out of the bathroom and into the bedroom. She knew without her gaze sweeping over the bed that Logan wouldn't be there—and he wasn't. Not having him present would make her task much easier.

Caryn dressed quickly, pulling on a faded sweatshirt over pair of jeans. She methodically removed everything which could indicate that she had occupied the space. It took two trips, but she managed to load her car without making a sound. Each time she made her way up the staircase, she expected to find Logan standing at the top staring down at her. But the door to his bedroom remained shut, permitting her to slip away from him and Marble Island like an apparition.

Logan felt her loss as soon as he awoke. The sun was high in the heavens, but there was an unnatural stillness that whispered to him that she was gone.

It taunted him as he pulled on a pair of shorts and made his way to her bedroom. His frantic gaze swept around the room, lingering on the corner where she had placed her bags. They were gone. She had left without saying goodbye.

His movements were jerky and uncoordinated when he walked over to the double dresser, opening drawers to verify what he already knew They were empty. The bathroom was next. All of her bottles bearing sensual scents were also gone.

Numbly, blindly, he stumbled back to the bed where only hours before he had spilled his passion into her willing body, and fell across the mattress. The lingering fragrance of her body wafted in his nostrils, offering him his last opportunity to hold on to her.

He wanted to scream, bellow out his frustration and pain. He'd thought, hoped he would be successful, successful enough to batter down the wall she had erected to keep him out.

She had fled, not giving him the opportunity to offer sharing his life with her. She had rejected him enough in the past so if she did reject him again he would've added it to the mounting list.

But, dammit, she hadn't given him the chance!

Rolling over on his back, he stared up at the ceiling. His mind was blank, and he marveled how he could be so calm. The woman he loved had just walked out of his life, and he lay there like someone numbed by a powerful narcotic.

Throwing a muscled arm over his face, he shook his head in amazement as a smile twitched at his mouth. The smile widened followed by a rumble of laughter. He laughed and laughed until spent. Then he sat up, knowing what it was he had to do. He stood up to walk out of the room, but something caught his eye. The drawer to the bedside table wasn't closed. Reaching down, he pulled it open and withdrew a small, tapestry-covered book.

He fanned the pages, scanning one or two. He froze when he saw his name. Peering closer, he read the entry, his gaze widening. He'd found Caryn's journal. She had left Marble Island without taking it with her.

Floating back down to the bed, he read one entry, then another. He hadn't realized he was holding his breath until he felt the constricting band around his chest.

Then his breathing quickened until he was hyperventilating. Putting the journal aside, he lay down to compose himself. "She loves me," he whispered over and over like a litany.

"Hot, damn!" he shouted. "She loves me!"

Logan sat up, bracing his back against the bed's headboard and began reading the first entry. The writing was just like Caryn—neat and delicate.

His expression changed, hardening with a loathing as he read how Thomas Duff had abused her with the methodical atrocities of an oppressor. He read of her pain and humiliation, and how she had kept it all inside as it slowly ate away at the very fabric of her being.

He read the entry three times when Tom Duff had pushed her down the stairs and she lay bleeding, the life of her unborn child seeping out of her body and onto the expensive fabric of a Persian rug.

Logan threw the journal across the room, it bouncing off a wall and landing on the floor. "The son of a bitch! I'll kill him!" he shouted to the empty room. His gaze, flooded with rage, shifted and he stared at Domino standing outside the bedroom.

Gasping, as if he had run a grueling race, he stood up and walked over to the dog. "It's okay. I'm okay." Domino's tail wagged as he took a few steps, stopped, then looked back at his master.

He smiled. He had to let the dog out.

Logan spent the morning reading Caryn's journal—twice. Four cups of strong black coffee had fortified him as he memorized her gentle confessions, her tender words of love.

He glanced at his watch, noting the time, then reached for the small cellular phone on the table. Pressing a button, he listened for the speed dial to connect him with Jace Prescott's private line.

"Jace, here," came a strong masculine voice.

"Have you taken to answering your own phone now?"

"Edith is sitting here with me, taking dictation. I'm replying to a query from Wainscott and Llewellyn."

"Good news?"

"It is, son. Your proposal was excellent. It appears as if they're ready to finance the Fairview project."

"That is good news, Dad. I'm calling to let you know I'll be back sooner than I'd first planned. I'm just going to need a few more days to close up the house."

"Thanks, Logan."

"Dad?"

"Yes?"

"Tell Mama to book that cruise."

"Why don't you call her and tell her yourself. She's been complaining that she hasn't heard from you in a while."

"She's right. I'll call her as soon as I hang up."

He depressed a button, ending the call. But he didn't call his mother—not right away. He dialed a series of numbers, listening for the break in the connection.

"Raleigh Police Department. Lieutenant Robinson."

"Robbie, Logan. Brother, I need a favor."

"What's up, Logan?"

"Can you run a plate through DMV for me?"

"Someone hit you and take off?"

"Nothing like that. I need an address on a Caryn Edwards in Asheville."

There was a pause before Jerome Robinson's authoritative voice came through the wire again. "What did she do to you?"

"Nothing." A smile softened Logan's stern features. "I just need to know where she lives so I can return a personal journal she lost."

"You're not putting me on, are you?"

"No."

"Can you wait for me to check the computer?"

"Yes." And he would wait until hell froze over if it meant seeing Caryn Edwards again. It was another three minutes before Jerome returned, giving him Caryn's address in Asheville.

"Thanks, Robbie. I owe you."

"This is personal, isn't it?"

"Yes, it is."

"If I hear of any trouble between you and the lady, I'll deny any involvement."

"Don't worry, brother. There won't be any trouble."

He rang off, then made his third phone call of the morning. What he thought of as the darkest day of his life had suddenly become one of the best. And he knew there were better days to come. Days he would share with Caryn Edwards.

Chapter Twenty

Caryn turned off the two-lane highway and onto a narrow local road leading to her house. It was only the second day of classes, and she felt as if she had been back in the classroom for months. She had been assigned a group of students whose intent it was to see how hard a time they could give her. She had begun the first day with staring down a girl who had openly challenged her authority. The sixteen-year-old stood at least three inches taller and probably outweighed her by more than fifty pounds, but she had held her ground. No one, regardless of their age, would ever intimidate her ever again.

She had changed, even Marcia had commented on it, but she liked what she had become. It was as if she'd grown up the five weeks she had stayed on Marble Island.

She could not think about Marble Island without thinking about Logan. Each time she conjured up his arresting face and magnificent body she smiled. And it was at night that her body betrayed her whenever she recalled the smell, taste, and feel of his lovemaking.

Slowing, she maneuvered into the driveway. Her foot hit the brake when she saw the sleek lines of a gleaming black Ferrari with JP2 on a North Carolina license plate parked ahead of her.

He's come for me. She knew the car belonged to Logan even before she saw him rise from the rocker on the porch.

Caryn put her car in park, turned off the ignition, and sat waiting for him to come to her. Her gold-green gaze caressed his tall body, silently admiring the expertly tailored charcoal-gray suit floating over his body.

Her gaze moved from his short barbered hair, clean-shaven lean jaw, to the stark white shirt collar contrasting with the velvety darkness of his strong neck. He was impeccable, perfect, as evidenced by his professional and personal success.

Leaning down, he smiled at her. "Good afternoon, Caryn."

Her heart pumped uncontrollably in her chest. "Hello, Logan."

He arched an eyebrow. "I've been waiting for you."

"So I see." Her voice was soft, calm, belying her inner turmoil

Reaching in through the open window, he unlocked the door and pulled it open. "May I help you out?"

She placed her hand in his as he gently pulled her to her feet. It was as if they were strangers; two very polite strangers.

Logan took in her appearance with one sweeping look, his smile mirroring his approval. Her curly short hair was brushed off her face, accentuating the delicate hollow of cheekbones in her small face. She wore a minimum of makeup—a muted eyeshadow, mascara, and lipstick.

He liked her professional look. She wore a linen gabardine suit in a flattering burnt-orange shade with a pair of black patent leather pumps. Her only jewelry was a watch and the diamond studs in her pierced lobes.

Tilting her chin, she gave him a challenging stare. "Why have you come?"

"I'm surprised you have to ask me that."

"Why?"

"Because there's something I need to hear from you, Caryn. You write beautifully, but I want you to tell me what I need to hear without having to read it in your journal."

Her jaw dropped as her eyes widened until he saw into their mysterious depths. "You took my journal!"

"I *found* your journal. You left it at the house. You were in such a hurry to run away that you forgot it."

"You had no right to read my personal—"

"I had every right," he countered, cutting her off. "I have a right to know that you love me as much as I love you. I have a right to know whether I can, based on my feelings for you, ask you to marry me."

Cradling her face between his large hands, he brushed his mouth over hers. "I'm no Thomas Duff, sweetheart. Any man who loves a woman would never abuse her."

Her fingers curled around his wrists. "He was a monster, Logan."

"He's your past, baby. I'm your present and your future." He increased the pressure of his mouth. "The passion you arouse in me is frightening, unbelievably frightening, because there are times when I want to scream out how much I've come to love you."

Pulling back, Caryn stared at him as if she'd never seen him before. He'd memorized her journal entries. Her eyes filled with unshed tears, tears of love and joy.

"And I do love you, Logan Prescott."

"As I do love you, Caryn Edwards."

Reaching up, she curved her arms around his neck and pressed her lips to his smooth jaw. "Let's go in the house. I have something I want to give you."

He pulled back, giving her a questioning look. "What's that?"

"An in-home demonstration of how much I've missed you."

Logan released her long enough to reach into her car to retrieve her handbag from the console between the front seats. He handed her the leather bag, grinning.

"How much will this demonstration cost me?"

She made her way to the little house, glancing over her shoulder. "Only the next fifty years of your life as Mrs. Logan Prescott."

He picked her up and spun her around. A tender expression filled his eyes, a tenderness that had never been there before. "Sold to the woman who stole my heart the day I walked into the beach house on Marble Island."

"I don't give refunds, darling."

"I don't want one," he crooned as she leaned over and opened the door.

Logan lowered her to her feet, but did not release his hold on her body. "We have a lot to talk about. When and where we'll marry. Where we'll live. How many babies you want."

She held his hand, pulling him in the direction of her bedroom. "We'll talk about that later. Right now I need you to show me how much you love me."

"Of course, sweetheart."

He walked into her bedroom, seeing only the woman standing before him as he undressed slowly, knowing this joining would be different, special. As special as the love they'd found on Marble Island. As special as the love that would bind them together for the rest of their lives.

Epilogue

Two years later . . .

October fourteenth—

Logan and I celebrated our second anniversary and the birth of our first child today. The only thing I can say about our daughter is that she's beautiful. She wasn't due until the end of the month, but decided she wanted to make her special appearance on her parents' anniversary. There's no way Logan will ever forget our anniversary or Angela's birthday.

We've decided to name her Angela because she is our angel—our miracle baby. Maeve and Jace have taken grandparents' status to another level—lunacy. And because my parents are experienced grandparents, they are much more sophisticated about this repeat performance.

Our vacation residence is scheduled for completion next week. Logan and I are hoping to celebrate Angela's first Christmas at the new house on Marble Island. We've invited the Wheatons and their son, both sets of in-laws, and my brother, sister in-law, and their children. The house is tre-

mendous—five bedrooms, so there's enough room for everyone.

I will always be grateful to Terry and Marcia for letting me use their house so I could heal. It was a summer of storms and a summer of passion. It is a time that will stay with me forever.

I must close because I see my husband standing in the doorway smiling at me.

And I'm not afraid to let him know that I love him now and will love him forever.

Dear Readers:

Summer—a season of sun, fun, and a time for falling in love. And I hope the love, laughter, and passion shared by Caryn and Logan will linger with you this summer and many more to come.

My next novel will introduce the HIDEAWAY Legacy's second generation. It will be the heroines who continue the Cole, Sterling, and Kirkland tradition of sexy men and women who dare risk everything for love.

Regina Cole's HARVEST MOON is scheduled for an December 1999 release.

I look forward to hearing from you. Please include a self-addressed stamped envelope for a reply.

Sincerely,

Rochelle Alers

Rochelle Alers

Post Office Box 690
Freeport, NY 11520-0690

E-mail: Roclers@aol.com
Web Address: http://www.infokart.com/rochellealers

COMING IN JUNE 1999 . . .

PIECES OF DREAMS (1-58314-020-4, $4.99/$6.50)
by Donna Hill
Tragedy brought Maxine Sherman and Quinten Parker together years ago, until another woman stole Quinn away from her. Since then, her nights were filled with dreams of his return. When Quinn returns to rekindle their love, Maxine has a new life. But a secret binds them forever.

SUDDEN LOVE (1-58314-023-9, $4.99/$6.50)
by Angela Winters
Author Renee Shepherd decides to visit her sister in Chicago and is drawn into an investigation surrounding the suspicious death of her sister's colleague. The executive director of the company, Evan Brooks, is somehow involved in all this, and it'll take much trust and faith for Renee to risk everything for sudden love.

A MAGICAL MOMENT (1-58314-021-2, $4.99/$6.50)
by Monica Jackson
Atlanta lawyer Taylor Cates is dedicated to helping battered women at a non-profit shelter. When the shelter's reputation is threatened by a series of mysterious deaths, private detective Stone Emerson must uncover the truth while pursuing an unexpected love.

LOVE BY DESIGN (1-58314-022-0, $4.99/$6.50)
by Marcella Sanders
Interior designer Daniella Taylor returns to New Jersey to bury herself in work and avoid romantic relationships. But working at Parker's Art she'll have to face the owner, Brant Parker, who will not let her forget the passion and the love they once shared.

Available wherever paperbacks are sold, or order direct from the Publisher. Send cover price plus 50¢ per copy for mailing and handling to BET Books, c/o Kensington Publishing Corp., Consumer Orders, or call (toll free) 888-345-BOOK, to place your order using Mastercard or Visa. Residents of New York, Washington D.C., and Tennessee must include sales tax. DO NOT SEND CASH.